THE FOX

THE FOX

Frederick Forsyth

CORGI BOOKS

TRANSWORLD PUBLISHERS
61–63 Uxbridge Road, London W5 5SA
www.penguin.co.uk

Transworld is part of the Penguin Random House group of companies
whose addresses can be found at global.penguinrandomhouse.com

First published in Great Britain in 2018 by Bantam Press
an imprint of Transworld Publishers
Corgi edition for sale in the Indian subcontinent only published 2018

A CIP catalogue record for this book
is available from the British Library.

.9780552175852

Typeset in Bembo by Jouve (UK), Milton Keynes
Printed and bound in India by Thomson Press India Ltd.

Penguin Random House is committed to a sustainable
future for our business, our readers and our planet. This book
is made from Forest Stewardship Council® certified paper.

MIX
Paper from
responsible sources
FSC
www.fsc.org
FSC® C018179

1 3 5 7 9 10 8 6 4 2

With grateful thanks to my ace researcher Marcus Scriven, who traced so many hidden experts, and to Jamie Jackson, whose knowledge of all things military is awesome. And to those others who talked behind the hand on the basis of anonymity.

Chapter One

NO ONE SAW them. No one heard them. They were not supposed to. The black-clad Special Forces soldiers slipped unseen through the pitch-dark night towards the target house.

In most town and city centres there is always a glimmer of light, even in deepest night, but this was the outer suburb of an English provincial town and all public lighting had ceased at one in the morning. This was the darkest hour, 2 a.m. A solitary fox watched them pass but instinct bade him not interfere with fellow hunters. No house lights broke the gloom.

They encountered two single humans, both on foot, both drunk after late-night partying with friends. The soldiers melted into gardens and shrubbery, disappearing black on black, until the wanderers had stumbled towards their homes.

They knew exactly where they were, having studied the streets and the target house in intimate detail for many hours. The pictures had been taken by cruising cars and overhead drones. Much enlarged and pinned to the wall of the briefing room at Stirling Lines, the headquarters of the SAS outside Hereford, the images had been memorized to the last stone and kerb. The soft-booted men did not trip or stumble.

There were a dozen of them, and they included two Americans, inserted at the insistence of the US team that had installed itself in the embassy in London. And there were two from the British SRR, the Special Reconnaissance Regiment, a unit even more clandestine than the SAS and the SBS, the Special Air Service and the Special Boat Service respectively. The authorities had elected to use the SAS, known simply as 'the Regiment'.

One of the two from the SRR was a woman. The Americans presumed this was to establish gender equality. It was the reverse. Observation had revealed that one of the inhabitants of the target house was female and even the British hard squads try to observe a little gallantry. The point of the presence of the SRR, sometimes referred to in the club as 'Her Majesty's burglars', was to practise one of their many skill sets – covert entry.

The mission was not only to enter and subdue the target house and its denizens but to ensure they were not seen by any watcher inside and that no one escaped. They approached from all angles, appeared simultaneously around the garden fence, front, back and sides, crossed the garden and ringed the house, still unseen and unheard by neighbour or inhabitant.

No one heard the slight squeak of the diamond-tipped

glass cutter as it described a neat circle in a kitchen window, nor the low crack as the disc was removed with a suction pad. A gloved hand came through the hole and unlatched the window. A black figure climbed over the sill into the sink, jumped quietly to the floor and opened the back door. The team slipped in.

Though they had all studied the architect's plan, filed with the registry when the house was built, they still used head-mounted penlights in case of owner-installed obstructions or even booby-traps. They began with the ground floor, moving from room to room to confirm there were no sentries or sleeping figures, trip wires or silent alarms.

After ten minutes the team leader was satisfied and with a nod of his head led a single-file column of five up the narrow staircase of what was evidently a very ordinary detached four-bedroom family home. The two Americans, increasingly bewildered, remained below. This was not the way they would have subdued a thoroughly dangerous nest of terrorists. Such a house invasion back home would have involved several magazines of ammunition by now. Clearly, the Limeys were pretty weird.

Those below heard startled exclamations from above. These quickly ceased. After ten more minutes of muttered instructions the team leader uttered his first report. He did not use internet or cellphone – interceptible – but old-fashioned encrypted radio. 'Target subdued,' he said softly. 'Inhabitants four. Await sunrise.' Those who listened to him knew what would happen next. It had all been pre-planned and rehearsed.

The two Americans, both US Navy SEALs, also reported in to their embassy on the south side of the Thames in London.

The reason for the 'hard' takeover of the building was simple. Despite a week of covert surveillance, it was still possible, bearing in mind the amount of damage to the defences of the entire Western world that had come out of that harmless-looking suburban house, that it might contain armed men. There might be terrorists, fanatics, mercenaries hiding behind the innocent façade. That was why the Regiment had been told there was no alternative to a 'worst case' operation.

But an hour later the team leader communicated again.

'You are not going to believe what we have found here.'

In the very early morning of 3 April 2019 a telephone rang in a modest bedroom under the eaves of the Special Forces Club in an anonymous townhouse in Knightsbridge, a wealthy district of London's West End. At the third ring the bedside light came on. The sleeper was awake and fully functioning – the outcome of a lifetime of practice. He swung his feet to the floor and glanced at the illuminated panel before putting the apparatus to his ear. He also glanced at the clock beside the lamp. Four in the morning. Did this woman never sleep?

'Yes, Prime Minister.'

The person at the other end clearly had not been to bed at all.

'Adrian, sorry to wake you at this hour. Could you be with me at nine? I have to greet the Americans. I suspect they will be on the warpath and I would appreciate your assessment and advice. They are due at ten.'

Always the old-fashioned courtesy. She was giving an order, not making a request. For friendship she would use his given name. He would always call her by her title.

'Of course, Prime Minister.'

There was nothing more to say, so the connection ended. Sir Adrian Weston rose and went into the small but sufficient bathroom to shower and shave. At half past four he went downstairs, past the black-framed portraits of all the agents who had gone into Nazi-occupied Europe so long ago and never come back, nodded to the night watch behind the lobby desk and let himself out. He knew a hotel on Sloane Street with an all-night café.

Shortly before 9 a.m. on a bright autumn morning, 11 September 2001, a twin-jet American airliner out of Boston for Los Angeles designated American Airlines 011 swerved out of the sky over Manhattan and slammed into the North Tower of the World Trade Center. It had been hijacked in mid-air by five Arabs in the service of terrorist group al-Qaeda. The man at the controls was an Egyptian. He was supported by four Saudis who, armed with box-cutter knives, had subdued the cabin staff and hustled him on to the flight deck.

Minutes later, another airliner, flying far too low, appeared over New York. It was United Airlines 175, also out of Boston for Los Angeles, also hijacked by five al-Qaeda terrorists.

America and, within moments, the entire world watched in disbelief as what had been presumed a tragic accident revealed it was nothing of the sort. The second Boeing 767 flew deliberately into the South Tower of the Trade Center. Both skyscrapers sustained terminal damage in the mid-sections. Aided by the fuel from the full tanks of the airliners, savage fires erupted and began to melt the steel girders that held the buildings rigid. A minute before 10 a.m. the South Tower collapsed into a mountain of red-hot rubble, followed by the North Tower half an hour later.

At 9.37 a.m. American Airlines flight 77 out of Washington Dulles International Airport, also bound for Los Angeles with full tanks, dived into the Pentagon, Virginia. It had also been hijacked by five Arabs.

The fourth airliner, United Airlines 93, out of Newark for San Francisco, again hijacked in mid-air, was recaptured by a passenger revolt, but too late to save the aircraft, which, with its fanatical hijacker still at the controls, dived into farmland in Pennsylvania.

Before sundown that day, now known simply as 9/11, a fraction under 3,000 Americans and others were dead. They included the crews and passengers of all four airliners, almost all those in the World Trade Center's two skyscraper towers and 125 in the Pentagon. Plus the nineteen terrorists who committed suicide. That single day left the USA not simply shocked but traumatized. She still is.

When an American government is wounded that badly, it does two things. It demands and exacts revenge, and it spends.

Over the eight years of the George W. Bush presidency and the first four years of that of Barack Obama, the USA spent a trillion dollars constructing the biggest, the most cumbersome, the most duplicated and possibly the most inefficient national security structure the world has ever seen.

If the nine inner US intelligence agencies and the seven outer agencies had been doing their jobs in 2001, 9/11 would never have occurred. There were signs, hints, reports, tip-offs, indications and oddities that were noted, reported, filed and ignored.

What followed 9/11 was an explosion of expenditure that is literally breathtaking. Something had to be done, and be seen to be done by the great American public, so it was. A raft of new agencies was created to duplicate and mirror the work of the existing ones. Thousands of new skyscrapers sprang up, entire cities of them, most owned and run by private-sector-contracted enterprises eager for the fathomless dollar harvest.

Government expenditure on the single pandemic word 'security' detonated like a nuke over Bikini Atoll, all uncomplainingly paid for by the ever-trusting, ever-hopeful, ever-gullible American taxpayer. The exercise generated an explosion of reports, on paper and online, so vast that only about ten per cent of them have ever been read. There simply is not the time or, despite the massive payroll, the staff to begin to cope with the information. And something else happened in those twelve years. The computer and its archive, the database, became rulers of the world.

When the Englishman seeking an early breakfast off Sloane Street was a young officer in the Paras, then in MI6, records were created on paper and stored on paper. It took time, and the storage of archives took space, but penetration, the copying or removal and theft of secret archives – that is, espionage – was hard and the quantity removable at any one time or from any one place was modest.

During the Cold War, which supposedly ended with the Soviet reformer Mikhail Gorbachev in 1991, the great spies like Oleg Penkovsky could abstract only as many documents as they could carry about their persons. Then the Minox camera and its product microfilm enabled up to a hundred documents to be concealed in a small canister. The microdot made copied documents even smaller and more transportable. But the computer revolutionized the lot.

When defector and traitor Edward Snowden flew to Moscow it is believed he carried over one and a half million documents on a memory stick small enough to be inserted before a border check into the human anus. 'Back in the day', as the veterans put it, a column of trucks would have been needed, and a convoy moving through a gate tends to be noticeable.

So, as the computer took over from the human, the archives containing trillions of secrets came to be stored on databases. As the complexities of this mysterious dimension called cyberspace became more and more weird and increasingly complicated, fewer and fewer human brains could understand how they worked. Matching pace, crime also changed, gravitating from shoplifting through financial embezzlement to today's daily computer fraud, which enables more wealth to be stolen than ever before in the history of finance. Thus the modern world has given rise to the concept of computerized hidden wealth but also to the computer hacker. The burglar of cyberspace.

But some hackers do not steal money; they steal secrets. Which is why a harmless-looking suburban house in a provincial English town was invaded in the night by an Anglo-American team of Special Forces soldiers and its inhabitants detained. And why one of those soldiers murmured into a radio-mic: 'You are not going to believe what we have found here.'

Three months before the raid a team of American computer aces working at the National Security Agency in Fort Meade, Maryland, discovered what they also could not believe. The most secret database in the USA, probably in the world, had apparently been hacked.

Fort Meade, as the word 'fort' implies, is technically an army base. But it is a lot more than that. It is the home of the fearsome National Security Agency, or NSA. Heavily shielded from unwanted view by forests and forbidden access roads, it is the size of a city. But instead of a mayor it has a four-star army general as its commanding officer.

It is the home of that branch of all intelligence agencies known as ELINT, or electronic intelligence. Inside its perimeter, rank upon rank of computers eavesdrop the world. ELINT intercepts, it listens, it records, it stores. If something it intercepts is dangerous, it warns.

Because not everyone speaks English, it translates from every language, dialect and patois used on planet Earth. It encrypts and decodes. It hoards the secrets of the USA and it does this inside a range of super-computers which house the most clandestine databases in the country.

These databases are protected not by a few traps or pitfalls but by firewalls so complicated that those who constructed them and who monitor them on a daily basis were utterly convinced they were impenetrable. Then one day these guardians of the American cyber-soul stared in disbelief at the evidence before them.

They checked and checked again. It could not be. It was not possible. Finally, three of them were forced to seek an interview with the general and destroy his day. Their principal database had been hacked. In theory, the access codes were so opaque that no one without them could enter the heartland of the super-computer. No one could get through the protective device known simply as 'the air gap'. But someone had.

Worldwide, there are thousands of hacker attacks per day. The vast bulk are attempts to steal money. There are endeavours to penetrate the bank accounts of citizens who have deposited their savings where they believed they would be safe. If the 'hacks' are successful, the swindler can pretend to be the account holder and instruct the bank's computer to transfer assets to the thief's account, many miles and often many countries away.

All banks, all financial institutions, now have to encircle their clients' accounts with walls of protection, usually in the form of codes of personal identification which the hacker cannot know and without which the bank's computer will not agree to transfer a penny or a cent. This is one of the prices the developed world now pays for its utter dependence on computers. It is extremely tiresome but better than impoverishment and is now an irreversible characteristic of modern life.

Other attacks involve attempts at sabotage stemming from pure malice. A penetrated database can be instructed to cause chaos and functional breakdown. This is generally done by the insertion of a sabotage instruction called 'malware' or a Trojan horse. Again, elaborate protections in the form of firewalls have to be wrapped around the database to frustrate the hacker and keep the computerized system safe from attack.

Some databases are so secret and so vital that the safety of an entire nation depends upon them remaining safe from cyber-attack. The firewalls are so complicated that those who devise them regard them as impossible to breach. They involve not just a jumble of letters and figures but hieroglyphs and symbols which, if not in exactly the right order, will forbid entry to anyone but an officially 'cleared' operator with the precise access codes.

Such a database was at the heart of the National

Security Agency at Fort Meade, housing trillions of secrets vital to the safety of the entire USA.

Of course, its penetration was covered up. It had to be. This sort of scandal destroys careers – and that is the good news. It can topple ministers, gut departments, shiver the timbers of entire governments. But though it may have been hidden from the public, and above all from the media and those wretches of the investigative press, the Oval Office had to know . . .

As the man in the Oval Office finally comprehended the enormity of what had been done to his country he became angry – spitting angry. He issued a presidential order. *Find him. Close him down. In a supermax, somewhere far beneath the rocks of Arizona. For ever.*

There was a three-month hacker hunt. Very aware that the British equivalent of Fort Meade, known as the Government Communications Headquarters, was also of world quality and the Brits were, after all, allies, GCHQ was asked to collaborate at an early stage. The Brits created a dedicated team for that single task, headed by Dr Jeremy Hendricks, one of the best cyber-trackers they had.

Dr Hendricks was on the staff of the British National Cyber Security Centre, or NCSC, in Victoria, central London, an offshoot of the Government Communications HQ at Cheltenham. As its name implies, it specializes in hacker prevention. Like all guardians, it had to study the enemy: the hacker. That was why Sir Adrian sought the advice of Mr Ciaran Martin, the director of the NCSC.

He reluctantly and nobly permitted Sir Adrian to filch Dr Hendricks from him on what he was assured was a temporary loan.

Jeremy Hendricks, in a world where teenagers were becoming leading lights, was mature. He was over forty, slim, neat and reserved. Even his colleagues knew little about his private life, which was the way he preferred it. He was gay but made no mention of it, choosing a private life of quiet celibacy. He could thus enjoy his two passions: his computers, which were also his profession, and his tropical fish, which he bred and nurtured in tanks in his flat in Victoria, walking distance from his workplace.

He had graduated from York University with a First in computer sciences, gone on to a doctorate, then another at the Massachusetts Institute of Technology, before returning to an immediate post with GCHQ in Britain. His particular expertise was his ability to detect the most minute traces hackers often leave behind, which reveal, eventually and inadvertently, their identity. But the cyberterrorist who had penetrated the Fort Meade computer nearly defeated him. After the raid on the house in that suburb to the north of London he was one of the first allowed access, as he had played a major role in finding the source of the hack.

The trouble was, there had been so little to go on. There had been hackers before, but they were easily traced. That was before increased and improved firewalls had made penetration all but impossible.

This new hacker had left no trace. He had stolen

nothing, sabotaged nothing, destroyed nothing. He seemed to have entered, looked around and withdrawn. There was no vital IP, the Internet Protocol that serves as an identification number, a source address.

They checked all known precedents. Had any other database been penetrated in this way? They factored in some seriously clever analytical data. They began to exclude, one by one, known hacker factories across the world. Not the Russians, working out of that skyscraper on the outskirts of St Petersburg. Not the Iranians, not the Israelis, not even the North Koreans. All were active in the hacking world, but they all had their hallmarks, like the individual 'fist' of a Morse code sender.

Finally, they thought they detected a half-IP in an allied database, like a smudged thumbprint discovered by a police detective. Not enough to identify anyone but enough to 'match' if it ever occurred again. For the third month they sat back and waited. And the thumbprint occurred once more, this time in the penetrated database of a major world bank.

This penetration posed yet another enigma. Whoever had achieved it had, for the duration of his presence inside the bank's database, had at his disposal the means to transfer hundreds of millions to his own account far away, and then cause it to disappear for ever. But he had done no such thing. He had, as with Fort Meade, done nothing, wrecked nothing, stolen nothing.

To Dr Hendricks, the hacker was reminiscent of a curious child wandering through a toy store, satisfying their curiosity and then wandering back out again. But this time, unlike Fort Meade, they had left one tiny trace, which Hendricks had spotted. By this time the tracker team had given their quarry a nickname. He was elusive, so they called him 'the Fox'. Still, a match was a match.

Even foxes make mistakes. Not a lot, just now and again. What Hendricks had spotted was part of an IP, and it matched the half-print discovered in the allied database. It made a whole. They reverse-engineered the trace and, to the considerable embarrassment of the British contingent, it led to England.

For the Americans, this proved that the UK had sustained an invasion of some sort, a takeover of a building by foreign saboteurs of unimaginable skill, possibly mercenaries working for a hostile government, and very likely armed. They wanted a hard building invasion.

The British, as the guilty hacker seemed to be housed in a detached suburban home in a peaceful suburb of the provincial town of Luton, in the county of Bedfordshire, just north of London, wanted a silent, invisible, no-alarm, no-publicity attack in the dark of night. They got their way.

The Americans sent over a team of six SEALs, lodged them in the US embassy under the aegis of the Defense Attaché (himself a US Marine) and insisted that two at least go in with the SAS. And so it took place, and no neighbour suspected a thing.

There were no foreigners, no mercenaries, no gunmen. Just a fast-asleep family of four. A thoroughly bewildered chartered accountant, already identified as Mr Harold Jennings, his wife, Sue, and their two sons, Luke, aged eighteen, and Marcus, thirteen.

That was what the SAS staff sergeant had meant at three in the morning. 'You are not going to believe . . .'

Chapter Two

A LL THE CURTAINS on the ground floor were drawn.
Light would come with dawn and there were neighbours front and back. But a house with curtains still across
the windows would attract no suspicion up and down the
street. Late wakers are simply envied. The downstairs
team crouched below the window level, just in case someone chose to peer inside.

Upstairs, the captured family of four was instructed to
dress normally and wait after packing suitcases, one each.
The sun rose on a bright April day. The street began to
come alive. Two early leavers drove off. A newsagent's lad
delivered the day's papers. Three landed with a thud on
the doormat, and the teenager turned and went on down
the street.

At ten minutes to eight the family was escorted downstairs. They looked pale and shaken – most especially the
older son – but did not resist. The two Americans, still
black-masked, stared at them with enmity. These were the
agents/terrorists who had caused such damage to their

country. Surely no-release jail time awaited. The upstairs team, including the woman from SRR, came with them. They all waited silently in the sitting room, curtains still closed.

At eight a people-carrier clearly identified as a taxi drew up. Two of the SAS men had changed from black coveralls into formal dark suits with shirt and tie. They each had handguns under the left armpit. They escorted the family, with luggage, to the taxi. There was still no attempt to resist or escape. If any neighbour was interested, the family was simply going on holiday. The car drove away. Inside the house, the team relaxed. They knew they would have to wait out the hours of daylight, immobile and silent, then vaporize into the night the way they had come. The empty house, all systems switched off, would remain closed until much later.

The team leader received a short message to confirm that the arrested family was safely in custody elsewhere, and acknowledged it. He was a warrant officer, a very senior NCO and a veteran of operations inside the UK and abroad. He was in charge because the Regiment uses only NCOs for in-country ops. The officers, mockingly known as 'Ruperts', plan and supervise but do not go active inside the UK.

At ten a large van arrived. It was marked with the livery of a house-decorating company. The six men it disgorged wore white overalls. They took dustsheets and stepladders into the house. Neighbours saw it but took no real notice. The Jenningses were simply having some work done while they were on holiday.

Inside the house, the equipment was left on the floor of the hall while the men, led by Dr Hendricks, went upstairs to undertake their real task. It was to scour and gut the house of electronic equipment. They rapidly zeroed in on the attic, to discover an Aladdin's cave of computer equipment and associated devices. The loft space seemed to have been converted into a private eyrie.

Beneath the beams that sustained the roof someone had created a personal retreat. There was a desk, and tables and chairs, seemingly acquired cheaply from second-hand stores, ornaments, knick-knacks of some personal significance, but no pictures. Pride of place went to the desk, the chair that addressed it and the computer that stood on it. Dr Hendricks examined it carefully and was amazed.

He was accustomed to the finest and most complex equipment on the computer market, but this was simply ordinary. It was shop-bought, available in the out-of-town superstores owned and run by the common chains. It seemed a father had indulged a son with what he could afford. But how on earth had anyone defeated the best cyber-brains of the Western world with this kit? And which of the boys had it been?

The government scientist hoped he would have the time and opportunity to find out who had penetrated the database at Fort Meade, and to interview this computer geek – a wish Sir Adrian would soon fulfil.

It had taken no time to recognize that this was not a super-computer of the type they were used to out at GCHQ, the huge doughnut-shaped mini-city outside Cheltenham, in the county of Gloucestershire. But although shop-bought and available to anyone, what they discovered, examined and removed had been ingeniously altered and amended, presumably by the owner.

By late morning they were finished. The attic was what it had once been, a hollow shell beneath the rafters of the house. The cyber-team left with their booty. Behind still-drawn curtains the assault-team soldiers sat out of sight and whiled away the hours until 2 a.m. Then they, too, slipped into the darkness and vanished. No neighbour had seen them come, and none saw them go.

Adrian Weston had never, as a boy, intended to be a spy, let alone a spymaster. The son of a veterinary surgeon and raised in the countryside, he had lusted to become a soldier. As soon as age permitted, released from a minor public (boarding) school, he had volunteered for the army and, once accepted as 'officer material', gained entry into the Royal Military Academy at Sandhurst.

He did not get the Sword of Honour for his passing-out year but was well up the gradings and when offered the regiment of his choice selected the Parachute Regiment. He hoped it would provide more chance of combat. After two years against the IRA in Northern Ireland, he opted for a chance at university, on an army scholarship, and secured a 2:2 in history. It was after graduation that he was approached by one of the dons. A private dinner, perhaps? There were two other men present; no one else.

By the end of the melon starter he realized they were

up from London, the Secret Intelligence Service, or MI6. The history don was a spotter, a talent scout, a trawler. Weston ticked all the boxes. Good family, good school, good exams, the Paras, one of us. He entered 'the Firm' a week later. There was training and, later, assignment. During school holidays he had spent time with a German family as an exchange student and now spoke fluent and rapid German. With an intensive three-month course at the Army Language School, he had added Russian. He went to the Eastern Europe desk; it was the height of the Cold War – the Brezhnev and Andropov years. Mikhail Gorbachev and the dissolution of the USSR were still to come.

Technically, Sir Adrian was no longer on the government payroll, which had certain advantages. One of them was invisibility. Another, accorded by his retention as the Prime Minister's personal adviser on matters concerning national security, was access. His calls were taken, his advice accepted. Before his retirement he had been deputy chief of the Secret Intelligence Service at Vauxhall Cross, serving under Richard Dearlove.

When Sir Richard retired in 2004 Adrian Weston chose not to make a bid for the successorship because he did not wish to serve under Prime Minister Tony Blair. He had been disgusted by the foisting upon Parliament of what came to be known as the 'Dodgy Dossier'.

This was a document that sought to 'prove' that Saddam Hussein, brutal dictator of Iraq, possessed weapons of mass destruction and was prepared to use them so therefore his country ought to be invaded. There was, Tony

Blair assured Parliament, proof 'beyond doubt' that these weapons existed. Parliament voted to join Britain to the American invasion of March 2003. It was a disaster, leading to chaos sweeping the entire Middle East and the birth of the terror machine ISIS, still globally active fifteen years later.

To substantiate his claim, Mr Blair quoted as the source for all this the respected Secret Intelligence Service, and the claim formed the basis of the Dodgy Dossier. It was all bunkum. All the SIS had from inside Iraq were 'single source' allegations and, in the world of intel, single-source claims are never acted upon unless backed by documentary evidence of huge persuasiveness. There was none.

Nor were there any such weapons, as the subsequent invasion and occupation of Iraq proved. The source was a single lying Iraqi, code name Curveball, who fled to Germany, who also believed him. The British government, when the fiction was exposed, blamed MI6 for misinformation, though it had warned Downing Street repeatedly that the claims were highly unreliable.

Loyal to a fault, Sir Richard Dearlove remained silent, in the tradition of his service, until his retirement, and long after that. When he left, Adrian Weston chose also to retire. He did not even wish to remain as Number Two, knowing that the successorship would go to a Blair crony.

While Sir Richard moved on to become Master of Pembroke College, Cambridge, Adrian Weston took his knighthood, his 'K' from a grateful queen, and withdrew to his cottage in rural Dorset, reading, writing and occasionally visiting London, where he could always stay at the Special Forces Club in one of its small but comfortable and modestly priced guest rooms.

As a career-long Kremlinologist specializing in Moscow's iron rule of the European satellites, and with several hazardous missions behind the Iron Curtain under his belt, in 2012 he wrote a paper which came to the attention of the then-newly appointed Home Secretary in the Cameron government. Out of the blue in his rustic retirement he received a handwritten letter asking him if he would lunch with her outside the ministry in a private meeting.

Mrs Marjory Graham was new to Cabinet rank but very astute. At the Carlton Club – traditionally men-only but permitting ladies as associate members – she explained that her new remit included the Security Service, or MI5. But she wished to have access to a second opinion from a different stream of the intelligence world and had been impressed by his paper on the increasingly aggressive Russian leadership. Could she consult him on a very private basis? Three years before the raid on the house in Luton, David Cameron resigned and she became premier.

The privately circulated paper that had attracted her attention was entitled simply 'Beware the Bear'. Adrian Weston had spent a career studying the Kremlin and its successive masters. He had watched with approval the rise of Mikhail Gorbachev and the reforms he introduced, including the abolition of world Communism and the

USSR, but had regarded with dismay the pillaging of a humiliated country under the alcoholic Boris Yeltsin.

He despised the liars, cheats, thieves, rogues and thinly veiled criminals who had stripped their homeland of its assets, made themselves billionaires, and now flaunted their stolen wealth with mega-yachts and huge mansions, many of them inside Britain.

But as Yeltsin sank deeper into booze-fuelled stupor Weston noticed in his shadow a cold-eyed little former secret-police thug with a taste for homoerotic photos of himself riding bare-chested through Siberia with a rifle across his chest. His paper warned of the substitution of Communism with a new hard-right aggressiveness posing as patriotism that appeared to be infesting the Kremlin as the ex-*chekisti* replaced the drunk and it noted the close links between the Vozhd – a Russian word meaning 'the Boss' or, in the crime world, 'the Godfather' – and the professional criminal underworld.

The man who had achieved the complete mastery of Russia had started as a diehard Communist and had been privileged to join the KGB in the foreign branch, the First Chief Directorate, being posted to Dresden in East Germany. But when Communism fell he returned to his native Leningrad, renamed St Petersburg, and joined the staff of the mayor. From there he graduated to Moscow and the staff of Boris Yeltsin. Constantly at the side of the drunken giant from Siberia who took the presidency after the fall of Gorbachev, he became more and more indispensable.

As he did so, he changed. He became disillusioned with

Communism, but not with fanaticism. One simply replaced the other. He swerved to hard-right politics, masked by religiosity and devotion to the Orthodox Church and to ultrapatriotism. And he noticed something.

He saw that Russia was utterly controlled by three power bases. The first was the government, with its access to the secret police, Special Forces and armed forces. The second had come after the rape of Russia and its assets under Yeltsin: the corps of opportunists who had acquired from corrupt bureaucrats all the mineral resources of their native land at give-away prices. These were the new plutocrats, the oligarchs, instant billionaires and multimillionaires. Without money and uncountable masses of it, one could be nothing in modern Russia. The third was organized crime, known as 'thieves in law', or Vori v Zakone. These three formed an interlinked brotherhood. After a doddering Yeltsin stepped down and handed over the reins without opposition to the man at his side, the one now known as 'the Vozhd' became the master of all three, using them, rewarding them and commanding them. And, with their help, he became one of the richest men in the world.

Sir Adrian noted that those who had quarrelled with the new Vozhd appeared to have very short life-spans if they stayed in Russia, and a record of fatal accidents if they settled abroad but continued to criticize. The warning he uttered was back then prophetic and not popular in all quarters, but it seemed to have impressed Mrs Graham. Over coffee he accepted her request.

★

He arrived at the familiar black door of Number Ten, Downing Street, at five to nine. It opened before he had time to touch the ornate brass knocker. There are watchers inside. He knew the doorman who greeted him by name and was shown up the curving staircase, which was flanked by portraits of previous occupiers. At the top he was invited into a small conference room a few yards from the premier's working office. She joined him on the dot of nine, having been at work since six.

Marjory Graham did not waste time, explaining that the American ambassador was due at ten and Sir Adrian needed to be brought 'up to speed'. He already knew about the breaching of US cyber-security three months earlier but not about the recent events on his home territory. She gave him a short but thorough run-down on what had happened in a northern suburb of Luton.

'This family, where are they now? he asked.

'At Latimer.'

He was familiar with the small and picturesque village on the border of Buckinghamshire and Hertfordshire. Just outside the village limits is an old manor, taken over by the government during the Second World War as a lodgement for captured senior German officers. They had lived in genteel surroundings and chatted among themselves out of sheer boredom. Every word had been recorded and the information had proved very useful. After 1945 the manor was retained and operated as a safe house for Eastern Bloc defectors of importance and as such was run by MI5. In that world the word 'Latimer' was enough.

Sir Adrian wondered if the Director General of MI5 would be best pleased to have a problem family with no security clearance dumped upon him at short notice. He doubted it.

'How long will they be there?' he asked.

'As short a time as possible. The problem is twofold. What on earth can we do with them? And then, how shall we play it with the Americans? Let us start with the first. Reports from the house say that the residents are four and, given the set-up of the computer room in the attic and the initial impression given by the elder boy, it is likely that he is responsible. He is, let us say, mentally fragile. He seems to have withdrawn into an almost catatonic state and we shall have to have him clinically examined. Then it will be a legal question. What can we charge him with, if anything at all, with a hope of conviction? So far, we just do not know.

'But the Americans are not in a forgiving mood. If precedents are anything to go by, they will want a rapid extradition followed by a US trial and a very long custodial sentence.'

'And you, Prime Minister, what do you want?'

'I want to avoid a war with Washington, especially given the man who now sits in the Oval Office, and I want to avoid a scandal over here with the public and the media taking the side of a vulnerable teenager. What do you think? So far?'

'So far, Prime Minister, I do not know. As an eighteen-year-old, the boy is technically an adult but, given his state, it may be that we need to consult his father, or both parents. I would like to have a chance to talk to them all. And to listen to what the psychiatrist says. In the short term, we have to ask the Americans to give us a few days before going public.'

There was a knock, and a head came round the door. A personal secretary.

'The American ambassador is here, Prime Minister.'

'In the Cabinet Room. Five minutes.'

The Americans were three, all seated, and they rose as the Prime Minister and her small team of four entered. Sir Adrian came in last and sat at the back. He was there to listen, and to advise later.

Like many US ambassadors in prize posts, Wesley Carter III was not a professional career diplomat. He was a big-time Party donor to the Republicans, scion of a family owning a commercial empire in cattle feed based in Kansas. He was big, bluff, genial and steeped in old-world courtesy. He knew the real negotiations would devolve upon the two men with him. These were his number two, the minister-counsellor from the Department of State, and his legal attaché, a position always filled by a member of the FBI. Greetings and handshakes occupied several minutes. Coffee was served and the white-jacketed staff withdrew.

'Good of you to see us at such short notice, Prime Minister.'

'Oh, come now, Wesley, you know you are always

welcome here. So, the bizarre events out at Luton. Two of your own people were there. They have reported to you?'

'They have indeed, Prime Minister. And "bizarre" must surely be an example of your British understatement.' This came from the State Department man, Graydon Bennett. It was clear the two professionals would now take over. 'But the facts are still the facts. This young man has wilfully inflicted staggering damage on our database system at Fort Meade that will cost millions to repair. We believe he should be extradited without delay to face justice.'

'Very understandable,' said Mrs Graham. 'But your own legal system mirrors ours in this sense. The mental state of the accused can have a powerful effect on any case. So far, we have not had a chance to ask a psychiatrist or neurologist to meet with this teenager and assess his mental state. But your own two SEALs saw him at the house. Did they not mention that he seems – how shall I put it? – fragile?'

It was clear from the expressions across the table that the two SEALs who had spoken out of the Luton house by radio to the embassy had reported exactly that.

'And we have the question of the media, gentlemen. So far they have not latched on to what happened out there, what we discovered. We would like to keep it that way for as long as possible. When they do find out, I think we both know we will face a media storm.'

'So what are you asking, Prime Minister?' said the legal attaché, John Owen.

'Three days, gentlemen. So far, the father has not – what is the phrase? – "lawyered up". But we cannot prevent him from doing so. He has his rights. If he hires a lawyer, the story will break. Then the trench warfare cannot be prevented. We would like three days of silence.'

'Can you not keep the family in seclusion?' asked Carter.

'Not without their consent. That would make matters ten times worse in the longer term.' The Prime Minister had once been a corporate lawyer.

Due to the time zones, it was still before dawn in Washington. The embassy team agreed they would confer and consult, secure a decision on a three-day delay and inform Downing Street by sundown, UK time.

When they had gone Mrs Graham gestured to Sir Adrian to stay behind.

'Your take, Adrian?'

'There is a man, Professor Simon Baron-Cohen, out at Cambridge. Specialist in all forms of mental fragility. Probably the best in Europe, maybe the world. I think he should see the lad. And I would like to talk to the father. I have an idea. There may be a better option for all of us than simply sending the boy to a cell deep under Arizona for the rest of his life.'

'A better option? What have you in mind?'

'Not yet, Prime Minister. Could I go out to Latimer?'

'Do you have a car?'

'Not in London. I come up by train.'

The Prime Minister used the phone. There was a

Jaguar from the ministerial car pool at the door in ten minutes.

Far away by the still-frozen White Sea is the Russian city of Archangel. Nearby is the shipyard of Sevmash in Severodvinsk. It is the biggest and best equipped in Russia. That day, muffled against the cold, the work teams were putting the finishing touches to the longest and most expensive refit in Russian naval history. They were completing and preparing for sea what would become the largest and most modern battlecruiser in the world; indeed, apart from the American aircraft carriers, she would be the world's biggest surface warship. Her name was the *Admiral Nakhimov*.

Russia has only one carrier to the USA's thirteen, the clapped-out *Admiral Kuznetsov*, attached to the Northern Fleet headquartered at Murmansk. She once had four huge battlecruisers, headed by the *Peter the Great*, or *Pyotr Velikiy*.

Two of these four are no longer in commission, and the *Peter the Great* is also old and barely functional. In fact, she was waiting out in the White Sea for the work at Sevmash to be completed so that she could take her place where the *Nakhimov* had lain for ten years while her multibillion-ruble refit was completed.

That morning, as Sir Adrian motored comfortably through the burgeoning spring countryside of Hertfordshire, there was a party in the quarters of the captain of the *Admiral Nakhimov*. Toasts were raised to the ship, to her new skipper, Captain Pyotr Denisovich, and to her triumphal pending voyage from Sevmash around half the world to flagship the Russian Pacific Fleet at its HQ at Vladivostok.

The following month she would fire up her mighty nuclear twin engines and cast off to emerge into the White Sea.

Chapter Three

WHEN THE ENTIRE Jennings family was detained at three in the morning, the attitude of the parents was one of utter bewilderment but also of obedience and cooperation. Not many people are jerked awake at that hour to find their bed surrounded by men in black with submachine carbines, their faces distorted by ghoulish night-vision goggles. They were frightened and did as they were told.

With the coming of daylight and the ride out to Latimer, that mood changed to anger. The two soldiers who rode with them could not help, nor the polite but non-committal staff at the Latimer manor house. So when Sir Adrian arrived at noon on the day of the house invasion at Luton, he met the full force of the pent-up rage. He sat quietly until it had blown itself out. Finally, he said:

'You really don't know, do you?'

That had the effect of silencing Harold Jennings. His wife, Sue, sat beside him, and they both stared at the man from London.

'Know what?'

'Know what your son Luke has actually done?'

'Luke?' said Sue Jennings. 'But he's harmless. He has Asperger's syndrome. That's a form of autism. We've known for years.'

'So, while he has been sitting above your heads in the attic, you don't know what he has been doing?'

The earlier anger of the Jenningses was now replaced by a sense of foreboding. It was in their faces.

'Tapping away at his computer,' said the boy's father. 'It's about all he does.'

It was clear to Sir Adrian that there was a marital problem. Harold Jennings wanted a fit, boisterous son who dated girls, could join him for a round of golf and make him proud at the club, or play football or rugby for the county. What he had was a shy, withdrawn youth who did not function well in the real world, and was only really at home in semi-darkness staring at a screen.

Sir Adrian had not yet met Luke Jennings, but a short telephone call from the limousine to Dr Hendricks, who was still posing as a decorator while he and his team gutted the Luton house, had convinced him that the problem did indeed derive from the elder son.

Now he was beginning to understand that the blonde forty-year-old mother was hugely protective of her fragile offspring and would fight for him tooth and claw. As they spoke it became clear that this totally enclosed teenager was emotionally dependent on his mother and was only comfortable when communicating with the outside world

34

through her. Were they to be separated – as by extradition to the USA – he would be likely to disintegrate.

'Well, I'm afraid he seems to have managed the impossible, given the equipment he had at his disposal. He has broken into the heart of the American national security system, causing many millions of dollars' worth of damage and frightening the living daylights out of all of us.'

The parents stared back at him open-mouthed. Then Mr Jennings put his face in his hands and said, 'Oh God.'

He was a fifty-three-year-old chartered accountant in a private practice with two partners, making a good if not spectacular living and enjoying his weekend golf with his mates. He clearly did not understand what he had done to deserve such a fragile son, who had enraged his country's principal ally and could be facing extradition and jail. His wife exploded.

'He can't have done! He's never even left the country. He's hardly left Luton, or barely the house, apart from to go to school. He has a terror of being moved from the only place he knows. His home.'

'He did not have to,' said Adrian Weston. 'The world of cyberspace is global. It looks as if the Americans, in their present mood, which is not a happy one, will demand that we extradite him to the States for a trial. That would presume jail time for many years.'

'You can't do that.' Mrs Jennings was close to hysteria. 'He would not survive. He would take his own life.'

'We'll fight it,' said the father. 'I'll get the best lawyer at the London Bar. I'll fight it through every court in the country.'

'I'm sure you will,' said Sir Adrian. 'And you will probably win, but at enormous cost. Your house, your pension, your life savings – all gone in legal fees.'

'It doesn't matter,' snapped Sue Jennings. 'You cannot take my child away and kill him – and that is what it would amount to, a death sentence. We'll fight you up to the Supreme Court.'

'Mrs Jennings, please understand I am not the enemy. There may be a way to prevent all this. But I will need your help. If I do not get it, then I will fail.'

He explained to the Jenningses the legal position, which he had just learned in the back of the Jaguar. Until only a few years earlier, computer hacking had not even been on the statute book as a crime in Britain.

Then the law had changed. A hacking case had arisen that caused Parliament to act. Hacking was now an offence in law, but with a maximum penalty of four years and, in the case of a vulnerable defendant with a good lawyer and a humane judge, probably no jail time at all. The American penalties were far harsher.

Extradition might therefore not succeed – there had already been two cases where extradition had been refused, to the great chagrin of the USA. In addition, massive publicity could not be avoided. The national mood would become emotional. A crowd-funding appeal mounted by a daily newspaper could well cover the legal bills, despite the scare he had implanted in Harold Jennings.

But it would mean two years of trench warfare with the US government, and precisely at a time when international trade, the fight against terrorism, the departure from the European Union and the ever-rising aggressiveness of Russia meant that a united Anglo-American front was crucial.

The Jenningses listened in silence. Eventually, Harold Jennings asked:

'What do you want?'

'It is more what I need. And that is a bit of time. So far, the damage perpetrated on the American cyber-systems has not reached the press. But the USA has a ferocious investigative media. They will not remain in the dark for long. If the story breaks, it will be enormous. Even over here, the media frenzy will mean your family is hounded night and day, making your life a misery. We may be able to avoid all of that. I need a week. Maybe less. Can you give me that?'

'But how?' asked Harold Jennings 'People will notice that we seem to have disappeared from our home.'

'As far as your neighbours in Luton are concerned, the Jennings family has gone on a brief holiday. Mr Jennings, could you contact your partners and explain that a family problem has caused your departure at very short notice?'

Harold Jennings nodded.

'Mrs Jennings, the Easter school holidays begin on Monday. Could you contact the school and explain that Luke has been taken ill and that he and Marcus will be starting their holidays a few days early?'

Another nod.

'And now, may I please meet Luke?'

Sir Adrian was led to another room, where both the Jennings boys were engrossed in games on their smartphones, which they had somehow been allowed to keep and bring with them.

If Sir Adrian had expected a highly impressive figure of the youth referred to as a cyber-criminal or a computer geek, he was to be disappointed. And yet he was not. It was the very ordinariness of the boy that impressed.

He was tall, rake-thin and gangling with an untidy mop of blond curls over a pale, sun-deprived face. His manner was of extreme shyness, as of one withdrawn inside himself looking out at a presumably hostile world. The security adviser found it hard to believe that Luke Jennings had really done what he was accused of doing.

And yet, according to initial evaluations by the top experts from GCHQ, Luke could do things and go places in cyberspace that had never been managed before. In their judgement, he was either the most talented or the most dangerous teenager in the world . . . or maybe both.

Luke sat hunched over his smartphone, totally absorbed in another world. His mother embraced him and murmured in his ear. The lad broke his concentration and stared at Sir Adrian. He appeared in part terrified, in part truculent.

He clearly found it hard to make eye contact with strangers or even to talk to them, and it became obvious that light conversation and small talk were beyond him. From his research during the drive from Downing Street to Latimer, Sir Adrian had learned it was a symptom of Asperger's syndrome to be possessed of fanatical neatness, an obsession that everything must be in its exact and accustomed place, never moved, never disturbed. In the course of the previous day, everything had been dislocated and, therefore, in Luke's perception, wrecked. The boy was in trauma.

After Sir Adrian had initiated the conversation, Luke's mother intervened frequently to explain what her son meant, and to prompt Luke to answer questions. But the boy was interested in just one thing.

It was only at this point that he looked up and Sir Adrian noticed his eyes. They were of different colours, the left eye light hazel brown and the right one pale blue. He recalled having been told the same about the late singer David Bowie.

'I want my computer back,' he said.

'Luke, if I get you your computer back, you have to make me a promise. You will not use it to try to hack any American computer system. Not one. Will you give me your promise?'

'But their systems are flawed,' said Luke. 'I have tried to point that out to them.'

It was part and parcel. The youth had been trying to be helpful. He had discovered something out there in cyberspace that, in his mind, was simply not right. Something that was less than perfect. So he had gone to the heart of it to expose the flaws. The 'it' was the National Security Agency database at Fort Meade, Maryland. He genuinely had no idea how much damage he had caused – both to cyber-systems and certain egos.

'I have to have your promise, Luke.'

'All right, I promise. When can I have it?'

'I'll see what I can do.'

He borrowed an office, shut the door and contacted Dr Hendricks. The guru from GCHQ had now left Luton. Having gutted the attic under the rafters with his team, Hendricks now had Luke Jennings's personal computer in front of him back at the National Cyber Security Centre in Victoria, London. He was hesitant about doing what Weston asked because he needed to examine the PC and its contents in minute detail before he could make his report. Eventually, he said:

'All right. I'll download everything on it to another machine and send it—'

'No, hang on there. I'll send a car to collect it.'

Sir Adrian's next call was to the Prime Minister. She was on the front bench in the House of Commons. Her Parliamentary Private Secretary whispered in her ear. When she could get away, she withdrew to her House of Commons office and called Sir Adrian back. He made his request. She listened carefully and posed a couple of questions. Finally, she said:

'It is very short notice. He may not agree. But I'll try. Stay at Latimer. I'll call you back.'

It was late afternoon in London, almost noon in Washington. The man she wanted was on the golf course, but he took her call. To her surprise, he agreed to her request. She had an aide ring Sir Adrian back.

'If you drive to Northolt, Sir Adrian, I believe the RAF will try to help. As soon as they can. The request is in.'

Technically, Northolt is still a Royal Air Force base on the north-western outskirts of London, just inside the M25 orbital motorway, but it has long shared its functions with the private sector as a host to the executive jets of the rich and privileged.

Sir Adrian spent six hours in the departure lounge availing himself of the café for a very delayed lunch and the news-stand for an array of papers to read. At midnight, a young RAF man summoned him to one of the departure gates. Outside on the pan his flight was being refuelled for the transatlantic crossing. It was a BAe125 twin-jet executive airplane which could make Andrews Air Force Base outside Washington in eight hours against the headwinds, but gaining five on the time zones.

After half a lifetime of grabbing sleep where and when he could, Adrian Weston accepted a sandwich and a glass of moderate red wine from the steward, tilted back his seat and fell asleep as the jet cleared the Irish coast.

They landed at Andrews Air Force Base at just after four in the morning. Sir Adrian thanked the steward who had served him breakfast and the crew who had flown him. The squadron leader in the left-hand seat assured him that their instructions were to wait until whatever he had come to do was done, then bring him back home.

There were more hours to wait in the arrivals reception area for his transport. Because his entire journey was off the books, the British embassy was not involved. The White House sent an unmarked Crown Victoria with a young West Wing staffer beside the driver. There were no passport formalities, though he always carried his with him.

The journey took an extra hour, but much of that was spent crawling in the commuter stream to cross the Potomac into downtown DC. The driver knew his trade. He had been told to minimize any chance of a stray pressman with a camera spotting the car and its passenger so he came into the White House grounds from the back.

The limo came up Constitution Avenue and right into 17th Street, then right again on State Drive within the lee of the Eisenhower Executive Office Building. Here four steel pillars jutting up from the roadway withdrew into the tarmac as the escorting officer flashed his identity at the gatehouse, and they were in the short drive called West Exec that runs straight to the West Wing, where the President lives and works.

At the awning that marked the access to the West Wing from the lower level, the car stopped and Sir Adrian descended. A new escort took over, leading him inside. They turned left and up the stairs that brought them to the door of the National Security Adviser's office. No journalists can roam freely up here.

He was led down another walkway to a reception area with two desks where his briefcase was passed through a scanner. He knew hidden cameras had already done a body-search, as at an airport. At the rear of the area was one last door – to the Oval itself. One of those at the desks went and tapped on it, listened, opened it and gestured Sir Adrian inside. Then he came back and closed it.

There were four in there, all seated, and a spare chair facing the desk of the President of the United States, universally known in the building as the POTUS but, to his face, always Mr President.

One of the seated men was the Chief of Staff, another the Defense Secretary and the third the Attorney General. The POTUS sat ahead of him, facing the door, glowering behind the *Resolute* desk, the ornate carved-oak bureau cut from the timbers of the British warship HMS *Resolute* and presented by Queen Victoria to another president over a hundred years ago. Close to his right hand was a red button, not to summon a nuclear war but a succession of Diet Cokes.

The Chief of Staff made the unnecessary introductions. All the faces but that of Sir Adrian were well known via many camera lenses. The atmosphere was courteous but hardly convivial.

'Mr President, I bring you the warmest regards of the British Prime Minister and our thanks to you for agreeing to see me at such short notice.'

The big coiffed blond head nodded in gruff acknowledgement.

'Sir Adrian, please understand it is only out of regard for my friend Marjory Graham that I have agreed to this. It seems one of your fellow countrymen has done us enormous damage and we believe he should face justice over here.'

Sir Adrian was convinced that squirming would do no good. He simply said:

'Broken glass, Mr President.'

'Broken what?'

'This young cyber-genius, about whose existence we had not the faintest idea, has broken into a major US database like a burglar, smashing glass to get in. But once inside he looked but then left alone. He seems to have destroyed nothing, sabotaged nothing and, above all, stolen nothing. This is not another Edward Snowden. He has offered absolutely nothing to our countries' enemies.'

At the mention of the name Snowden the four Americans stiffened. They recalled too well that Edward Snowden, an American working for the state, had stolen over a million classified documents in the form of a memory stick and flown to Moscow, where he was now residing.

'He still did a huge amount of damage,' snapped the Attorney General.

'He did what was thought to be utterly impossible. But it was not. So, what if a diehard enemy had done it? Broken glass, gentlemen. We have glaziers. We can mend. But all your secrets are still there. I repeat: he stole nothing, took nothing away. Surely the fires of hell are for traitors?'

'So you have flown across the Atlantic to ask us to repair all the damage he caused and to be merciful, Sir Adrian?' said the President.

'No, sir. I have crossed the Pond for two reasons. The first is to make a suggestion.'

'Which is?'

In answer, Sir Adrian drew a slip of paper from his breast pocket, crossed the carpet between himself and the *Resolute* desk and placed it in front of the leader of the Western world. Then he resumed his seat. They all watched the blond head lean forward to study the sheet of paper. The POTUS took his time. Then he straightened and stared at the British emissary. He held out the sheet to the Attorney General, who was closest to him. In sequence, all three other men read it.

'Would it work?' asked the POTUS.

'Like so much in life, Mr President, we'll never know if we don't try.'

'You mentioned two purposes to your visit,' said the Defense Secretary. 'What was the second?'

'To try and cut a deal. I think we have all read *The Art of the Deal*.'

He was referring to the President's own book about the realities of business. The POTUS beamed. He could not get too much praise for what he regarded as his masterpiece.

'What deal?' he asked.

'If we are allowed to go ahead with this' – Sir Adrian gestured at his sheet of paper – 'we will put him on the payroll. He signs the Official Secrets Act. We keep him in a sealed environment. Supervise his activities. And if it works, if there is an intel harvest, you share the product. All of it.'

The Secretary of Defense interjected. 'Mr President, we have not a shred of proof that this could ever work.'

There was a deep silence. Then the big blond head rose and turned to the Attorney General.

'John, I'm going to go with it. Deep-six the extradition request. Not necessarily for ever. But we'll give this a try.'

Two hours later Sir Adrian was back at Andrews. The return journey from there was easier, with following westerly winds. His car was waiting at Northolt. He phoned the Prime Minister from the back seat. It was nearly midnight and she was about to turn in, her bedside alarm set for 5 a.m.

But she was sufficiently awake to give him the permissions he needed. And far away, close to Archangel, the sea ice was beginning to splinter.

Chapter Four

I N THE AFTERMATH of that visit to Washington things
went well. From the press point of view, the story died
because it had never existed, leaving those on the inside to
continue repairing the damage at Fort Meade, installing a
newer and better defensive system, while consideration in
Britain was given to what the future held for the deeply
troubled boy now known as the Fox.

In Washington, the US kept her word and the request
for extradition was quietly dropped, which made no rip-
ples on the water because it had never been announced.
But there was one downside.

Working inside the Justice Department was a Russian
agent, a low-level sleeper. It was a woman, one hundred
per cent American but prepared to betray her country, like
the long-imprisoned Aldrich Ames, for money.

She noted the rescinding of the request to the British
government for the extradition of a British youth for data-
hacking and wrote a short report for her employers. She
gave it no priority, but systems are systems and greed is

greed. So she passed it on to her handler inside the Russian embassy, who passed it back to Moscow and thus to the Foreign Intelligence Service of the Russian Federation, or SVR. There it was simply filed.

Sir Adrian had his second conference with Mrs Graham, who was much relieved that there would be no long war in the courts with the USA and agreed with the latter part of his idea. This would involve Sir Adrian moving from Dorset to London at least for the duration. He was allocated a small grace-and-favour flat not far from Admiralty Arch and a workaday saloon car with a driver on twenty-four-hour call.

It had been years since Adrian Weston had lived in London, and he had become accustomed to the peace, the quiet, the solitude of his Dorset country life. It had been a long time since he had run an operation and, back then, it had been against the old USSR and, covering the whole Soviet empire and the Eastern European satellite states, his enemy, the KGB.

Then came Gorbachev and the end of the USSR, but not of the Russian Federation and certainly not of the Kremlin. Until his retirement, the SIS Division, which he had finally commanded as Deputy Chief, had kept an eagle eye on the sprawling land east of Poland, Hungary and Slovakia.

He knew the KGB had been split up under Gorbachev but did not fool himself it had ceased to exist. The Second Chief Directorate, the internal secret police, had become the FSB, but his career opponent had been the First Chief Directorate, targeted at the West. This had become the

SVR, still based at Yazenevo, south-west of Moscow city, and he knew who now ran it.

Even during his decade in the peace of Dorset he had maintained his comprehensive list of contacts throughout the British establishment. After Downing Street he had his driver take him across the West End to the Special Forces Club and from there called a good neighbour who agreed to rent a van with a driver and clear out those items from his cottage that he would need in his government flat behind Admiralty Arch. The lady in Dorset would send two large trunks with enough possessions to turn a functional but heartless apartment into a kind of home and she would look after his dog while he was away.

Above all, he would need his family photographs. He would, as each night before turning into sleep, gaze at the face of his late wife, five years gone to leukaemia, whom he still grieved. Staring at the departed face of that calm, wise woman, he would recall the day she had met a traumatized young Para officer back from Northern Ireland and determined within an hour to marry him and make him whole again. Which she had done.

In a ritual no one else would ever see, he would tell her about his day, as he used to do for forty years, until the cancer took her. Beside her he would put the picture of their son, the only one the God she worshipped had allowed her. He was a naval commander on a cruiser in the Far East. With his treasures around him, Weston could again present the world with the steel-tough spymaster.

★

His first visit was to Latimer, to see the Jennings family, who chafed in their detention.

Harold and Sue Jennings had done as they had been asked. They had telephoned their friends and colleagues at Luton to explain that their son Luke had been taken unwell and that they had removed the whole family for a spring break at a rented cottage on the coast of faraway Cornwall. After that they took no phone calls, letting each of two or three further enquiries go to voicemail and stay there.

Marcus, the younger boy, had discovered sets of bows and arrows in a storeroom, with a target, and practised archery on the front lawn, tutored by the gardener, who was an adept. Harold read the papers, which were delivered daily, did numerous crosswords and raided the manor's copious library, puzzled that much of it was in German or Russian, the tastes of earlier of Her Majesty's guests.

Luke was in a miserable state, pining for his room in the attic at Luton and all his old familiar surroundings. The centre of his existence was his returned computer. He had traced every single online file and restored them all to the way they had been, the way he wanted them, the way they had to be. His mother comforted him continuously, promising that soon he would have a room of his own, if not the one at Luton, then certainly an exact replica.

Dr Jeremy Hendricks had visited from the NCSC in Victoria, so that Luke could explain step by step how he had avoided all the firewalls and supposedly impenetrable access codes to infiltrate the NSA database at Fort Meade. He was still there when Sir Adrian arrived, so he was able to explain in layman's language some of the complexities of the only world in which it seemed the boy could exist and which was a closed galaxy to the vast majority of the human race. Also Professor Simon Baron-Cohen had kindly visited from Cambridge for a four-hour seminar with Luke. He was now back at the university preparing a copious report on both Asperger's syndrome in general and on how it affected Luke Jennings in particular.

The whole family had been relieved to learn that there would be no attempt to extradite the elder son to face jail time in the USA. But Sir Adrian was adamant that the Jenningses' part of their bargain was unfulfilled. Further senior staff from GCHQ would visit to enrol Luke, who was in law fully adult, as a member of their staff to be directed as they saw fit.

What none of them knew was that they were crucial ingredients in the contents of the slip of paper that Adrian Weston had slipped to the President of the USA the previous day; the execution of his plan, now endorsed by two heads of government.

He named it Operation Troy in tribute to Homer, who in his classic *Iliad* had described the ancient Greek deception of the wooden horse. He had in mind to create the greatest deception in the history of the cyber-world. But it all depended on the unusual brain of a diffident British teenager, the like of which had never been seen before.

It had become obvious within ten minutes that if Operation Troy were ever to succeed, it would be Sue Jennings, not the ineffectual father, whom Weston had to win over. She would have to accept Luke's enrolment into the service of GCHQ. And she would also have to be engaged in a technical role, since without her constant reassurances her fragile son did not seem able to function in the adult world. Clearly, she was a more forceful character, the one who had taken charge of the family and held it together, one of those calm but fiercely determined women who are the salt of the earth.

Weston knew from the briefing notes handed to him by one of the Prime Minister's staffers in Downing Street that she had been educated at Luton Grammar School, the daughter of a local printer and his wife. In her teens she had met and married her husband, who was then at accountancy college. So far, so banal. She was twenty-two when their first son was born.

She did not look forty, apparently spending time in the gym and during the summer at the local tennis club. Once again, so far so ordinary. There was nothing about the Jennings family to attract a flicker of interest, except the pathologically shy, withdrawn boy of eighteen who sat in a corner while his parents negotiated with this man from London. He, it seemed, despite or perhaps because of his difficulties, was a computer genius.

Sir Adrian tried to engage the youth in the adult conversation, but it proved fruitless. Luke could not, or would not, connect with him on a personal level. At all attempts, his mother answered for him, the tigress protecting her cub. Sir Adrian had no experience of Asperger's syndrome but the briefing notes that had been rapidly put together during the morning of the family's detention indicated that there were various levels of severity. A phone call from Professor Baron-Cohen had just confirmed that Luke was a severe case.

Periodically, if Sue Jennings sensed that her son was becoming distressed when the adults discussed something he had done but did not know he had done, she would wrap a comforting arm around his shoulders and whisper reassurances into his ear. Only then would he calm down.

The next stage was to find a place for that young man and his family to live and work in a safe but closed environment. Back in Whitehall, Weston began the search among hundreds of government-owned establishments. For two more days he researched and travelled. He hardly slept. Apart from snacks, he hardly ate. He had not been under such pressure since, back in the Cold War, with his fluent Russian and flawless German, he had flitted through the Iron Curtain as the deranged Yuri Andropov had almost brought the world to nuclear war. After three days he believed he had found the place.

Stopping passers-by on any British street, the number discovered who had ever even heard of Chandler's Court would have been about zero. It was a very clandestine place indeed.

In the First World War its owner had been a cloth manufacturer who had obtained a contract to supply khaki serge uniforms to the British Army. That was when it was confidently expected the war would be over by Christmas 1914. As the slaughter mounted, the contracts for more uniforms became bigger and bigger. The manufacturer got very rich indeed and, in 1918, as a multimillionaire, he purchased the seventeenth-century manor house set in a forest in Warwickshire.

During the Great Depression, when the queues of unemployed snaked for miles, he created work by having teams of workless bricklayers and labourers build an eight-foot wall to surround the entire 200 acres. Dubbed a war profiteer, he was not a popular figure, and he wanted and needed his privacy. With his wall and just two guarded gates, he got it.

When he died in the early fifties, having neither widow nor offspring, he gifted Chandler's Court to the nation. It became a retirement home for badly wounded ex-soldiers. Then it was abandoned. In the late eighties it achieved a new use. It was converted into a research laboratory, shrouded in secrecy and banned to the public because it delved into some of the most fearsome toxins known to man.

Much more recently, after the poisoning with Novichok of the former Soviet spy Colonel Sergei Skripal and his daughter, Yulia, it was Chandler's Court rather than the much better known Porton Down that came up with the antidote that saved their lives. For obvious reasons, the credit in the media went to Porton Down.

The sprawling manor at Chandler's Court had been allowed to stand idle, maintained but not inhabited. The research laboratories were scattered through the wood-land, as were the comfortable modern apartment blocks where the junior staff lived. Only senior scientists lived off site. There were two gates in the wall, one for commercial deliveries and the main gate for personnel. Both were manned and guarded.

Within a week, teams of artisans and decorators arrived to work on shifts spread throughout the twenty-four-hour day to restore the manor to human habitation. The Jennings family was shown around and, just over three weeks after the White House meeting, moved in. Dr Hendricks had agreed that the huge mini-city of GCHQ Cheltenham would not be right for Operation Troy. Too big, too con-fusing; for Luke Jennings, too intimidating and too populated. He and a team of two would also transfer to Chandler's Court to monitor the programmes and mentor the juvenile genius at the centre of it.

There was one flaw, and Sir Adrian had attended a tense family parting at Latimer the day before the Jenningses left for Chandler's Court. For a decade, the marriage had been on the rocks. The parents had tried to shelter their sons from the breakdown of the relationship between them, but it had become harder and harder, up till the point of impos-sibility. In short, they wished to part.

It had been decided that, at Chandler's Court, Luke would live and work on assignments issued by GCHQ. His mother would live with him and assist in his dealings with others. The younger brother, Marcus, could attend any of two or three excellent local schools within easy driving

FREDERICK FORSYTH

distance. Harold Jennings did not wish to live there and, with the marriage at an end, did not even wish to return to Luton to resume work at his old accountancy practice.

What he really wanted had surprised Sir Adrian. He wished to emigrate to the USA and become a citizen of New York. It was a dream he had nurtured for years, since attending a conference there.

Sir Adrian had mentioned that he had friendly contacts in the USA and might be able to help by arranging some official assistance in fast-tracking the bureaucracy and formalities of residence and work permits.

With great speed, it was done. Harold Jennings had left his Luton practice and resigned from his golf club. The house was put in the hands of a local estate agent. In New York, he had a post with a British finance company just off Wall Street with a good salary. After a period in a hotel he would acquire a comfortable apartment and start his new life.

And now came the parting. It would have appeared unusual to a stranger inasmuch as it was so unemotional, as indeed was Harold Jennings. Had he had feelings and been prepared to show them, he might have saved his marriage years earlier. But it seemed the man's spirit was as dry and lifeless as the accounts and figures that he had spent his career poring over.

He forced himself to embrace his two sons and, finally, his wife, but awkwardly, as if they were acquaintances at a cocktail party. His sons had caught the mood many times before and responded in kind.

Marcus, the younger boy, said, 'Goodbye, Dad, and good luck in America,' which evoked a panicky smile from his father and an assurance of 'I'll be fine.' The lack of warmth in the embrace of the parents indicated why the soldiers a month earlier had found separate beds for the parents on the first floor of the Luton house.

There was a cab waiting in the forecourt of the manor. He left his family in the hallway, went outside and was gone to the airport.

Sir Adrian, hearing this later that evening, presumed that this was the last he would hear of Harold Jennings. He was wrong.

The following morning Sue Jennings and her sons moved into a spacious suite on the first floor of the manor at Chandler's Court. It still smelt of fresh paint, but the weather was mild for the beginning of May and, with the windows open, the odour soon evaporated.

In the south wing, Dr Hendricks, who was single and lived alone, installed himself and supervised the completion of the computer room, the heart of Operation Troy. All the equipment came from GCHQ at Cheltenham, and it was the best. Two other mentors installed themselves in apartment blocks in the forest from which they could easily walk to work inside the manor. Marcus Jennings was enrolled at a very good school just four miles from Chandler's Court.

Luke Jennings had a room of his own and contentedly began to convert it into an exact replica of the room he once had under the roof at Luton. Because of his mindset, every single detail had to be one he was accustomed to. A furniture van brought the contents of the Luton room to Warwickshire so that every chair and table, book and ornament could be placed precisely where it had to be. Luke even objected to the clock, because it ticked. He wanted a silent clock. He got one.

And his mood brightened. The stress and the consequent tantrums and tears of the weeks since the night raid abated. With his personal space restored and his computer in front of him, just as it ought to be, he could resume his preferred life. He could sit in half-darkness, wander through cyberspace and look at things.

In the far north of Russia, the final hawser cables were thrown down to the quay and the mighty *Admiral Nakhimov* eased her way out of Sevmash yard to the waiting sea. From their elevated viewpoint on the bridge, Captain Denisovich and his officers could see the distant spires of the nearby port of Archangel as the prow of the world's most fearsome surface warship turned to the north. Behind her, Severodvinsk dropped away. The captain and officer corps were beaming with pleasure and pride.

They were gazing down from the bridge at the pride of the Orlan-class battlecruisers, the biggest non-carrier warship in the world, a floating fortress of steel and missile power. The *Nakhimov* was 827 feet long, almost 100 feet wide and displacing 24,300 tons, with a crew of over 700 mariners.

These Russian cruisers are armed-to-the-teeth mobile platforms capable of taking on any enemy warship in the world. As she steamed out of Sevmash yard, the *Nakhimov* was the most ultra-modern of her class, her every function fully computerized with touch-screen technology.

Below the water her echo sounders would find the hundred-fathom line and guide her along that line so that she never ventured nearer to the shore unless so bidden. Every detail would be reported to the bridge on one of the high-tech controls that governed her. And there was more.

Many years ago, a novel was published in the West called *The Hunt for Red October*. It was the debut novel of Tom Clancy and proved very popular. It told the story of a Soviet naval captain who defected to the West, taking his nuclear-missile submarine with him. It was immediately banned in the USSR and read only by a core of very senior men, for whom its plot was an abiding disaster.

In the Soviet Union, defections, especially of high-ranking officials, intelligence or military officers, were a nightmare, and the thought of one disappearing to the West with a large piece of ultra-modern equipment was beyond even that. Clancy's novel was taken extremely seriously through the Soviet Navy and up to the Politburo.

Now, it was not merely unthinkable but immediately preventable. Every function in the *Nakhimov* was computerized, and every function could be duplicated in the master database in the Northern Fleet headquarters at Murmansk. Thus, at a stroke, Murmansk could override the computers on board the *Nakhimov* and take back complete control. That put paid to treachery.

As for malfunction or interference, these too were out of feasibility. Her steerage system was not the more common US-designed Global Positioning System, or GPS, well known to every satnav user on the roads, but the Soviet-designed GLONASS-K2 system, inherited by the post-Soviet Russian state. It was owned and operated by the military.

GLONASS will define a Russian naval ship's position to ten to twenty yards anywhere in the world. It relies on twenty-four satellites spinning in inner space. Any hacker seeking to disrupt the system would have to suborn five separate satellites simultaneously, which is clearly impossible.

The course of the *Nakhimov* was pre-ordained. She would cruise out of the White Sea and north to the Barents Sea, then north-west. With Norway's North Cape to port, she would turn again, easing out of the Barents Sea into the North Atlantic, then south down the length of Norway. There would always be a helmsman at the controls, but he would not be needed. The computers would keep her on the hundred-fathom line and perfectly on course. For five days, that was exactly what she did.

The ice and bitter cold of the White Sea and North Cape receded and the sun shone through. Between duties, her seamen strolled the decks and took in the bracing air. To port, the mountains surrounding the Tromsø Fjords, where, in 1944, the RAF finally sank the mighty *Tirpitz*, came and went in the mist. The Lofoten Islands slipped away.

At this point, the *Nakhimov* could have turned west, deeper into the North Atlantic, to skirt the British Isles to the east as she ploughed south to round the Cape of Good Hope and headed for the Orient. But her orders had been decided weeks earlier in Moscow, by the Vozhd himself.

She would continue south into the North Sea with Denmark to port and Scotland to starboard until she left the North Sea behind and entered the busiest shipping lane in the world: the English Channel. Staring out from his office above the Alexandrovsky Garden below the west-facing wall of the Kremlin, the Vozhd had made his wishes very plain to the commanding admiral of the Northern Fleet.

As scores of vessels scattered to get out of her way, the *Admiral Nakhimov* would cruise down the Channel and through the pinch-point of the Strait of Dover. Let the blasted British sit at their picture windows in Ramsgate, Margate, Dover and Folkestone and gaze at the might of the new Russia cruising past them, towering over them and their puny navy escorting the mighty *Nakhimov* south.

On day eight after the departure from Sevmash the sailors on the *Nakhimov* were staring at the sea foaming past them. Far to port, Denmark had blended into Germany and Germany into the Netherlands. Also out of sight and to starboard, the flat fens of Lincolnshire were hidden behind their banks of mist.

In a small apartment behind Admiralty Arch a phone rang. Sir Adrian picked it up. It was a breathless Dr Hendricks on the line.

'For the second time this year, I do not believe what I am seeing,' he said. 'He's done it. It can't be done, but the boy has done it. We are in. Inside GLONASS-K2. Five satellites. And here is the really weird thing. They have not even noticed the entry.'

'Well done, Doctor. Hold position, if you please. Stay within feet of the phone until further notice. Night and day.'

When he had finished the phone call, Sir Adrian dialled again. The Royal Navy HQ beneath the suburb of Northwood in north-west London. They had been forewarned.

'Yes, Sir Adrian.'

'I am coming out to visit you. Tomorrow may be a busy day.'

Heading, as she was, to become the flagship of the Russian Pacific Fleet, the *Admiral Nakhimov* could easily have skirted the British Isles by keeping to the west of Ireland in deep, clear water and out of sight of land. But the Vozhd had clearly made a deliberate decision to insult the British by driving her straight down the North Sea and through the Strait of Dover, at twenty-two miles wide one of the most overcrowded sea passages in the world.

With two streams of marine traffic, one heading north and the other south, the Dover Strait is governed by strict rules to prevent collisions. As predicted, at her size, the *Nakhimov* could make it only by driving right down the centre. Russian warships had done this before as a deliberate provocation by Moscow to the United Kingdom.

The Admiralty did not need to be told where the *Nakhimov* was. There were two frigates escorting her and a relay of observer drones out of RAF Waddington over-head. She was off the coast of Norfolk but slowing to let the night pass before she went through the Strait of Dover. The shoals of the Dogger Bank were behind her in the North Sea. Her echo sounders told her she still had over a hundred feet of clear water beneath her keel. Her course predicted that she would never have less than eighty feet.

At dawn she was opposite Felixstowe in Suffolk and she increased her power to optimum cruise. The Channel was narrowing, with Belgium coming into view to port. The radio waves were alive with the chatter of merchant-men in this traffic jam of a Channel as the Russian mastodon broke all the rules.

Ahead lay the narrowest part – the Strait of Dover – and she tucked close to the Essex and Kentish shore on the Goodwin Sands. Wise mariners avoid the Goodwins like the plague. They are so terribly shallow. But the com-puters were adamant. The *Nakhimov* would ease past them with plenty of sea room towards the French shore.

Chapter Five

IT WAS A beautiful spring dawn. The sun rose to shine from a cloudless blue sky. The early risers of the coastal towns and villages of north-east Kent were up and walking the seashore with their dogs, binoculars and cameras. Out of the north the vast grey shape of the battlecruiser slid through the Strait of Dover. Via fully automated visual media, the world was watching.

In the pretty waterside town of Deal, separated from the just-invisible Goodwin Sands by a small lagoon of navigable water where local fishermen take blue mussels and peeler crabs, breakfasting citizens sat at their sea-facing windows, unaware of the hulking monster cruising towards them.

On the bridge, Captain Denisovich and his officers stood behind their consoles and looked down at the smaller vessels scattering before them. Far away in Moscow, the Vozhd also watched on a huge screen a live feed from an aeroplane chartered by RT (formerly Russia Today), the state-funded television network, which was circling the Kentish coast.

As the *Nakhimov* began to inch to the right, the helmsman corrected her course immediately. She continued to
slip towards starboard.

Staring straight forward over the prow, the officers and
crew could see the painted cottages of Deal. Below them in
the engine room the revs of the nuclear-powered turbines
began to increase. The chief engineer presumed the order
had come from the bridge.

'Five degrees port!' snapped Captain Denisovich to the
helmsman, but the helmsman was already tapping the
screen to make the correction. The prow swung through
Deal and the ship's pace increased. The *Nakhimov* simply
refused to obey the command. The navigation officer
shouldered the helmsman aside and took over. He ham-
mered in the necessary corrections. Nothing happened.

To the north, in Murmansk, the admiral commanding
the Northern Fleet gazed in disbelief at his wall-sized TV
screen.

'Take back command!' he shouted. At his side, the fingers of a technician flew across his console. If the controls
of the *Nakhimov* were malfunctioning, then Murmansk
would retake command and bring her back to her pre-
destined course. Russian technology would not fail.

In Northwood, a young Royal Navy officer stared at
his screen as his fingertips gave the Russian warship her
new orders. Beads of sweat ran down his face. Behind
him, four admirals gaped at the TV screen. One of them
murmured, 'Bloody hell.'

In Moscow, the cold-eyed little man who controlled

the biggest country in the world did not yet realize something had gone wrong. He was not a mariner. The bright façades of the cottages of Deal should not be straight ahead of the prow. They should be well to the right. There should be miles of clear, sparkling seawater ahead.

At low tide, the soft, clinging sands of Goodwin are just visible as the Channel washes over them. At high tide, those sands are ten feet below the surface. The *Admiral Nakhimov* drew thirty-two feet. At 0900 hours GMT, the nuclear engines of the *Admiral Nakhimov* drove her 827 feet and 24,300 tons at warp speed on to the Goodwin Sands in front of the eyes of the world.

Far below the stern the huge twin propellers drove her forward as the prow rose in the air. In the engine room the controls were set at full astern, but that command did not reach the drive shafts. It was at that point that the man in the Kremlin realized something had gone very wrong indeed. He began, alone in his private office, to scream with rage.

As the *Nakhimov* finally came to a complete halt, command and control were restored to the onboard systems. Everything functioned perfectly. The engines went into full astern mode and the propellers responded, slowing to motionless and then starting to turn in the reverse direction. There are no rocks in the Goodwins, and the sand is soft, but it clings. The front half of the battlecruiser was deeply embedded, and she would not move. After half an hour of vain effort Captain Denisovich closed her down.

★

Hundreds of millions of watchers across the world stared in amazement. Those to the west awoke, turned on their TVs and saw the image of the motionless *Admiral Nakhimov* fill the screen. Those to the east left their desks as the word spread and crowded round their televisions amid an excited buzz of comment. No one could understand it. But it had just happened.

In Russia the start of the inquiry occurred within minutes. Streams of queries flowed out of the private office of the Vozhd to Murmansk, but Northern Fleet HQ could not respond with a logical explanation.

In Washington, the President was woken and studied the TV images as every channel covered the story. Then he began to tweet. He also put in a call to Marjory Graham in London.

She was trying to raise Sir Adrian. He was in his car, being driven back from Northwood to his flat at Admiralty Arch. He had been up all night taking command of a Russian battle-cruiser. At Chandler's Court, Dr Jeremy Hendricks gazed at the screens in the computer room and swore softly.

In another wing the teenager who had delivered the codes that enabled the penetration was fast asleep. He was not all that interested.

It did not take the cyber-experts at Murmansk more than twenty-four hours to report back to the Kremlin. This was not a malfunction. Against unimaginable odds, their system had simply been penetrated and, for seven vital minutes, had been under the command of a malign stranger.

The voice from the private office in the Kremlin was not forgiving. They had assured him that their technology was unassailable, based on a trillion-to-one likelihood of infiltration. There would be multiple dismissals, even criminal charges, on the grounds of culpable negligence.

Technical officers at Murmansk began to plan the huge operation that would be necessary to get the mass of inert steel off that sandbank. The Moscow-based and government-controlled TV and radio media, which by noon had not even carried the story, tried to work out how to explain what had happened even to a docile Russian public. Word was spreading; even in a controlled dictatorship the power of the internet cannot be repressed for very long.

In his seventh-floor office at Yazenevo the man controlling the foreign intelligence arm of the Russian Federation gazed out of the plate-glass picture window that gave on to the birch forest beneath him. Far away he could see the glitter where the spring sun touched the onion domes of St Basil's Cathedral on Red Square. He knew the call was imminent. It came at noon on the day after the grounding. Yevgeni Krilov knew who would be on the line. It was the red phone. He crossed the room to pick it up at the second ring. The SVR man listened briefly then ordered his car.

Like the self-effacing Englishman currently installing himself in a small flat in London, Krilov was a career-long intelligence officer, beginning under Communism. He too had been talent-spotted at university and intensively interviewed before being accepted for the KGB.

Another in his intake was the man whose call he was now answering, the former secret policeman who had become master of all Russia. But while the Vozhd had been assigned the Second Chief Directorate (internal) and posted to Dresden in Russian-run East Germany, Yevgeni Krilov had shown a flair for languages and secured a posting to the First Chief Directorate (foreign espionage), which was regarded as the cream of the cream.

He had served in three overseas embassies, two of them hostile: Rome and London. He spoke workable Italian and excellent English. Like the Vozhd, he later parted from Communism without hesitation when the moment came, for he had long seen its numerous flaws. But he never lost his passion for Mother Russia.

Though at that point he had no idea how the disaster at Goodwin Sands had occurred or who was behind it, over two extensive careers in espionage, he and the Englishman had, ironically, clashed swords before.

Krilov's ZiL limousine entered the grounds of the Kremlin as always by the Borovitsky Gate, banned to all but senior officials. Although no underling could possibly be riding in a ZiL, the fanatically loyal FSO guards stopped Krilov's car and examined him through the windows. Then they lifted the barrier and waved his driver forward.

The Vozhd has three offices. There is the big outer one, large enough to receive delegations; the smaller inner one, functional, workaday, with the crossed flags behind the desk, one the Russian national flag, the other the black, double-headed eagle. Almost no one ever gets to the smallest and innermost room, where there are intimate family portraits. But it was here that Krilov was received.

The man who totally controlled the gangster-impregnated regime of the new Russia was white with rage. He could barely express himself for emotion.

Krilov knew him well. Not only were they of similar age, their careers had run in parallel. He knew that the Vozhd had never wholly got over the disintegration of that Russian empire, the USSR, which had accompanied the tenure of Mikhail Gorbachev, whom he had never forgiven. He had watched the Vozhd seeth as the USSR was disbanded and humiliation after disgrace were heaped upon his beloved Mother Russia. He had not betrayed Communism; it was the other way round: Communism had betrayed his country. The Vozhd had returned from Germany just before the German Democratic Republic had vanished to be reunited with West Germany. He had climbed through the ranks of the bureaucratic structure that governed his native St Petersburg, then transferred to Moscow. In the capital he had attached his career to the star of Boris Yeltsin, riding the old drunk's coat-tails until he became Mr Indispensable.

It was no secret that he had never respected the ageing alcoholic, but he had been able to manipulate him to the point where, retiring from the presidency to withdraw and die in peace, Yeltsin had anointed him successor.

During the Yeltsin years the present chief had fumed with anger as he watched his homeland being systematically stripped of every mineral and natural asset, to be handed over by corrupt officials to opportunists and gang-sters. But there was, back then, nothing he could do to stop it. By the time he attained the presidency, he had learned and understood the three cornerstones of power in Russia. They had not changed since the time of the Tsars.

Forget democracy. It was a pretence and a sham, and the Russian people did not really want it anyway. The three pillars of power were the government with its secret police, mega-money and the criminal underworld. Form an alliance of these three and you could rule Russia for ever. So he did.

Through the FSB, not Krilov's service but the newly named KGB, you could have anyone who got in your way arrested, charged, tried and convicted. That sort of power meant you would win any election, rigged if need be; it meant that the media would do and publish what they were told; and it meant that the Duma, the parliament, would pass any law you told it to. Throw in the armed forces, the police and the judiciary, and the country was yours.

As for cornerstone two, tackling mega-money was easy. The angry ex-secret policeman may have seethed as he watched his country denuded of its natural assets and in its wake the emergence of a network of five hundred multimillionaire oligarchs, but he had no hesitation in joining them. Yevgeni Krilov knew he was in a room with the richest man in Russia, possibly the world. No one did a ruble's worth of business in Russia without paying a per-centage fee to the supreme boss, albeit through a complex network of shell companies and front men.

And the third factor, the ruthless 'thieves in law', this alternative society had existed under the Tsars and had, effectively, run the labour camps, the fearsome Gulag, from within right across the country. In the era of post-Communism, the Vori v Zakone had spread to establish large and lucrative branches in most cities of the developed world, and especially in New York and London. They were very useful for 'wet work', the obedient infliction of violence as and where needed. (The 'wet', of course, refers to human blood.)

The Vozhd kept his conversation and his instructions short. He had no need to mention the name *Admiral Nakhimov.*

'It was not an accident or a technical malfunction. It was sabotage. That is very clear. Whoever did it – and my suspicions lie with our friends in the UK – has inflicted a truly massive humiliation on our country. The entire planet is staring at our ship marooned on an English sandbank. There must be retribution. I am placing it in your hands. Your orders are three.

'Discover who it was. Trace that person or persons. Eliminate them. You may go.'

Krilov had his orders. As the biggest tugs in the Russian navy and the maritime world were being assigned or chartered to proceed to the English Channel, he drove back to Yazenevo to begin a manhunt.

In espionage, few things are this simple, but Krilov had a stroke of luck. As the new orders filtered down the floors at Yazenevo, a sharp-eyed archivist recalled having seen a minor item filed out of Washington. For unknown reasons, some weeks back, the American government had lodged with the British a request for the extradition of a computer hacker. A few days later, also for no given reason, the USA had cancelled the request. It might be nothing, reasoned Krilov, but even in the intelligence world, once described by CIA veteran James Angleton as a wilderness of mirrors, two and two still made four. Two major computer hackers in a month? He sent for the file.

There was little enough that could be added to the snippet from the Attorney General's department, but the once-wanted offender was called Luke Jennings and he came from Luton.

Yevgeni Krilov had two chains of agents inside the United Kingdom. One was official, the network inside the Russian embassy, or what remained of it after the devastating expulsions following the Skripal affair. Its reconstruction was ongoing. Leading this network was the recently appointed Stepan Kukushkin, posing as the assistant commercial counsellor but probably fooling no one.

Krilov's other chain was made up of the 'illegals' or 'sleepers' passing themselves off as legitimate British citizens and speaking perfect English. The agent heading these masqueraded as a shopkeeper in the West End of London whose British name was Burke. His real name was Dmitri Volkov.

Broadly speaking, sleeper agents fall into two categories. Some are born and raised in the countries they are now prepared to betray. They can pass easily for a native of that land because that is exactly what they are. As for motivation, there are several.

During the Cold War the bulk of those in the West betraying their own homeland were dedicated Communists for whom the lust to see the triumph of Communism worldwide overcame any loyalty to the country in which they lived. On the other side of the Iron Curtain, those who were prepared to work for the West were so almost always because of a profound disillusion, maturing into loathing, of the Communist dictatorships into which they had been born. There were other motivations – greed, resentment at their treatment, the wish to earn an assisted escape to a better life in the West. But the main one was a desire to help bring down a regime they had come to despise. These usually volunteered their services as a one-off in exchange for an aided escape but were persuaded to stay as an agent-in-place until they had earned an exit.

The other category consists of quite different patriots inserted at great risk to themselves to pretend to be natives of the target country and, being fluent in both the language and the culture of the target country, to live there and serve their real love back home. These are known as 'illegals' and also as 'sleepers'.

In their use, there are also two choices. Some simply and regularly pass on information that comes their way by virtue of the job they do. This is usually low-level data, and its extraction poses little risk. But such agents have to be 'serviced' or 'handled', meaning they need a constant channel along which to pass their gleaned information so that it eventually reaches the intelligence HQ of the country they are serving.

This was the function the sleeper inside the US Justice Department served when she noticed that the USA had rescinded without explanation a request to the British for the extradition of a British teenager called Luke Jennings from a town called Luton on an accusation of hacking classified US computers.

The other use is to keep completely unnoticed an agent who can be called on for one-off missions – an errand now and again, a bit of detective work. This was what the Russian agent Dmitri Volkov was tasked to do in fulfilment of the mission imposed by Krilov.

Two days later, Volkov, or Mr Burke, noticed a small advert in the usual place in the usual paper. It contained the usual harmless wording which meant that he was wanted in Moscow. He closed up his shop and headed east, diverting to three different countries, all in the European Union and signatories of the Schengen Agreement, meaning that they had virtually no border checks. He arrived as a tourist at Sheremetyevo airport after a total of twenty hours in transit. In the cab on the way to downtown Moscow he reverted to his Russian passport.

The briefing was short and to the point. He did not even go out to Yazenevo. The meeting was in town, just in case of an unfortunate recognition at HQ. He had worked there once, and former colleagues still did. Caution was always worthwhile.

Krilov gave his UK operative all that he had. The target was Luton, the family name Jennings, and one of them was a computer addict. Where was he now? Within twenty-four hours, Dmitri Volkov was heading back to London. Nothing was committed to paper and absolutely nothing to the airwaves or the internet.

On his way back to the UK, Dmitri Volkov, another lifelong 'spook' and veteran of the old days, mused on the irony that all this modern technology simply meant that total security now demanded the old methods, a personal 'meet'. He also decided who among the twenty sleepers he could call upon he would use. He finally decided upon four.

He intended that each of his British nationals need know nothing about the other three. All would report to him with harmless phone calls.

One would establish which Jennings family was the one containing a Luke and where they lived, or had lived, if they had moved. He would pass this information on to Agent B. That was all. This second agent would investigate the house. If it was now vacant, he could, posing as a prospective buyer, question the estate agent and maybe the neighbours. The third would investigate the social life of the target. The fourth would remain in his hotel room in reserve.

The reason for choosing four sleepers was security. The same man making enquiries all over the town might be spotted, if, perchance, Luke Jennings himself was also a subject of interest to British counter-intelligence.

*

In separate cars, from the separate small hotels in which they were lodging, the four agents slipped into Luton two days later. Résumé – their instructions were: move fast.

Agent A was tasked to have a look at the electoral register. In the UK, this is a public document. Political constituency officials study it. It also includes addresses. Agent A reported back within a day. There were nine Jennings families in Luton but only one contained someone named Luke. He was listed as being eighteen, just on the electoral register after qualifying on his last birthday. The register showed him as living with his parents. There was an address for the now three voters who lived there. Two parents, Harold and Sue, and the teenager.

Agent B was told where to go and cruised past. In the garden a placard on a post announced that the house was for sale. The estate agent was listed. Agent B went there and secured a viewing that afternoon.

On his visit he could see that the house had clearly been gutted and professionally cleaned. There was not even an old envelope, an invoice or a bill indicating where the family might have gone. Until the cupboard under the stairs. Agent B insisted on peering everywhere and in the small area off the hallway, up against the far wall, lay a discarded golf tee. It was possible the dark cupboard had once played host to a set of golf clubs, a hobby of the father, perhaps.

The next day Agent C took over. There are three golf clubs serving the town of Luton. From his hotel bedroom the Russian rang the first then hit gold with the second. His patter was perfectly inoffensive.

'Look, I wonder if you can help me. I have just moved into the Luton area and I'm trying to make contact with an old mate who lives here. He sent me his card but, like an ass, I've lost it. But he did tell me at the time that he had joined a terrific golf club. Would that be you? Fella called Harold Jennings.'

It was the assistant secretary on the line.

'We do have a Harold Jennings on file, sir. Would that be him?'

'Yes, that would be him. Would you have a number for him?'

It was a landline number and it was disconnected. Almost certainly the number of the abandoned house. Not that it mattered any more. Agent C drove out to the golf club.

He chose the lunch hour, asked to see the secretary and enquired after a membership.

'I think you may be in luck, sir,' said the affable official. 'We are normally jammed full, but we recently lost a couple of members. One went to the great nineteenth hole in the sky and I believe the other has emigrated. Let me introduce you to the bar while I go and check.'

The bar was crowded and jolly, with members coming in off the eighteenth hole in twos and fours, leaving their kit in the changing room and ordering a stiffener before lunch. Agent C began to circulate. His patter was the same as on the phone.

'I've just moved out here from London. Used to have a very good mate who was a member here. Harold Jennings. Is he still here?'

Toby Wilson was at the bar, and his large, veined nose indicated he was no stranger to it.

'He was until a month ago. Are you joining? Good show. Yes, Harold's gone and emigrated. Oh, don't mind if I do. Gin and tonic. Many thanks.'

The barman knew his man. The fizzing glass was on the bar before its predecessor was empty. The secretary returned with forms to fill in. Agent C complied. They would never trace him anyway; the address he gave was completely phoney. Just a formality, explained the secretary. It would have to go before the committee, but he foresaw no problem for a chum of Harold Jennings, playing off ten. In the meantime, why not enjoy the bar as his guest? Then he was called away. Agent C returned to Toby Wilson.

'Yes, sad, really. His marriage broke up. Mind you, I wouldn't have minded taking that wife off him. What a cracker.'

'Sue, wasn't she?'

'That's right. Gorgeous girl. Anyway, they've parted, and he's gone off to New York. Good job, nice flat, new life, last I heard.'

'He's been in touch, then?'

'Gave me a call the other day.'

An hour later Agent C helped Toby to his car and, in the process, a mobile phone found itself transferred from Wilson's pocket to that of the agent.

When Agent C reported to Dmitri Volkov, he was able to be very helpful. If the hacker was the boy, he and his mother had definitely disappeared from Luton. But if anyone would know where they were, it would be the father. He was now in New York, but the agent had his mobile-phone number.

The SVR has another chain of agents in New York City and, with modern tracing technology, a mobile-phone number is as good as an address. The colony of Russian gangsters in New York was duly contacted.

Chapter Six

THERE WAS NOTHING unusual about the garbage dumpster on the dingy New York street that morning in mid-May, except for the human leg dangling out of it.

If the skip had been empty, the body would have been at the bottom of it and out of sight, for days or even weeks. It wasn't. Had an apartment owner high above looked down, that person might have seen the limb of the cadaver hanging out of the dumpster, but there were no such apartments.

The skip was on a patch of waste ground off a dingy alley in Brownsville, not far from Sheepshead Bay, Brooklyn. Flanking the alley were old and empty warehouses; the whole area was an industrial slum. The only reason the police patrolman had seen the leg was because he had entered the waste ground to relieve himself.

He zipped up and called his partner. The two young men stared at the limb then peered into the interior. The remainder of the corpse lay on its back: a middle-aged white man, eyes open, staring sightlessly upwards in death.

The partner called it in to their local precinct station. After that, the usual machine went into operation.

After ascertaining that life was extinct the street cops left the body alone. It was a matter for the detective branch and the medical examiner. Awaiting their arrival, the patrolmen scouted the immediate area and, in a nearby warehouse, rank and empty apart from scattered trash, one found ropes tied to some heating pipes. It looked as if – and the ME would confirm this from rope burns on the wrists – the victim had been tied to the pipes, apparently to take a beating.

An unmarked sedan arrived, carefully picking its way down an alley strewn with debris. Two detectives got out to join the uniforms and have a look at the body. A crime team came to fence off the dumpster and the surrounding area with tape. Passers-by would be forbidden from entering, but there were none. The thugs who had done this had chosen well.

Next came the ME himself. He took very little time to pronounce death, presumably murder, and permit the removal of the body. His team hauled it out of the dumpster and on to a stretcher, then to their van, and thence to the morgue. By this point the ME had been able to establish only that the body was fully clothed but had been stripped of valuables. There were pinch marks either side of the nose, but no eyeglasses. These were later found near the ropes in the warehouse. So, also, was a discarded handkerchief.

There was the mark of a signet ring on one finger, but

no ring. All pockets were empty. No billfold and no identification. A more thorough examination would have to be done at the morgue.

It was there that the examiner, during the removal of the cadaver's clothes, noticed two more oddities. There was a ring around the left wrist where a watch would have been, but no watch. Even stranger, the maker's tags on the clothing indicated that none of it was American. The clothes looked to be British. The ME's heart sank. A dead tourist, snatched and murdered in a slum, was bad news. He called down a senior detective.

For the rest, he could establish cause of death. It was heart failure. The victim had been punched hard in the face. The blow had broken his nose and there was congealed blood in the nostrils and around the mouth. He had also been punched in the solar plexus. It was clear, with the chest cavity open, that the victim had had a weak heart, although he might not have been aware of this, and the trauma to which he had been subjected – the terror, the pain, the beating – had provoked cardiac arrest. The detective from upstairs joined him.

He too examined the clothing labels. Jermyn Street. Was that not in London? The victim was middle-aged. A tad overweight, but not obese. Soft hands. He ordered the face to be cleaned up and photographed. And fingerprints taken, of course, plus a DNA sample. If he was a Britisher and a recent arrival, he must have come through immigration control, probably at Kennedy Airport.

What Detective Sean Devlin wanted was a name. Did

the dead man have a residence in the city? Was he staying at an uptown hotel? With friends? In addition to the British clothes, there were other oddities. This had not been a street mugging gone wrong. Muggers pounced, struck, incapacitated, robbed and ran. This man must have been snatched from miles away, brought to this slum, tied to metal pipes and beaten. Why? Punishment? Information?

When he had the pictures Detective Devlin ran them to three state agencies: Immigration and Customs Enforcement, known simply as IC; the omnipresent Department of Homeland Security; and, of course, the Bureau, the FBI. It took a day, and it was facial-recognition technology that clinched it. In the Brownsville precinct house to which Detective Devlin was attached, it suddenly rained FBI. The dead man was a new arrival as a resident and was under the protection of the Bureau. This was going to be embarrassing. But not for Detective Devlin. It went way upstairs to the FBI offices in New York.

Their records showed that Mr Harold Jennings had been granted permission to move to and settle in New York City and that the necessary and copious paperwork had been fast-tracked by the Bureau as a favour to the British Prime Minister, via Scotland Yard. The Yard had to be informed, with apologies.

Over in London, a man called Sir Adrian Weston was also informed. He motored out to Chandler's Court and sadly relayed the information to Mrs Sue Jennings and her two sons. The younger one, Marcus, shed tears; the older one noted the death of his father as a fact, along with many others that he stored.

Sue Jennings asked if the body of her husband could be repatriated for burial in England. This was promised. The British consulate in New York was charged to liaise with the FBI so that this would happen as soon as the cadaver could be released. She mentioned a watch that she would like returned. It had sentimental value.

She explained it was a Rolex Oyster in gold. She had presented it to her husband on their tenth wedding anniversary and it was inscribed. On the reverse were the words 'To Harold, with love from Sue, on our tenth anniversary'.

New York replied that there was no watch but the hunt for the killers was ongoing and the New York Police Department would put out a BOLO (Be On the Look-Out) for a gold Rolex inscribed in that manner. There was a list that went regularly to pawnbrokers and jewellery shops, and the BOLO went on it but yielded nothing.

Sir Adrian was troubled by the New York incident. It was too coincidental. If Moscow had made a connection between the disaster of the *Admiral Nakhimov* and the United Kingdom, they had done so incredibly fast – that was worrying. He called the FBI in New York and asked to speak with the detective who had been assigned to the case.

With the Bureau's help, he had a long talk with Detective Devlin in Brooklyn, who was as helpful as he could be, which was not much. And there, for a week, the trail died.

★

On the day that the body found in the New York dumpster was identified as Harold Jennings, eight of the most powerful oceangoing tugs in the West assembled in the Strait of Dover and were hooked up to the stranded battlecruiser. Steel cables the thickness of a man's waist snaked from their sterns to the immobile leviathan. At the height of the spring tide they hauled together. The two massive propellers of the *Nakhimov* churned up tons of fine sand beneath her stern. Inch by inch, then foot by foot, then yard by yard, she slipped backwards off the Goodwins into deep water.

For ten days, the *Admiral Nakhimov* had been a tourist attraction. Enterprising owners of launches up and down the Kent coast had run trips out into that patch of safe water between the Goodwins and the shore known as the Downs. Visitors took millions of photos, usually of themselves standing, beaming, with the battlecruiser in the background.

Once she was free, the eight tugs unhitched and scattered to their bases; the Russians set off for the Baltic and the Dutch and French who had been summoned to help to their respective ports. The *Nakhimov*, however, did not get far in her journey to the Russian Far East. She needed a hull examination. Once under way again, she turned north, back towards Sevmash, in perfect working order. For the Kent locals, the spectacle was over. That was not the view of the Kremlin.

As so often with police inquiries, the break, when it came, was a fluke. A mugger was arrested and he was wearing an inscribed gold Rolex watch. And he was Russian.

There are 600,000 Russians in New York City, and half of them live and work in the zone known as Brighton Beach. This is a community in the southern section of the borough of Brooklyn, running along the shore of the Coney Island peninsula. It contains a vigorous and violent crime world made up of several known gangs. The NYPD has a large team of Russian-speaking officers for whom Brighton Beach and its gangs are the sole concern.

The arrested man was called Viktor Ulyanov, and he was making it plain he intended to say nothing. He was clearly a gang-fringe lowlife and extremely stupid.

He had tried a solo mugging in leafy Queens, miles from home, selecting a respectable-looking executive type walking down the street where he lived. But it had not been Viktor's day. The middle-aged businessman had boxed at light-heavyweight for the USA in the Atlanta Olympics and his right fist was still an impressive assemblage of muscle and bone.

Before Ulyanov could use his knife his target's fist had made acquaintance with his jaw and he had woken up on the sidewalk to find several blue-clad legs around him. Down at the station house he was an object of mockery and lapsed into sullen misery. And all his possessions were confiscated before he went into his cell.

On an upper level a bright young recruit looked at the watch and recalled a BOLO that had gone out a week earlier that mentioned an inscribed gold watch belonging to a dead Brit. He raised the matter with his sergeant and was duly praised for his sharp wits. Then the detectives took over and alerted the FBI.

Mrs Sue Jennings was shown a picture of the watch as she returned to Chandler's Court from her late husband's funeral at a nearby church and confirmed it had been his. Over in New York, Ulyanov was informed that the charge against him was being raised from street assault to murder in the first.

He recalled perfectly clearly what had happened. He had been recruited into the gang assigned to undertake the snatch of the British accountant only at the last minute because a smarter gang member had fallen out. There had been five of them, and it was a contract job. They had had no idea they had been contracted by a Russian agent working for the SVR in Moscow.

The job was to go to an apartment in Queens, ring the bell and, when it was answered by the sole tenant of the flat, march him at gunpoint out to the sidewalk and into their van. This duly happened, with the terrified prisoner doing exactly what he was told. It had been dark, close to midnight, and no one had noticed a thing.

As per orders, they had driven to an empty warehouse in a slum not far from Sheepshead Bay, tied the weeping foreigner to some pipes and prepared to complete the assignment. Their orders were very simple. Knock him about a bit and ask him one simple question: where is your son?

Then it had gone wrong. At the second punch from the gang leader, the man had convulsed, his eyes had bulged and he had slumped in the ropes. They thought he had lost consciousness and tried to revive him. But he was dead. Apart from the word 'please' over and over, he had said not a word. They had been more worried about the reaction of their boss than about the stiff.

Three of the five went outside to find a place to dump the body. The fourth and Ulyanov stayed to untie the corpse and see if the man had anything worth taking. The other Russian took the signet ring and the billfold; Ulyanov took the watch and stuffed it in his trouser pocket. Later, he put it on his wrist in place of his cheap Timex.

Sitting facing two steely-eyed detectives, the Russian thug realized that if he named his fellow killers he was a dead man. So he was stunned when they offered him a quite different deal. Though, privately, they knew a murder charge would not stand, they told him they were interested in one thing only and that they may be able to drop the charge if they got it. What did the Limey say before he died?

Viktor Ulyanov thought it over. Answering seemed harmless enough. Set against twenty to life?

'He didn't say nothing.'

'Nothing? Nothing at all?'

'Not a word. Just took the second punch, choked and died.'

The detectives had their answer. They passed it on to the FBI HQ in Washington, which passed it on to London.

For Sir Adrian, the sudden death of Harold Jennings in New York and the assurance from the NYPD that he seemed to have uttered not a word about his son or, more vitally, about his son's new location, was a partial relief. But only partial.

More to the point was a nagging worry. How had the Russians ever heard the name Jennings or found the right Harold Jennings in a New York apartment 3,500 miles away? Somewhere – he had no idea where – there had been a leak.

It was self-evident that Moscow would not take the global humiliation of her grounded battlecruiser as just a bit of bad luck. Even without traditional Russian paranoia, they would work out that their computers had been penetrated. Back-engineering on board the *Nakhimov* and in the Murmansk database would have proved there had been a hack, and a very successful one, so clever that it had gone unnoticed until too late. That would entail a massive inquiry. And Sir Adrian had a pretty clear suspicion as to whom it had been entrusted.

That is one of the things about the aces of the intelligence world. Like chess players, they study one another. Outwitting rather than outshooting is the ideal. Shooting is for men in camouflage uniforms. Checkmate is more satisfying. Sir Adrian had worn the camo in the Paras and the dark suit in the Firm.

Though he was ten years older than the man at Yazenevo, he had noted the rising star of the SVR when he had been deputy chief of MI6. Yevgeni Krilov had been subtle and tenacious as head of his service's Western Europe Division back in the day, and he had not disappointed in his subsequent career. He had gone on rising through the ranks to the seventh-floor office.

It is reported that during the desert campaign in North Africa in the Second World War the British general Bernard Montgomery had spent hours in his caravan staring at a picture of his opponent, the German Erwin Rommel. He was trying to work out what his enemy would do next. Sir Adrian had kept a file on Yevgeni Krilov. It too contained a portrait. He went back to his ex-colleagues at Vauxhall Cross and was allowed, for old times' sake, to sit in a closed room and study the Krilov file.

Krilov had, in the late nineties, spent two years serving under the Rezident, or chief of station, in the SVR unit inside the Russian embassy in London. He was non-declared, meaning he was posing as a harmless junior cultural attaché, but the British knew exactly what he really was.

In that strange *danse macabre* that is espionage it is common for agents on opposite sides to attend embassy cocktail parties – conversing, beaming, clinking glasses and pretending to be all jolly diplomats together, while behind the mask privately intending to outwit and destroy the opponent. Sir Adrian believed he might have met the (then) junior Russian spy at one such Russian reception.

What he could not know was that there had nearly been another meeting. It would have been in Budapest, on that occasion when he turned away from a meet with a defector Russian colonel because he sensed it had been 'blown'. He discovered later he was right. The tortured colonel had given everything away before he was executed. Because the traitor was a Russian, the ÁVO, Hungary's secret police, had invited a man from the Russian embassy to be present at the capture of the British agent. Budapest was Krilov's third foreign posting. He had been sitting inside the ÁVO trap, waiting for the British spy who never appeared.

Closing the file and leaving Vauxhall, Sir Adrian's suspicion grew stronger. Krilov had not climbed from Russian embassy gofer to the seventh floor at Yazenevo for nothing. He must be the man tasked to trace the super-hacker.

Weston also knew that Moscow had learned two names: Jennings and Luton. He did not know how. But it no longer mattered. The Jennings family had disappeared from there, but he had every right to presume that Moscow had never heard the name Chandler's Court. And yet . . . and yet. He had that gut feeling again. That was why he wanted a small but expert squad of armed men around the boy. A few soldiers at Chandler's Court might not be a bad idea.

In a miserable back alley in Brownsville, Krilov's chosen minions had failed him, but if Moscow had really decided that the heads and hands that had created the humiliation of the *Admiral Nakhimov* dwelt in that small island off the north-west coast of Europe which the Vozhd loathed so heartily, he would not stop there. He would try again.

Sir Adrian would have been even more disquieted if he could have hovered, spectre-like, in the office of his adversary above the birch forest at Yazenevo.

★

Spread out across Krilov's desk was a large print-out of a photograph. The original had been taken by a Russian space satellite rolling unseen over central England, diverted off its original planned course at his request. The machine had followed the coordinates programmed into it from far below. It had taken the picture then resumed its original orbit. The next time it was over Russia it had beamed down the image it had been asked for.

Yevgeni Krilov took a large magnifying glass and studied the image at the centre of the aerial map. It showed a walled, forested estate known as Chandler's Court.

Chapter Seven

Yevgeni Krilov did not work for a squeamish organization. In its time and recently under his direction the SVR had organized repeated foreign assassinations, but Krilov always preferred to use surrogates to accomplish the wet work.

Staring at the print-out of the satellite photo, he realized he had resolved the first two problems set him by the Vozhd. The gut instinct of the President had been right after all. It was the British, not the Americans, who had inflicted this humiliation upon Mother Russia, in revenge for the Skripal affair.

In the early spring of 2018 a Russian living quietly in the British cathedral city of Salisbury was very nearly assassinated by Russian agents. Sergei Skripal had once spied for Britain against Russia. He had been detected, tried, sentenced and imprisoned in Russia. On his release, he had been allowed to emigrate to the UK and settle there.

He was living quietly, indeed invisibly, when a Russian agent had smeared the deadly nerve agent Novichok on his door handle. Both Skripal and his visiting daughter, Yulia, had touched the agent and been almost mortally poisoned. A hitherto unknown British antidote had just saved them both. The credit had gone to Porton Down.

Personally, Yevgeni Krilov had been against the business, but he had been overridden by the Vozhd. It turned out that Krilov had been right. In the aftermath, thirty-six Russian diplomats had been expelled, and the Britishers had chosen well. All thirty-six were embassy-based spies and their departure had savaged Krilov's network in the UK.

It had all been a disastrous mistake, but he knew it was more than his job was worth to say so again. Now, a fresh catastrophe had occurred in the grounding of the pride of the Northern Fleet and Russian revenge was mandatory. At least he was two-thirds of the way there.

The British had discovered a secret weapon and they were prepared to use it with a ruthlessness he intended to match. It was not a piece of machinery. It was a human brain possessed by an autistic youth that could do the impossible. Like the cyber-scientists of Fort Meade, the Russians at Murmansk had presumed that the complexity of the firewall around the Murmansk database was impenetrable, and they had been proved wrong.

Thanks to an agent in Washington, the youth had acquired a name. Thanks to detective work in Luton, he had located the father of the genius, but he had proved useless. Now a new source had named the target – the place where the British had squirrelled away their secret weapon, out of sight and out of mind. Except he was very much on Krilov's mind. He now had to accomplish the Vozhd's third demand. Eliminate him; avenge the insult.

There were five pools of trained killers in Russia on which Krilov could draw. His real quandary was which one to use.

On the government payroll are two. There are the Spetsnaz – Special Forces soldiers to match the British SAS, the SBS and the almost invisible SRR, or the American Green Berets, Delta Force or Navy SEALs. All the soldiers were trained to the ultimate, with slightly varying skill sets, according to their particular talents or areas of expertise.

Inside the Spetsnaz was a secret unit trained to operate abroad. They attended a totally covert school which taught them how to move in civilian clothes unseen through various foreign societies, how to acquire their weapons from secret 'drops' where the embassy – importing in the cannot-be-touched diplomatic bag – had left what they needed, then to complete their mission and return to their regular life as invisibly as they had come. They practised foreign languages to high fluency levels and the most studied was the world's common language, English.

Also in government service and under Krilov's control was the old Department 13, expanded now and renamed Department V, or Otdel Mokrie Dela, the 'wet affairs' unit, a relic of the old KGB that had never been lost when the organization was split up and renamed under Gorbachev.

It had been two operators from Department V, one as team leader and the other to watch his back and drive the rented car, who had visited Salisbury to smear Novichok on the traitor's door handle. Even the joke Russian ambassador in the UK, Yakovenko, knew nothing about them. That was why he had been able to stand up and tell the British press that the affair had nothing to do with Russia without even going pink.

Outside the SVR, Krilov could call on the organized criminal underworld, the Vory v Zakone. The Vory could always be relied upon to do favours for the government, secure in the knowledge that the favours would be repaid in Russia with contracts and concessions for their pandemic business empire.

Pretty much unknown in the West were the bikers, the Night Wolves, who operated at a level of violence that made California's Hells Angels look like off-duty curates. Professing a savage patriotism, the Night Wolves specialized in attacking and crippling foreign football fans who travelled in Europe to support their teams. Among them were a sprinkling of ex-Spetsnaz veterans and English-speakers.

Finally, there were two non-Russian groups who could be relied upon to do 'contract' work for Moscow, each of whom had networks of criminal gangs notorious for extreme levels of violence – the Chechens and the Albanians.

Non-state contractors would need funding, but this, too, was not a problem. The Kremlin had the closest links with the network of industrial and commercial billionaires who had become unimaginably rich by scalping the assets of their homeland and then moving abroad to live in luxury. Some, the foolish ones, had split with the biggest gangster of them all, and there were vicious vendettas between these and the Kremlin. But they had to live in their foreign estates surrounded by teams of bodyguards, and even that did not always save them. Those who knew what was good for them would always provide the funding.

After two days of cogitation Yevgeni Krilov decided he would use the bikers, an elite team drawn from the Night Wolves, all well travelled and all English-speaking.

There was logic in his choice. The blame for the Skripal affair had landed squarely on Russia and been endorsed by the entire intelligence world because Novichok was very specifically a Russian development. But non-state crime was universal. The bikers could have been hired by any-body. After the death of the computer hacker, the British at official level would know who had sent the assassins but, unlike the Novichok trail, they would never be able to prove it.

Sir Adrian liked to think that he was a pragmatic man, prepared to accept and face reality, however disagreeable it might be. But he also had no contempt for intuition.

Twice in his life he had refused to ignore a gut instinct that things were not right; twice he had scented the odour of danger and removed himself as fast as he could. Once, in the late seventies, the East German Stasi had closed their trap just after he slipped through the border into safety in the West. On the other occasion, in the early 1980s, the

KGB raid on the Budapest café where he was due to meet a 'contact' had occurred minutes after he slipped away. It later transpired that the contact had already been taken and would die in Siberia.

Years of putting himself in harm's way for his country had taught Adrian Weston not to mock gut feeling, nor confuse it with the nervousness of a coward, which he was not.

After Budapest, there had been a defection from the ÁVO, and he had interrogated the man in a safe house outside London. By chance, the Magyar had been one of those waiting at the rendezvous for the British spy who never showed up. He was able to confirm that because the arrested traitor was a Russian, a KGB man had attended and his name was Yevgeni Krilov. Subsequently, Weston had not unnaturally followed from afar the steady rise through the ranks of this Krilov and, after his own retirement, had learned of the Russian's eventual elevation to the captaincy at Yazenevo.

As a professional, he knew how the mass expulsions of SVR agents from the London embassy after the Skripal affair must have gutted the man who was once nearly his nemesis. That was why another of his bedside portraits was the face, gleaned from the archives of all those diplomatic cocktail parties of long ago, of the man who now ran the SVR.

After studying the FBI reports from New York, he caught the same scent again.

Something was not right. Moscow was moving too

fast. Sir Adrian knew nothing of a Russian mole inside the Department of Justice in Washington, but somehow Krilov had got that name, and it was the right one. And, according to the Bureau, the men contracted by the SVR had failed in New York only because of a fluke – Harold Jennings's weak heart.

He became more and more convinced that Krilov would try again. There was an aroma of frenzy about all this. The orders must be coming right from that inner office in the Kremlin, and they would be obeyed. He had poked a bear and the bear was angry. So the old mandarin of Vauxhall Cross asked for another private meeting with his Prime Minister and made his request. When he told her what he suspected and what he wanted, she closed her eyes.

'You really think it may be necessary?'

'I pray not, but I would prefer to be safe than sorry, Prime Minister.'

Politicians seldom have to be convinced of the need for caution. There are medal-awarding ceremonies at Buckingham Palace, but they never involve politicians.

'If you can clear it with the DSF. But I will take his advice if he goes against you,' she said.

The Director of Special Forces is a senior army officer, usually of Brigadier-General rank, and he has an office off Albany Street, Regent's Park. He received Sir Adrian that afternoon with no delay at all. The request had come from Downing Street. The DSF looked, thought Sir Adrian, terribly young, but then they all did nowadays. He explained his problem. The brigadier had no trouble understanding it. He had spent years in the Regiment before his promotion.

The Regiment has no trouble with close protection, the technical term for bodyguard work. It has carried out CP missions all over the world, assisting friends of Britain and very often training those heads of state's own fellow nationals. It is able to charge generous fees to those it enables to raise their CP level and has spent a long time in the oil-rich Persian Gulf. Indeed, it may be the only unit in the armed forces that makes a profit for the country.

'You are expecting an attack, Sir Adrian?' asked the soldier.

'Not expecting. Just preferring to be on the safe side.'

'We rarely carry out CP work inside this country.'

Both men knew that, though the Metropolitan Police has highly capable armed units, occasionally, those surrounding the queen are from the Special Forces. It remained unsaid.

'I suppose we could treat it as a training mission,' mused the brigadier. 'How many men would you need?'

'A dozen, perhaps. Plenty of sleeping room in the old staff quarters. Regular scoff from the kitchen staff. TV room for the off-duty.'

The brigadier grinned. 'Sounds like a holiday. I'll see what I can do.'

They arrived at Chandler's Court two days later and they were twelve – three sergeants and nine troopers – commanded by a thirty-nine-year-old captain, Harry

Williams. He would be allotted a room on the first floor and would eat with the family and the GCHQ team.

Sir Adrian made a point of being there to meet them, and that also provided an opportunity to assess them. He liked what he saw. No one needed to tell him that the men of the Special Forces are called 'special' for a reason. Broadly speaking, they have a very high IQ level and multiple skill sets. Extreme physical fitness and mastery of a wide range of weaponry go without saying. Within the four-man units that form the basic components of the Regiment there is usually a linguist or two, a paramedic-level first-aider, an engineer/mechanic and an armourer.

Before motoring to Chandler's Court Sir Adrian had scanned the notes from the Director of Special Forces about the team leader. Harry Williams, like Adrian Weston years before, had been assessed as 'good family, good school, good exams and POM' (potential officer material) when he had volunteered for the army as a teenager, and he had worn the uniform for twenty years.

He had also gone through Sandhurst and had secured a commission in the Coldstream Guards, but at twenty-five, lusting for more combat, he had undergone selection for the Special Air Service. That selection, much of it in the Brecon Beacons of South Wales, is so gruelling that the percentage of candidates chosen is a small one. Harry Williams was one of them.

In the Regiment the permanent staff are the ORs, the Other Ranks, or non-coms and troopers. Officers, or 'Ruperts', come and go, and always on invitation. Captain

Williams was on his third tour. He had been on – and survived with one minor bullet wound in the left thigh – two covert missions behind the lines in Afghanistan and Syria, where, according to eyewitnesses, he had 'slotted' (killed) half a dozen terrorists.

Sir Adrian recalled the remark of the brigadier: 'Sounds like a holiday.' For this blooded warrior, Chandler's Court certainly would be. Before he left, the mastermind of Operation Troy made sure the commander of the protection squad had met his charges, the Jennings family. They took tea together in the family sitting room.

The boys reacted differently to Captain Williams. Luke was, as ever, shy and withdrawn, but Marcus was agog for details of past combat. Captain Williams just smiled and murmured 'Later . . . maybe.'

Sir Adrian was a practised observer. He noted with approval the gentleness of the soldier towards the older boy and he could not fail to notice the reaction of the very handsome Sue Jennings. His own beloved Fiona would have smiled her quiet smile and whispered, 'Bed bait.' This was certainly the unspoken reaction of the recently widowed Mrs Jennings. Sir Adrian could sense it across the tea cups. From his notes, he knew the soldier was a widower and suspected this would emerge later, after he had left.

Accustomed to deserts, moorland, jungles, the Arctic and swamps, the men were soon at home in the old staff rooms under the roof. Because they would be constantly seen by staff who lived off base and word spreads fast, they were not in camouflage kit but T-shirts, fleeces and trainers.

Two days were spent converting the immediate surrounds of the manor to the way Captain Williams wanted it. Bushes and shrubs were uprooted to create unbroken lawn around the walls of the building on all sides. This gave a fifty-yard-deep field of fire, should it be needed. In a thin strip of woodland nearest to the open grassland, body-heat sensors were hung in the trees. They switched off in daylight but at night, lights would glow on the console in the command room under the eaves. The brightness of the lights indicates the size of the heat source. The men watched, listened and waited, taking shifts through the days and nights. Of what went on in the computer centre, they had no idea. It was the principle of 'need to know'.

The Russians slipped into the country the next day. There were six and they were from the Night Wolves. They were all big and brawny, former soldiers from combat units, and all had seen action against the Afghans or rebel Chechens. They were fully briefed for the task ahead, acting under the remote supervision of Yevgeni Krilov.

Their passports were false, professionally forged, and indicated that they came from Slavic countries of Eastern Europe. All spoke English from halting and accented to fluent, in the case of the two former Spetsnaz. They came on different flights from different capitals, all within the European Union.

Upon landing at Heathrow they convened at the designated café in the concourse – a harmless-looking half-dozen tourists – and waited to be collected, which they were. They were driven to a large rented flat in an outer suburb, whence their escort departed, never to be seen again.

The weapons they had asked for were in suitcases in the second bedroom, supplied for a flat fee by an Albanian gang operating in London. The food cupboards and the fridge were stocked. On the second day a Ford people-carrier appeared in the car park with the ignition key under the rubber floor mat on the driver's side, as planned.

At the British end, everything had been provided and paid for by a Russian billionaire very much in the service of the Kremlin. Once settled in, the six, under the leadership of Anton, began to plan their assault.

They made one reconnaissance trip to the village next to Chandler's Court, then cruised around the estate. On a lonely stretch of narrow lane they stopped and two of them went over the wall. The scouts moved through the forest until they could see the walls and windows of the manor that housed their target. Anton made his plan; then the pair withdrew to the wall, went over it and they all drove away. It was the middle of the night. The research scientists were asleep.

Inside the house they had visited a red light had glowed on a console. In London an elderly man dined alone an easy stroll from Admiralty Arch.

In his breast pocket a smartphone throbbed softly. Sir Adrian glanced at the screen and said:

'Yes, Captain?'

'We have had visitors. Two. In the forest. Just watching. They have gone.'

'They will return. There will be more. I fear they will be fully armed. And they will break cover. They will almost certainly come at night.'

'My orders?'

Normally, only a senior officer could reply to that. But Captain Williams had been briefed that he should follow instructions from the voice on that number.

'Do you remember Loughgall?'

It is a small village in County Armagh, Northern Ireland. On 8 May 1987 a task force of eight of the IRA's top killers attacked the small barracks of the Royal Ulster Constabulary there. They arrived in darkness with a mechanical digger containing a bomb in its bucket. The bomb destroyed the main gate and the driver jumped down to join the other seven. All eight invaded the base. Their orders were to wipe out the entire garrison of RUC men. But there had been a leak. Some informer high in the ranks had made a call. Twenty-four SAS men were waiting, inside the barracks and in the surrounding woodland. They emerged and opened fire. All eight IRA men died. Since then the word 'Loughgall' has meant what Lawrence shouted to his men on the road to Damascus: no prisoners.

'Yes, sir.'

'Then, Captain, you have your orders.'

He disconnected and the sommelier refreshed his glass of claret.

To the wine waiter, the composure of his client did not flicker. Internally, Sir Adrian was seething. The fact that his enemy, Krilov, knew about Chandler's Court could mean only one thing – there had to be a second mole.

Chapter Eight

THEY RETURNED; THE Night Wolves came back the following night, and they were armed to the teeth. They thought they were taking on an undefended target. Their mission was to invade an old if sprawling house and eliminate a sleeping teenager in one of the bedrooms. Anyone else on that floor would also have to be taken down.

They wore black coveralls and black ski-masks. They parked along a deserted stretch of the boundary wall and, using the roof of their vehicle as a departure point, leapt down into the forest. In single file they padded through the wood until they saw in the moonlight the manor of Chandler's Court before them. They did not know that inside the manor red lights were flashing angrily on a console. And they did not know that thirteen sets of night-vision goggles were staring at them. And most of all, they did not know about the night-vision rifle sights. Worse, they had never heard of Loughgall.

The Special Air Service Regiment enjoys a privilege (among others) shared only by the other two SF regiments.

They are allowed to choose their weaponry from a worldwide menu rather than accept what is allotted to them by the Ministry of Defence.

For a combat rifle they prefer the C8 carbine by Diemaco, now made by Colt Canada. Its barrel is only 15.7 inches long but the gun is cold-hammer forged and very accurate. For a sniper rifle they choose the Accuracy International AX50 with a Schmidt and Bender scopesight. There were six of each concealed behind the curtains of Chandler's Court. The moon had not emerged, but it did not matter. The night-vision sights illuminated the intruders in a liquid-green luminescence. And the weapons pointed at them were silenced.

Anton led his comrades as they emerged from the trees on to the grassland. He was no stranger to violence, having put three England football fans on the streets of Marseille into wheelchairs. But he was still surprised when the hollow-point slug hit him in the chest. Half a second later he ceased to be surprised because he was dead.

Seeing him go down, his companions brought their assault carbines to the fire position, but too late. Hollow-point ordnance does not permit debate or post-trauma surgery. Two of the six, realizing they were in a killing ground, turned and tried to make the cover of the trees. They went face down and stayed there.

Within five minutes the six cadavers had been dragged into an outhouse belonging to the manor. They would be removed in a windowless van to the mortuary at Stirling Lines, until a decision could be made. Mother Nature and a long hose-watering would cope with the red splashes on the greensward.

In daylight the parked van outside the wall was traced, hot-wired, driven a hundred miles and torched. The local police in that county traced it to a second-hand-car dealer in London from whom it had been bought for cash by a man who did not exist. The burnt-out carcass went to a car crusher. The slaughter at Chandler's Court simply never happened.

At Yazenevo, Yevgeni Krilov waited in vain for news. In two days he would realize that his killers were not coming home. But he still had his ace. He would try again. He had to. The Vozhd would insist.

In London, Sir Adrian was woken by another pre-dawn phone call and given an elliptical report that would have meant nothing to any eavesdropper. Something about the weeds having been successfully cleared from the garden.

He sat in his flat as the rising June sun tipped the spire of Big Ben over the Palace of Westminster down the street called Whitehall and stared at the face in the frame. The eyes above the Slavic cheekbones, last seen at a meaningless cocktail party twenty years ago, stared back. The British spymaster seldom swore, but he swore now. With venom. His worst fears had come true.

The name Chandler's Court had never crossed the Atlantic. He would scan the records, uncover every occasion it had ever been used, where and by whom. Who had heard it? How had Yevgeni Krilov ever learned it?

This second mole, this hidden informant, must be in London, close at hand in the heart of the establishment. Moscow simply knew too much. The FBI had been adamant: the late Harold Jennings, father of the autistic genius, had had no chance to give up the name Chandler's Court. But they knew. There had to be a traitor. The hunter gene in Adrian Weston came back on-stream.

Back in the Cold War, even after the crushing of the Hungarian uprising of 1956 and the brutal suppression of the Czechs in 1968, when so many Western Communists, disgusted by the ruthlessness of Moscow, had abandoned their deranged faith, there were still diehards who clung to Karl Marx's dream right to the end.

But that end was well past. Even Moscow and the man who now controlled Russia had abandoned Communism for rabid nationalism. Even the most deluded intellectual – and Sir Adrian had never fooled himself that even a lauded intellectual could not also be as thick as a plank – would no longer spy for Communism. The traitor had to have a motive, and a powerful one. What could it be?

Wounded pride, resentment at ego-affronting treatment, self-importance? As a spotter and recruiter in the Cold War, Sir Adrian had exploited them all.

A life of freedom in the West worked as a motive for prisoners of the Communist world, but something else was behind this leak. Where and in what documents had the name Chandler's Court been mentioned? Only among a very select few, which would mean that the leak must have come from someone already high up in the British system, someone well paid, privileged, cosseted. He settled on two motives. Blackmail, perhaps to cover up career-destroying private behaviour? That could still work. Or old-fashioned money-greed. Bribery as old as humanity. Then he began to hunt for the leak. He used his influence to call for the transcripts; all the meetings concerning the relocation of the Jenningses had been recorded.

There was COBRA, the Cabinet Office Briefing Room. The 'A' might stand for 'Annexe' but probably does not. It was simply added to make a word beloved of the media. He remembered one meeting at the long oval table with squared-off ends in that silent room in the basement of the Cabinet Office. Being underground, you could not hear the rumble of traffic on Whitehall, as you could on the ground floor. The attendance list was clear: only five, and from the very top drawer. The transcript made no mention of Chandler's Court. He would have been the only one to know that he had made the choice of the manor house as the new home of the ultra-secret cyber-unit. And he had not mentioned the name.

There had been a restricted Cabinet meeting inside Number Ten, Downing Street, in the same room where he and the Prime Minister had confronted the US ambassador. Those present were Mrs Marjory Graham, the Home, Foreign and Defence secretaries, the Cabinet Secretary – the highest civil servant in the land – and two note-takers. Again, Chandler's Court had not been mentioned.

That left only one meeting: of the National Security Council, which he had attended as a guest. And yes, Chandler's Court had been mentioned once. Those attending were the Home and Foreign secretaries, the heads of GCHQ, MI6, MI5 and the Joint Intelligence Committee. And the Assistant Cabinet Secretary, whose superior was abroad with the Prime Minister on that day.

He decided to concentrate on that meeting. Everyone at it had security clearance to the highest level. But so did Kim Philby. There never was a human machine in history that could not make a mistake. In the Firm they had a saying: if you want to keep something secret and three men know, shoot two of them. He thought about the two possible motives.

Blackmail? He stared at seven faces. Could one be a victim of blackmail? A secret orgiast? A paedophile? An embezzler in an earlier career? All were possible.

Or bribery? Back in the Cold War, falling for pro-Communist ideology had been the British weakness. For the Americans, it had always been money. He recalled the Walker Family, Aldrich Ames – always traitors for money.

London is a world banking centre and has been for centuries. Add insurance, money management, international finance. Out of London tentacles spread to a thousand banks in a hundred countries, along with personal friendships and connections. Adrian Weston had some contacts in that world, centred on a single square mile of inner

London called simply The City. He knew some ex-spooks who had settled after the fray for a life on the board of a bank. He decided to call in some markers. Within days, he had a reply.

The question he had asked was simple. Had anyone noticed, probably in a tax or banking haven – meaning home to dubious transactions – a deposit account recently opened by the Russians? Opened, massively endowed then quickly emptied and closed?

A merchant banker called to say he had heard a murmur. Liechtenstein. The Vaduz Bank. A well-lubricated dinner in Davos not too long ago and a certain Herr Ludwig Fritsch who talked too much.

There is no international airport for Vaduz. Liechtenstein is tiny, a principality situated entirely within the Alps and by head of population the richest country in the world. Its capital, Vaduz, contains twelve large and secretive banks. Sir Adrian secured an interview with Herr Fritsch over the phone. The knighthood helped; he indicated he might be seeking a home for some money and that was enough.

He flew to Zurich, in next-door Switzerland, and rented a car. He always travelled with carry-on luggage, he flew economy class and he dropped the 'Sir' on his passport. Old habits die hard. He had had a career dedicated to invisibility, and it had served him well.

With the help of a satnav he arrived an hour early at the bank so he took an extended coffee at a café across the street. Vaduz is a quiet little town; sitting at his window table, he must have seen a dozen walkers on the pavements. People drive in Vaduz. Carefully.

Inside the bank he was escorted across the lobby, up two floors in the lift and into the office of Herr Ludwig Fritsch. His first task was to dispose of the idea that he had come to open a lucrative account.

'It is a delicate matter,' he said.

Fritsch was as smooth as a ball of butter and about as communicative. He indicated that he rarely concerned himself with matters that were not delicate. They sipped spring water from crystal glasses.

'How can I be of assistance, Sir Adrian?'

'In my country a very large sum of money has been stolen. One of those dispossessed is Her Majesty.'

That shook the buttery Herr Fritsch. In the cyber-age financial crime was pandemic and London could not expect to be immune. But Vaduz did not wish to become a depository for the proceeds of theft – at least not the provable sort. And anything concerning the British queen could go as high as his own head of state, Prince Hans-Adam II. That was serious.

'Outrageous.'

'It was, of course, financial. A swindle on a massive scale, involving money-laundering.'

'It is a scourge, Sir Adrian. Everywhere. I say again, how may I help?' This time, he meant it.

'We know the perpetrator. Scotland Yard's bank-crime division are not fools.'

'You think he resides here in Liechtenstein? Heaven forbid.'

'No, no, no. He is a Russian. We know the stolen wealth went to Russia. A very shady billionaire, far too many of whom are permitted to live in London.'

Herr Fritsch nodded earnestly. On that subject there was not a cigarette paper between the views of the two men.

'You British are very tolerant, Sir Adrian.'

'Perhaps more than we should be.'

'Indeed. But how can that affect Liechtenstein and the Vaduz Bank?'

'All barrels of apples, Herr Fritsch, risk a bad one. We think the fraudster had some help. From inside the barrel. In fact, we know it. And the rogue will insist on taking a very large financial reward. I know I can rely on your discretion . . .'

'This bank is known for it.'

'. . . when I say that phones have been tapped, communications intercepted.'

Ludwig Fritsch needed no convincing. The expertise of the British at that sort of thing had been established when Sir Francis Walsingham, spy-catcher to Queen Elizabeth I, had kept his monarch alive by intercepting the secret letters of conspirators.

'There is a possibility . . .' Herr Fritsch knew it was beyond a possibility. The bloody British had proof, or what was this obvious spook doing in his office? And the prince's palace was only a mile away.

'. . . that quite recently a person of Russian origin

opened a deposit account. That it was quickly endowed with a large sum of money. And that another person came to empty it, possibly to cash. We would, of course, be immensely grateful . . .'

Herr Fritsch excused himself and left the office. When he returned he held a slim folder.

'I have conferred with colleagues, Sir Adrian,' he began. Nothing flickered in Adrian Weston's face, but he knew he was being lied to. So the buttery Herr Fritsch was part of the scam. A bought man.

'A month ago a gentleman came here and sat exactly where you now are. He was from the Russian embassy in Bern, across the border. He opened a deposit account. A nominal sum was used for that. A week later the equivalent in euros of five million US dollars was paid in by electronic transfer. No source.'

'A tidy sum. And the beneficiary?'

'A week after that another man came. No name. It was not necessary. Under the terms of the account, only a sequence of letters and numbers was required. This man had exactly the necessary identification. But he was certainly a fellow countryman of yours.'

'And he withdrew it all to cash.'

'He did indeed. I am authorized to reveal this solely on the basis that I have your word it will go no further.'

'You have my word, Herr Fritsch. But as he crossed the lobby, the CCTV camera I noticed there would have secured a picture.'

'You are very astute, Sir Adrian.'

'One does one's best, Herr Fritsch.'

'You understand that I cannot permit this file to leave this room. But if you happened to glance at it, I could hardly prevent you.'

The file lay between them. Herr Fritsch rose and turned his back to stare out of the window at the town below. Adrian Weston leaned forward and flicked open the file. It contained a single print-out of the lobby and the man crossing it. He glanced, closed the file and pushed it back across the desk. Herr Fritsch resumed his seat.

'Herr Fritsch, I and indeed my country are enormously grateful. I assure you, what I have seen today will go no further. Steps will be taken, but nothing will come back to this bank.'

They shook hands in well-simulated camaraderie. An escort was summoned and the Britisher was accompanied back to the front door. He glanced up towards the mounted camera that had photographed the man carrying the bulging Gladstone bag containing $5 million in high-denomination euro bills.

His rented car was in the bank's car park. He began the long drive back to Zurich airport. From his second-floor office, Herr Ludwig Fritsch watched him go and reached for the phone.

On the drive, Sir Adrian mulled over what he had seen. The photo image showed a middle-aged senior civil servant in the lobby where he had been a few moments earlier. The face was unmistakeable and he knew it well. It was Julian Marshall, the Assistant Cabinet Secretary in London.

It had long occurred to Sir Adrian that the guilty party must have left London to visit Vaduz and retrieve his Judas money. But it was a needle-in-a-haystack shot. Virtually everyone at the very top of the tree had a country home, regularly visited at weekends. Any mandarin could slip away unnoticed, board a private executive jet, fly there and back, and reappear unspotted. Nothing had come up in his investigations. He stared again at the photo in his mind's eye. There was something wrong, some tiny detail. Then he saw it.

The Russian in Yazenevo who had concocted the photo had done a brilliant job. The shoes were probably from Lobb's in St James's, the beautifully cut suit undoubtedly from Savile Row. And the face that had been photoshopped on to the torso was certainly that of the civil servant who had chaired the meeting of the National Security Council when the name Chandler's Court had been mentioned.

The image-creator had been very clever, apart from a single error. The concocted figure was wearing the wrong tie.

Chapter Nine

FOR MOST MEN worldwide, the tie, if worn at all, is a strip of cloth wound around the neck under the collar, knotted at the front and allowed to fall down the chest. The pattern or motif, if any, is at the choice of the wearer. But in England they can be a bit more than that.

The pattern and colours of the stripes or the nature of the design woven into the cloth can indicate in a moment which school the wearer went to, the military unit he served with or the club he belongs to. It is a sort of code, a kind of recognition key.

Julian Marshall had undoubtedly attended Eton College, one of Britain's most exclusive private academies or 'public schools'. And those who have attended are entitled to wear the Old Etonian tie. Actually, there are three ties: the standard OE tie on black with slanting pale-blue stripes, and two even more exclusive because they indicate athletic achievement within the school.

There is the Eton Ramblers tie: magenta with purple and green stripes and fine gold lines, so carefully clashing it has to be deliberate. This is for those who have played cricket for their school. And this is what the figure in the photo was wearing.

And there is the Eton Vikings tie: dark red and black stripes with light blue lines, for those who have rowed for the college. The two sports occupy the summer term and thus exclude each other.

Sir Adrian recalled years ago standing on the banks of the Thames at Henley, weekending with an MI6 colleague who had a Thames-side cottage, watching Eton win the Princess Elizabeth Cup. Rowing at stroke in the Eton Eight was a very young Julian Marshall.

Before reaching Zurich airport, he realized he had been looking in the wrong place. He had presumed that a senior mandarin was the Judas. That was what Krilov had wished him to think and why they had gone to all that trouble to bribe Herr Fritsch to put out word of a fictional bank account and a fictional visit by a genuine British civil servant. He had been almost out-calculated. What he had forgotten is that there is another category of person who sits at the heart of the British establishment – the invisible underling.

As one of life's compulsive observers, he had noted that those styled as the great and the good often overlooked the army of good and loyal men and women who really made the machine of commerce, the professions and of government work: the drivers, the secretaries, the note-takers, the file copiers, the archive-keepers, the interpreters, even the white-jacketed coffee-servers.

They came, they went, they stood and served, and they were generally ignored. But they were not wooden statues. They had eyes and ears, brains to remember, deduce, and certainly a capacity to feel affronted, ignored, belittled by the snobbish and arrogant.

That the name Chandler's Court had been passed to the Russians there was no doubt. But which underling had broken ranks? As to the 'why?', he still clung to bribery, and nothing like $5 million's worth. But where in the haystack of Whitehall was this invisible needle to be traced? He recalled from his days at MI6 the exposure of a leak and the ruse he had employed to bring the mover in darkness to the light. He would have to use it again.

On the flight back to Heathrow his mind returned to the single conference when the name Chandler's Court had been fleetingly mentioned. Someone present had heard that, possibly noted the words, the name of the place where the youth nicknamed the Fox had been lodged for his safety.

Who had been present? Well, the heads of four Intelligence services: MI6, MI5, GCHQ and Joint Intel. All security-cleared to the eyeballs. But who had sat behind them, quietly note-taking?

And there were two Cabinet ministers, the Secretaries from the Home Office and Foreign Office, each with a small team of subordinates.

Four days had passed since the Russians' raid on Chandler's Court. Sir Adrian was certain that Krilov had by now concluded that the armed attack had been a total disaster. There at least it was they who had underestimated him. Perhaps they could be tricked into doing it again. It would be logical for him to move his hacking phenomenon somewhere else. So he would do the opposite.

He had in any case conferred with Dr Hendricks on this after the shoot-out. The computer wizard from Cheltenham had begged him not to relocate the family, if it was at all feasible. The academic had over a few weeks become like a surrogate father to the youth. Every time Luke Jennings was moved or his world disrupted, he descended into a mental crisis. And he had just been tasked with his second database-hacking exploration and was working on it.

Sir Adrian, on one of his visits, had noted with approval the developing relationship. After a lifetime in computers Dr Hendricks was, in technical terms, far ahead of the teenage boy. But neither he nor anyone else from GCHQ could match the seeming sixth sense of the youth when it came to penetrating the blinding complexity of the firewalls that the major powers used to protect their innermost secrets. Dr Hendricks might have resented this. Others probably would. But Jeremy Hendricks had a generosity of spirit that endowed him with a protective paternalism towards the young genius in his charge. Luke Jennings seemed to respond to this. He was receiving daily encouragement, something he had never had from his late father. Rejected, he had lived in his own private world. His mother could protect, shield his fragility as a mother hen with her chick, but she could not encourage, because his world was utterly incomprehensible to her, as it was to Sir

Adrian and would have been to all Luke's former school-teachers. Only with Dr Hendricks did he at last have a common language. So, for Sir Adrian, Hendricks's advice was important. If moving the entire hub from Chandler's Court somewhere else would send the boy into a frantic depression, it would be resisted. Luke Jennings would have to stay where he was.

So, with Hendricks's advice in mind, Sir Adrian began to work on his attempt to wrongfoot Krilov. He would pretend to move the lad and let it be known that he had. He would choose four targets. But first there was some research to do. He began with his copious contact list. Four country houses, all set in their own grounds.

In the days when he kept a pair of shotguns and accepted invitations to spend a day shooting pheasant and partridge he had made acquaintance with over a dozen of these home-owners. He rang four of them and asked for the favour he wished. All agreed. One even suggested 'it might be fun', which was certainly one way of putting it. He doubted the Night Wolves on their slabs in Hereford-shire would agree.

His second concern was to revisit the Director of the Special Forces.

The brigadier was courteous but reproving.

'The CO of the Regiment is not best pleased,' he remarked. 'He thought his men were on a training mission close-protecting a family of three and three boffins. They end up in a re-enactment of Stalingrad.'

'That was evenly balanced,' replied Sir Adrian. 'What happened at Chandler's Court was very one-sided. But please convey my apologies to the Regiment. I had no idea the killers had located the target. Had I known, the target would not even have been there. The house would have been empty. What is likely to follow will be wholly different.'

He explained his proposition. The DSF thought it over.

'I recommend the SRR. They're based in Herefordshire too. At Credenhill. I would suggest two men per house. Then they could spell each other.'

The Special Reconnaissance Regiment is, with the SAS and the Special Boat Service, one of Britain's three SF fighting units. High among its skill sets are covert entry and invisibility. Add to that close observation (unseen). Its members will usually seek to avoid close encounters but can be just as lethal as members of the other two units if needs demand.

There was another encrypted conversation between the commanding officer of SRR at his Credenhill base and the DSF. Once again the evocation of the wishes of the Prime Minister in assisting her security adviser clinched the matter.

The four pairs of unexpected house guests arrived at the residences of their hosts within twenty-four hours and were made welcome. The four residences were a manor, a grange and two farms.

All the houses were large and sprawling, set deep in the

countryside, where a wandering stranger, let alone a foreigner on a scouting mission, would be noticeable. The soldiers installed themselves in their quarters, patrolled the surrounding territory and selected their watching points. In each case they chose an elevated eyrie to give a good overview of the grounds of the residence. Then, turn and turnabout, they mounted guard.

Sir Adrian had picked four of those who had attended the crucial National Security Council meeting. These were the quite innocent Julian Marshall, the Home Secretary, the Foreign Secretary and the chairman of the Joint Intelligence Committee. He knew them all, though the two politicians less well.

He wrote to each a very personal private letter with the envelope so marked that it would not be opened except by the hands of the man named on the front. After perusal it would be seen by not more than one other, a confidential private or filing secretary trusted with classified correspondence.

He explained that there had been an incident at Chandler's Court and he felt it wise to move the young cyber-hacker at the heart of Operation Troy to a new location. He then revealed the new location, but each one was different. For clarity, Weston identified them to himself as A, B, C and D.

He knew about waiting. Much of espionage involves waiting, and he had spent his life in it. An angler knows the feeling: the hours trying not to nod off into a doze, to keep eyes on the floater, an ear cocked for the tinkle of the little bell at the rod-tip. When a trap has been laid it is similar, except that there are constant false alarms. Each call has to be attended to, but it is not the one the setter of the trap is really waiting for.

He did not have to wait long. The call came, as agreed, from the CO of the Regiment at Credenhill.

'My lads tell me they are under observation. Someone patrolling the woods, field glasses, staring at the house. My men have, of course, not been seen. Do you want the intruder taken? Just say the word.'

'Thank you, Colonel. I have what I need. I think you will find he will soon be gone.'

The colonel had named Residence C. That was Persimmon Grange, in Wiltshire. Years ago on a one-day shoot Sir Adrian had knocked down fifty pheasant as one of eight guns. A former ambassador from an embassy behind the Iron Curtain had retired there with his arthritic wife and plain daughter.

Persimmon Grange was the location mentioned in the letter to the Home Secretary. Weston needed to talk to him.

He got his chat after the minister finished a private lunch at Brooks's. They repaired to the library, where the portraits of the Dilettantes stared down at them.

'I really do need to know, Home Secretary, who would have seen that letter after you read it.'

The man was twenty years his junior, one of the up-and-coming thrusters, one of those to whom the Prime

Minister had given high office and who was proving worthy of it, despite his youth.

It was not a long conversation. There was no need to waste time.

'After I read it,' said the Home Secretary, 'it would have been filed. One copy only, the one you sent, no duplicates, filed under lock and key. By my personal private secretary, Robert Thompson.'

Unless something had gone badly wrong, Sir Adrian had his betrayer.

Robert Thompson was a civil servant on a civil servant's salary. He did not live in Chelsea, Knightsbridge or Belgravia but south of the river in Battersea. Records showed he was a widower with a daughter aged ten who lived with him. Sir Adrian knocked at the door of the flat just after 8 p.m. It was answered by the man whose file he had been studying.

Thompson was about forty, and he looked tired and strained. There was no sign of any daughter. Jessica might be on a sleepover with a schoolfriend. When Thompson saw Sir Adrian on the doorstep, something flickered in his eyes. Not surprise, not guilt, but resignation. Whatever he had been doing, it was over and he knew it.

The civilities were observed. Thompson invited Adrian Weston into his sitting room. Both remained standing. No need, again, to waste time.

'Why did you do it? Didn't we pay you enough?'

In reply Thompson slumped into an armchair and put his face in his hands.

'Jessica,' he said.

Ah, the daughter. A better school, perhaps. More exotic holidays. The tropics. Keeping up with better-off friends. He noticed a framed photo on a side table. A young girl: freckles, pigtails, a trusting smile. Daddy's little girl.

Then the younger man's shoulders began to shake. Sir Adrian turned away. The man was weeping like a child and Sir Adrian had a problem with crying men. He came from a generation and a military tradition that taught other things.

In triumph, modesty. In pain, stoicism. In defeat, grace under fire. But very rarely tears. Winston Churchill had been prone to tears, but he had been different in many ways.

He recalled two times when he had seen grown men break down. There was the agent in East Germany who had made it through Checkpoint Charlie into the West and safety and who had collapsed in sheer relief at being alive and free at last. And his own son, in the maternity ward, looking down at the wrinkled, outraged face of his first-born son, Sir Adrian's only grandchild, now at Cambridge. But a traitor caught red-handed? Let him weep. But then, everything changed.

'They have her,' sobbed the man in the chair. 'Snatched her on her way home from school. A voice on the phone. Threatening they would gang-rape her, strangle her . . . unless.'

An hour later Sir Adrian had the details. The child walking home alone after choir practice. A car at the kerb. A friend watching from fifty yards away the only witness. Jessica had got into the car – half pulled, half pushed by the man on the pavement. It drove off.

Then the phone call. So they knew his mobile number, but she would have given them that. There was a special nickname she used for her dad. The speaker knew that too.

The voice? Fluent English but accented. Russian? Possibly. There was a number retained by Thompson's phone, but it would be a buy-and-throw, a 'burner', long gone into the Thames.

Sir Adrian left the broken man with one last instruction. To tell his contact at the next call that there had been another letter. Weston had changed his mind. The youth would be moved, but to an army camp, not a private house.

He left the house in Battersea and walked home, back across the Thames to Whitehall and Admiralty Arch. He had spent a lifetime trying to avoid anger. It clouded judgement, defeated logic, obscured clarity. When things went wrong an intelligent man needed all three. But he was angry now.

He had lost agents and grieved comrades who would never come home. He had been in hard, merciless places, but there were still rules. Children were out of bounds. Now Moscow had again decided to abandon all rules, as with the attack on long-retired Colonel Skripal.

Adrian Weston had few illusions about the profession of espionage to which he had devoted most of his life. He knew it had its darker side. He had repeatedly put his freedom and his life on the line because experience in 'the job' had convinced him that in a thoroughly imperfect world it was necessary if the safe and free were to remain safe and free. He believed in his own country and in its tested standards. He believed that these were basically decent, but he also knew that on modern planet Earth decency was something to which only a small minority still held.

For years his main enemy had been the KGB and, since the fall of Soviet Communism, its successors. He knew that, across the divide, murder, torture and cruelty had been the norm. He had fiercely resisted the temptation to go down that route to cut corners, achieve results. He knew with regret that some allies had not resisted.

His own choice had always been to deceive the enemy, to outwit, to out-manoeuvre. And yes, there were dirty tricks, but how dirty? Servants of the global enemy had been suborned, persuaded to betray their country and spy for the West. And yes, by blackmail, if need be. Blackmail of thieves, of adulterers, of perverts in high office. It was repugnant but sometimes necessary, because the enemy from Stalin through to ISIS was far crueller and must not triumph. He knew that the man at Yazenevo now charged by the master of the Kremlin to avenge the *Nakhimov* humiliation, must, in his spectacular rise through the ranks, have endorsed or set into motion practices which Adrian Weston would not touch with a bargepole.

But this was different. A child had been snatched, possibly threatened with gang-rape, to blackmail a civil servant into committing treason. Krilov was using contracted killers, little more than animals. There would be retribution. There would be blood. He intended to ensure it.

Chapter Ten

THE COURTING COUPLE in the lay-by in the middle of the night were locked in each other's arms and took no notice when the saloon car shot by them, going well over the speed limit.

But they sprang apart with cries of alarm when, a hundred yards up the road, it came off the tarmac and slammed into a tree. They watched through the windscreen as the first flickering flames began to lick at the wreck at the foot of the trunk.

As the light level given off by the flames increased they could see the outline of a single figure silhouetted against the fire. Then the blaze took over as the petrol tank caught alight and the car exploded. The young man was on his mobile phone, dialling 999.

In due course there was an ambulance and two fire engines. The latter hosed the wreckage with white foam until the flames were gone, but there was nothing the paramedics could do for the slumped and fire-consumed figure in the front seat. What was left of him was removed and taken away to become yet another accident in a country-road statistic.

The mortuary team accomplished the distasteful job of identification. The rear trouser pockets of the victim had survived the worst of the blaze. There were credit cards, more or less undamaged. And a driving licence. The unfortunate who had been driving far too fast was identified as Robert Thompson, a civil servant resident in London, where he also worked.

Without the quiet influence that was brought to bear, the incident might not have hit the media, but it made the papers the following evening and the day after that. In fact it achieved more coverage on radio, TV and the papers than it might normally have merited. Such quiet influence is an aspect of British official life of which, like the iceberg, very little is ever observed.

The phone call followed the appearance of the morning papers. Sir Adrian had secured the fullest cooperation of both MI5 and GCHQ at Cheltenham. The first provided the telephone numbers, which would have proved a considerable surprise to those who actually owned those numbers and thought they were secure.

Thames House, home of the Security Service, is only a few hundred yards down the river from the mother of parliaments, but democracy invisibly ends on the doorstep. The mass expulsion of Russian spies posing as diplomats after the flagrant use of the Novichok nerve agent on the streets of Salisbury had caused chaos in the hitherto active espionage machine that Moscow operated in London.

Linkages were broken, ongoing operations stultified, relationships discontinued. The newcomer, Stepan Kukushkin, had lately become the Rezident inside the Russian embassy and he needed more time to work his way in. The same applied to his new deputy, Oleg Politovski, who had been a lowly press officer. Both men thought their private mobile phones were secure. They were not; they were tapped.

Outside the embassy were the on-contract servants of Krilov, among them Vladimir Vinogradov, a gang boss and professional criminal, and an oligarch and billionaire who had moved into London, bought a football club and lived in a £10 million apartment in Belgravia. He was the one who made the call. It was tapped. GCHQ had seen to that. Sir Adrian was not surprised. He knew that, behind his façade of football-match-attending bonhomie, Vinogradov was a thoroughly nasty piece of work.

Back in the Russia of Yeltsin, Vinogradov had been a fully paid-up member of the gangster underworld, racking up convictions for protection, racketeering, rape, murder and armed robbery. He had served time in Lefortovo prison in Moscow. When the rape of Russia's natural assets began, he was at freedom and raised several million dollars. With the help of corrupt bureaucrats, he was able to buy a small Siberian oil field at a peppercorn price. This made him a billionaire. Then he threw in his lot with the rising Vodzh. Mysteriously, his entire criminal record was voided, stricken from the record. Newly respectable, he emigrated to London and became a lavish host.

Even though Vinogradov thought the line was secure, he was circumspect in what he said. The call was to a notorious Albanian gangster who ran his mob in south London, where the Richardson gang, rival of the Krays, once ruled the roost. Bujar Zogu had worked for him before. Always contract work and always involving violence. Sir Adrian had a transcript of what they said within an hour of the call.

Vinogradov was giving the orders, and they were simple. The operation is over, finished, cancelled. Get a message to your friends. Do not use any means of telecommunication. Drive personally to their location. Get rid of all the evidence – I mean, all of it – leave no trace and return home.

Clearly, time was of the essence. Once Zogu reached the place his thugs were holding the girl, she would be killed.

The Driver and Vehicle Licensing Agency in Swansea had Zogu's car details in seconds. A modest dark blue Volvo saloon, registration number such-and-such. Weston's next call was to the Commissioner of the Metropolitan Police, Lucinda Berry.

'Lucy, can you help me?'

'If it is legal and possible. What is it?'

'There is an Albanian gangster motoring out of his south London base. Destination unknown.' He dictated the car details. 'I have reason to believe that when he reaches his destination a child will be murdered. Can we intercept him?'

'Good God, we must.'

London is ringed by the 117-mile-long M25 motorway. It is constantly cruised by patrol cars but most of all it is surveyed by thousands of HADECS-3 speed-control cameras, centrally linked and computer-obedient. One of them got the Volvo on the southern arc of the motorway, heading for the Dartford Tunnel under the Thames.

There are toll booths there and cameras. The passage of the Volvo through the tunnel and on to the northern arc was noted. Ten miles later a patrol car slid out of Junction 29 to take up the tail. It was warned to pull off at the next intersection.

Bujar Zogu noted the police car in his rear-view mirror but he also noted that it pulled off at Junction 28. By then a police helicopter had found the blue car beneath it. The chopper held station until the Volvo left Essex county, still orbiting London on the motorway.

An unmarked police car had the tail until Junction 16, when the Albanian pulled on to the M40 motorway heading north-west towards the Midlands and Wales. Thames Valley Police took over, then another police helicopter.

After two hours' driving it was plain the Albanian was heading into Wales, specifically north Wales, one of the most sparsely occupied portions of the UK mainland.

The easy way would have been to intercept Zogu and

flag him down. But Scotland Yard had drawn down their file on him. This said he was smart and cunning. He would know, having stuck to the speed limit all the way, that there was no reason to flag him down. And the authorities still did not know where he was going, in what isolated place he and his team had hidden their prisoner. He might have it on his satnav screen, but he could wipe that even as the officers were walking towards him. Months of interrogation would never drag it out of him.

Sir Adrian did not have months. The only good news was that Zogu had abided by his orders. He had made no attempt to use his mobile phone to warn his team that he was coming, or why. But he still had to be stopped before he got there. At that point, there might be only seconds to spare. That was when Sir Adrian called on help from the Special Reconnaissance Regiment at Credenhill.

By late afternoon the roads the Albanian was following were becoming narrower and more isolated. He was on the A5, heading for Bangor. He was just turning off, following the guidance of his satnav, towards Denbigh Moors, when the SRR helicopter came up behind him. It was high and in his blind spot. He did not see it, but the six troopers on board saw him.

The troopers had been told only that a kidnapped child was being held against her will and if the man in the blue Volvo beneath them reached the hideout she would be murdered. That was enough. Soldiers become really angry about people threatening children.

★

The Denbigh Moors are a wilderness of heath and scattered farmsteads. The Volvo pulled off on to a narrow track that led to such a farm two miles ahead. There was no other building on that lane.

From his vantage at a thousand feet, the pilot of the Dauphin drawn from the Joint Special Forces Aviation Wing could see that the track ended just beyond the farm and went nowhere. The farm appeared abandoned, a single van in the yard. A working farm would have more than that.

From behind his windscreen Bujar Zogu saw an unmarked helicopter sweep overhead in the same direction as himself then drop out of sight behind high ground that rose ahead of him. What he did not see was the chopper descending into the valley, or the two men in camouflage uniform with machine pistols leaping out.

Until he crested the rise. The helicopter was gone – off down the valley and out of sight. The two soldiers were in the road. He did not notice that their MP5s were silenced. He could not fail to notice that they were waving him down. He slowed and stopped. The men approached his car, one on each side. Beside him was his folded jacket. Under it was his handgun.

He really should not have reached for it. It was a silly mistake. And it was his last. It fulfilled the 'self-defence' condition. His colleagues in the farmhouse would never receive the Russian message.

One of the soldiers by the riddled car spoke briefly to the four further down the valley.

They were also now on foot, trekking back towards the farm. Before it came in sight they disappeared into the waist-high heather.

One of the skill sets of the SRR is known as CTR, or close-target recce. It means drawing up close to a building so stealthily that the occupants never spot you outside. Using the cover of the barns and outbuildings, the six men, with darkness now closing in, reached windowsill level still unspotted.

One of the windows was broken but boarded up. There were cracks between the boards. An eye was applied.

'Three inhabitants,' murmured a voice into a lapel-mic. It was heard by the other five on earpieces. 'Ground floor. Living room cum kitchen. Eating. All armed.'

Another skill is MOE, or method of entry. There was not much point in further stealth. There was going to be a firefight. One of the troopers slipped to the front door and gave an imperious knock. Then stepped aside.

The three eaters jumped to their feet with cries in Albanian. Seconds later four bullets tore through the front door from the inside. After that it was open season. Hitherto invisible troopers appeared at each glassed window. The two kidnappers still standing by the table never had a chance to fire or surrender. They were holding guns, and that was enough. At the front, the door came down and the third Albanian died in the hall.

It took seconds to clear the ground floor, which had only four small rooms. These contained a few sticks of furniture and, now, three smelly bodies leaking red stuff.

The team leader raced upstairs. Two rooms, neither a bathroom. He threw open the door of one. More stink of unwashed bodies. Three smelly bedrolls. The trooper did not know for sure how many Albanians might be mounting guard over the hostage. There might be a fourth with a gun to the girl's head. He eased open the door across the landing, MP5 at the ready.

Chapter Eleven

S HE WAS ALONE, in a chair at the far corner. The room was small and dark. A single low-wattage bulb with no shade hung on a flex from the ceiling.

There was a thin bedroll and a stinking bucket for a toilet. A food-encrusted bowl and a bottle of water from the yard. And one chair.

The single window had once looked out on rolling fields but planks had been nailed across it so that only tiny slivers of light came through the cracks between the boards. The overpowering impression for the soldier was the stench. Clearly, it had never been an elegant room, but it had become a hellhole.

Big black flies buzzed round the feeble bulb. Others crawled on the rim of the latrine bucket, gorged by its contents. The child had been forced to eat from the bowl and to lie on the stinking palliasse on the floor. Or to sit on the single chair, where she now was, still in her school uniform, unwashed, with matted hair, accustomed to the smell of the room. Her arms were clasped around her, the eyes huge saucers of trauma and fear. She said nothing.

The SRR man slowly laid down his gun and removed his black ski-mask. His sudden appearance could only have frightened her. She had had enough of that. He did not attempt to approach. Instead he slid to the floor, back against the wall. Then he said: 'Hello.' And he smiled.

There was no reply. She just stared.

'I wonder if you can help me. I'm looking for a girl called Jessica. Her daddy has asked me to bring her home.'

Her lips moved. There was a small squeak.

'It's me.'

He affected pleased surprise.

'Really? Oh, that's wonderful. I've found you. Your daddy is missing you. He asked me to fetch you home. Would you like that?'

She nodded. He looked around.

'This is a horrid place. I bet your room back in London is nicer.'

She began to cry. Tears welled out of the frightened, exhausted eyes and rolled down her grimy cheeks.

'I want to go home. I want to see Daddy.'

'Well, that's marvellous, Jessica. I'd like that too. I've got some friends downstairs and we have a helicopter. Have you ever been in one?'

She shook her head. He rose slowly and carefully and crossed the room. He held out one hand. She took it and he eased her out of the chair. She began to urinate and cried even more, in shame. The effects of profound trauma are several and none of them are pretty. He turned away and went to the door.

'Coming down!' he called. 'Clear the hall.'

No need for her to see what lay there, or in the kitchen. Outside, he saw the downlights of the Dauphin and heard the growl of its twin engines. It settled in the heather beyond the barns, where there was space.

The other men were waiting below. They had dragged the bodies into the kitchen and closed the door. They saw the girl holding their colleague's hand as she came tentatively down the stairs, taking them one by one. They looked up at her, and one said: 'Jesus.' If there had been any feeling for the men they had killed, it vaporized.

The team leader helped Jessica Thompson into the Dauphin for the flight back to Credenhill.

He tried to use his mobile phone, only to discover that the dead Zogu could not have contacted his men even if he had tried. That part of the Denbigh Moors has no reception. He climbed in beside the girl and nodded at the pilot.

The other men would stay behind to be collected later. In the meantime, they had some clearing up to do. Down on the road, they had not shot up the engine of the Volvo and it still worked. One of them set off to collect it. There would be five troopers to pick up and four dead gangsters in body bags. The helpful but no doubt puzzled police of

Conwy County would be asked to crush the ruined Volvo into a block of scrap.

At Credenhill they delivered Jessica straight to the medical unit. Two female troopers took over, fussing as the girl bathed and shampooed her hair. One of them emerged to tell the commanding officer:

'They didn't touch her, you know. They threatened to, and leered at her every time they brought food. So just in time. She's a clever girl. Head on her shoulders. She'll need counselling, but she'll recover.'

The CO rang Sir Adrian, and he told Robert Thompson, who was very much still alive. Sir Adrian had a car with a driver and despatched both on the long drive through the dawn to Hereford for the reunion.

When they arrived back in London Sir Adrian visited Thompson again at his Battersea flat.

'I doubt you can continue in the civil service after this. Or whether you would want to. Perhaps a change of scene. And guaranteed security for you both.

'I know a place that is very beautiful. Warm climate, sparkling blue sea. Wellington, New Zealand. Good schools, welcoming people. I think I could arrange something, if you'd like. I know their High Commissioner in London.

'A good job with the Kiwi government. Nice house. Easy commute – it's not a big place. New life, perhaps. I think it might be arranged. Let me know.'

A month later Robert Thompson and Jessica left for that new life by the waters of the Cook Strait.

★

Adrian Weston was a humane man, and he was concerned to find out the true identity of the man whose charred remains had been in the remote-controlled speeding car.

Back in 1943 the Western Allies had been preparing the invasion of southern Europe. It was of concern to try to dupe the Nazi high command, to convince them that the invasion was coming where it was not coming. The British took the body of an unidentified down-and-out, dressed it in the uniform of a major in the Royal Marines and cast it adrift off the shore of southern Spain.

Attached to one wrist by a chain was a briefcase containing documents, apparently top secret, indicating that the invasion would be via Greece. The body drifted inshore, was found on a beach and handed to the Guardia Civil. Franco's Spain, technically neutral, was actually pro-Axis. The papers were passed to German intelligence and thence back to Berlin.

Greece was massively reinforced. The Allies under Patton and Montgomery invaded via Sicily and Italy. Thousands of lives were saved. Later, a book was written and a film made, both titled *The Man Who Never Was*. That was where Sir Adrian had got the idea.

The body in the speeding car was also that of a down-and-out, a dweller on the streets and alleys, and also unidentifiable. He had been destined for a pauper's burial in an unmarked grave. The autopsy revealed that the man had died of pneumonia, probably caught from sleeping out in the rain. Tests showed he had been an irrecoverable alcoholic with an already badly damaged constitution. The only thing left on him that he had not pawned to buy booze was a signet ring.

But once, reasoned Sir Adrian, he had been a man, perhaps one who loved and had been loved, one who had a job, a family, a life. How had he ended up a wreck, dying in a gutter? He decided at least to try to find out.

He put a 'hold' on the pauper's grave. He called in favours, kicked backsides, rattled cages. A DNA sample was eventually retrieved. The national DNA database was consulted. But there was nothing. If the dead man had a criminal record, his sample should have been listed. There was no listing.

Weston was about to let officialdom take its course when a scientist working at the DNA database called him.

'There might be a sibling match,' he said.

The possible match on the database had been in a bar brawl years before and had been charged with assault causing actual bodily harm, or ABH, and had been convicted. And he had a name. Drake. Philip Drake. It took a bit of police time to find him through three address moves. But he was found. He was shown the signet ring and confirmed it had belonged to his brother Benjamin, known as Benny.

He had not seen his brother for twenty years, not since the older sibling, ravaged by post-traumatic stress disorder, had slipped through the welfare net and society's various charities into alcoholism and a life on the streets. But he recalled that Benny's problems had derived from combat in Afghanistan wearing his country's uniform.

He had been a Mercian, one of a regiment drawn from

the East Midlands, headquartered at Lichfield. Weston rang the commanding officer and told him. And the CO decided that, low as he had fallen, Corporal Benny Drake should have his soldier's funeral. He delved into the regimental reserve and found the funds.

A week later the funeral column came out of Main Gate Whittington Barracks and turned into the streets of Lichfield. A hearse topped by the Union Jack carried the coffin, and behind it came a limousine bearing both parents. The people of the city took off their hats and turned to face the road as it went by. The bearer party and a warrant officer brought up the rear. All moved at the slow march.

At Whittington village cemetery the column turned in and was directed to the prepared burial plot. The bearer party took over, six soldiers carrying the coffin the rest of the way, past St Giles's Church, to the grave. The regimental chaplain conducted the service. When it was over, the flag was removed from the coffin, folded and handed to the parents.

As the coffin was lowered into the ground the firing party stepped forward with the regimental bugler. The sextons waited with their shovels. The riflemen discharged three volleys over the grave and the bugler sounded the 'Last Post'. Mr and Mrs Drake stood very straight and very proud as their son Corporal Benny Drake was sent to rest. He may have died in a gutter, but he was laid down with fellow soldiers.

As the final note of the 'Last Post' drifted away, at the far end of the cemetery a single figure put away his field glasses. Sir Adrian climbed into his car and was driven back to London. There was a score to settle.

The following morning, his bank accounts frozen, Mr Vladimir Vinogradov was requested to leave the country. The formal explanation, which had no justification because, under law, it needed none, simply declared that, in the view of the British government, his continued presence was 'not conducive to the public good'.

He protested, threatening lengthy court appeals. A photo was laid on his desk. It showed the face, eyes closed, of a gangster he had commissioned to kidnap a child. He lapsed into silence, then rang his personal pilot at Northolt and instructed that his plane be made ready.

In the darkened computer room at Chandler's Court Luke Jennings crouched at a console, stared at the display, tapped several touch-screen symbols and stared again, locked into and lost in his private world. By his side, Dr Hendricks sat and watched. He knew what the teenager was doing, but not how he was doing it. There are moments when instinct defies and denies logic. The man from GCHQ had set a task that was deemed impossible . . . and yet.

Outside, it was pitch black, the middle of the night. Neither man at the console knew or cared. There are no hours in cyberspace. Somewhere, many miles away, a database silently fought back, seeking to protect its secrets. Just before dawn, it lost.

Dr Hendricks gaped in near-disbelief. Somehow, and

he had no idea how, it had been achieved: Luke Jennings had crossed the air gap and entered the right algorithms. The firewalls opened, the faraway database capitulated. There was no need to go on. They had the codes. He tapped the lad on the shoulder.

'You can close down now. We can come back. You have given us the access. Well done.'

In breaking into the database at Fort Meade, Maryland, Luke Jennings had unknowingly risked many years in an American jail. In doing the same to this one, there would be only praise. He did not care either way. There had been a challenge, and he had met it. That was all that mattered. Others could enter the foreign database and plant malware, Trojan horses, instructions that the equipment should destroy itself.

The foreign database lay under the deserts of the theocratic republic of Iran, a country that employed and propagated terrorism and wanted to build its own atomic bomb. There was another country, destined for annihilation if that atomic bomb ever became a viable weapon. If Sir Adrian had his way and could persuade the Prime Minister, the access codes to the Iranian database would be shared with the state of Israel.

But perhaps not entirely for free. The vast new natural gas field that had just been discovered off Israel's western shore might enter into the conversation.

Sue Jennings gazed up into the darkness as the first hint of day touched the east. She knew exactly what she was feeling, and she was enjoying every second of it. It had been so long.

Her marriage had, effectively, ended ten years earlier. The strains of raising the two boys, the additional needs of the elder one, had been part of it. But that was not the main cause. There had been no single blazing row with Harold. But he had eventually made plain that he had not a flicker of interest in the physical side of their marriage. At that point, they had not made love for weeks. He had then been in his mid-forties, she a very healthy thirty.

In the intervening decade there had been, for her, brief affairs, always wholly and only physical. But she and Harold had stayed together for the sake of the boys, especially Luke. There were practical considerations: a home, a constant income and all the things an income bought. But Harold was gone; she was now a widow.

What she was feeling in the coming dawn was raw lust, and it was for the touch of the man sleeping beside her. She knew he would not have risked crossing the length of the first floor to her and, anyway, her room was in between those occupied by Luke and Marcus. So she had finally come to him.

The door had been unlocked. She had entered, let her robe slip to the floor and climbed under the duvet beside him. Very little was said. They simply made love, he with his iron-hard strength, she with the passion of long-suppressed desire.

When Captain Williams and his men had been assigned to their small community, he had joined their communal

151

table: she, Dr Hendricks, two others from GCHQ and her sons. The civilities had been maintained, but the mutual attraction was in the eyes. Details slipped out. He was thirty-nine, single since his wife had died in a tragic canoe accident off the coast of the Algarve eight years earlier.

Sue Jennings had spent days considering what she should do. She could no longer even pretend to deny the powerful attraction she felt for the soldier who joined the family and the scientists at the meal table. When their gaze had met across the tea cups that first time, she sensed it was mutual.

But she was no skilled seductress. That had never been part of her life.

She waited for him to make a move but, scrupulously polite, he made no advances. Manners? Reserve? Damn them both. She knew she was falling in love. Why would he not make the first move? After three weeks she made her decision.

Just after midnight she had risen from her single bed, still quite naked. By moonlight, she had looked at herself in the wardrobe mirror. She was forty and her figure was full but in no way plump. She had kept herself in shape at the gym, but for whom? Not for lacklustre Harold, who had been more concerned with his golf handicap than making love.

She was still young enough to make another baby, and she wanted to do just that, but only with one man, and he was sleeping in a room at the opposite end of the house. Barefoot, she slipped a robe over her shoulders and opened the door, taking care to make no sound and wake the boys sleeping on either side of her room.

She had paused one last time outside his door, hearing the deep, regular breathing from within, before turning the knob and sliding inside. Now, they had spent their first night together. In the glimmer of dawn beyond the curtains she made up her mind. She was going to have him, and not for just a night. She intended to be the next Mrs Harry Williams, and she knew that a good-looking woman with a fixed determination would always make an Exocet missile look like a badly designed firework. As the late-June sun tipped the tops of the trees in the forest, she slipped back into her own room.

Chapter Twelve

IRAN HAS LUSTED for many years to have an atomic bomb. The idea was first mooted under the Shah, who was deposed in 1979. By then, he had been talked out of it by his friend and protector the USA. Under the ayatollahs, there was no such influence.

For many years, the technology was not the problem. A Pakistani scientist who had been at the heart of that country's successful research into and construction of atomic bombs traitorously sold the data to Iran. The problem had long been acquiring a sufficiently large stock of weapons-grade uranium.

Uranium ore, known as yellowcake, has been purchased for many years from various suppliers around the world. But in the form of ore, uranium-235 has a purity of five per cent or less. This is far too crude to be used in the production of a nuclear weapon. It has to be refined until it is close to ninety-five per cent pure.

The excuse for its purchase has always been to build electricity-generating power stations, for which five per cent purity is enough. The world has never believed this excuse. Why, runs the argument, should a country that is virtually floating on an ocean of crude oil and does not give a fig about the environment not exploit her own free raw material to keep the lights burning? The key has long been secret chemical plants, hidden from the world and denied, their function to refine the raw yellowcake into weapons-grade uranium-235.

The nuclear club of the USA, China, France, Russia and Britain, with non-nuclear Germany and the European Union, concluded an accord in 2015 to the effect that Iran would desist in her efforts in nuclear research in exchange for the relaxation of the many economic penalties inflicted because of her nuclear ambitions. In secret, the accord was not abided by.

The ayatollahs have long decreed that the state of Israel, not endowed with oil fields but technologically extremely advanced, is destined to be wiped from the face of the Earth. Israel thus has a considerable interest in the Iranian nuclear ambition. She also has the Mossad (the 'Institution'), her very effective secret intelligence arm. Espionage efforts to find out just what the Iranians in their dictatorship are up to and how far they have got have been unrelenting.

Iran was not the first neighbour of Israel to start a nuclear programme. That had been Syria, which learned its lesson in 2007. Israeli espionage and over-flights had detected a huge square building, nicknamed in Tel Aviv the Cube, being built near Deir Ezzor at a remote site in eastern Syria. It excited too much curiosity to be ignored. Further espionage revealed it was home to a North Korean-built nuclear reactor designed to supply the Syrian dictator with plutonium – the core of an atomic bomb.

On a single night in 2007 eight Israeli jets took off from bases in the south of Israel. They flew west, out over the Mediterranean, then north, then east, flashing over the Syrian coast unseen. They were flying at a height of 300 feet or so, virtually rooftop height, and at that speed required nanosecond-accuracy. They carried a variety of bombs to ensure absolute destruction of the target.

At 00.42 all eight launched their payloads. None missed. At 00.45 the team leader radioed the single word 'Arizona' – target obliterated. The squadron turned north, made the Turkish border and followed it west until they were back over the sea. Then they turned again for home, still hugging 'the deck'.

The destruction of the Cube did not concern Iran directly, but it taught a lesson. When the Iranians began a nuclear-bomb programme, they went deep underground, into a series of bomb-proof caverns. In these they began to purify uranium-235 to create a stock of bomb-grade uranium.

It is known that there were two purification plants. The smaller, called Natanz, was inside a hollowed-out mountain in the north of the country. The far bigger one was called Fordow, deep under the desert, so far down as to be immune to the most powerful of deep-penetration bombs.

Row upon row of centrifuges, called cyclotrons in the early days, are employed in the purification process. These are extremely dangerous machines to operate. They are vertical columns six to eight feet tall whose cores spin at a staggering 50,000 revolutions per minute. They stand in ranks called cascades. The estimate was that Iran had 20,000 of them, linked in cascades of 128 each in the main centrifuge hall.

The reason for having so many is that they purify the uranium ore extremely slowly, extracting only a few precious grains per day, which are carefully stored. The reason they are so dangerous is that they spin on bearings which have to be delicately balanced. The slightest variation in spin-speed or balance can cause them to either overheat or rip themselves off their bearings, or both. In that event, the entire hall would become a charnel house, with body parts of the attendant technicians flying in all directions and the deranged centrifuges tearing themselves and their neighbouring machines to molten fragments.

To prevent this, the entire operation was controlled by a master computer, guided by a database so skilfully protected by layer after layer of firewall that only the on-site Iranian operators, armed with the access codes, could enter it. It was these impossible-to-obtain access codes that the teenager sitting beside Dr Hendricks at Chandler's Court had secured.

No warning was spotted at Fordow, so nothing needed to be done. The possession of the access codes was enough. It was these that Sir Adrian, with the permission of the

Prime Minister, handed over to a senior nuclear official in the Israeli embassy at Palace Green, London.

A week or so later, at the beginning of July, something very strange happened far beneath the Iranian desert. A minuscule variation appeared on the master computer. The rotating speed of the bearings in one cascade of centrifuges began to increase. A white-coated engineer at the master console instructed the database to correct it. The technology took no notice. Other hands, in the Negev Desert, were issuing new orders. The rotation speed continued to accelerate.

The worried engineer at Fordow called a superior. Puzzled, the senior technician entered the corrector codes. They were ignored. The gauge monitoring the temperatures of the bearings began to rise. Concern became worry, then, finally, panic. The database refused to obey. The spin-rate escalated, as did the temperature of the bearings. A red line was passed. The senior technician punched a red button. In the vast hall housing the centrifuges a klaxon blared. Men in white coats scurried towards the enormous steel doors. The wail of the klaxon persisted. The scurry became a mad run, a life-saving race as the first cascade was wrenched from its bearings. Metal glowed scarlet from the uncontainable friction. The running men fought each other for the now open doors.

The initial report that reached the supreme authority of the republic, Ayatollah Khamenei, related that the last technician made it out just in time. The doors hissed and began to close, sealing the inferno in the hangar-sized hall. The men were saved, but the centrifuges, cascade by cascade, destroyed themselves as they spun from their bearings to bring down the next cascade in line.

The Ayatollah, venerated and bent with age, forced himself to read the last line of the report as a row of ashen-faced scientists stood in front of him in his modest residence on Pasteur Street in Tehran.

Twenty years was the estimate. Twenty years of unrelenting hard work and expenditure had been wiped out in one catastrophic hour. There would be an inquiry, of course. He would order it. The finest brains in Iran would delve and probe. They would report to him. They would tell him what had happened, how, why and, most importantly, at whose hand. He dismissed the scientists before him and retired to his private mosque to pray.

Of course, behind it must have been the Israelis, may Allah damn them to hell. But how had they gained access to the codes? They had tried for years and failed. The malware Stuxnet, developed by the Israelis and the Americans years earlier, had done damage, but it had not got past the codes. Now, someone had. Could it have been the Israelis themselves? The Iranians could not know it was in fact someone else far away, the greatest hacker the world had ever seen – or, in this case, never seen.

The Supreme Leader had not the faintest idea about computers and was thus wholly dependent on his experts.

What they told him after the detailed inquiry was that the hands that had typed the order into the master computer to instruct the bearings in the centrifuges to increase their spin-speed to manic levels, causing the centrifuges to auto-destruct, were probably Israeli.

But the key quandary concerned the access codes. These would have been vital. Without them, no one could give suicidal instructions to the controlling master computer. With them, all was possible.

The Iranian disaster did not remain secret for long. The news could not be contained. Men, even scientists, who have been subjected to a traumatic experience, talk. They talk to their colleagues, those present and those who were not there. They tell their families. Word spread. It leaked into that worldwide community of scientists whose life's work is to study, on behalf of their governments, the progress of others in the same field. What had happened at Fordow was too similar to the computer disaster at Murmansk.

In the end, the enigma was not solved in Tehran, but in Moscow: Moscow knew who it was and where he was.

Two days later the Russian ambassador in Tehran sought a private audience with the Supreme Leader. He bore a personal message from the Vozhd. It concerned an isolated manor house in the countryside of England and a teenage hacker who could do the impossible.

In fulfilment of a promise made by Sir Adrian a copious report reached the man in the White House. A similar report saying much the same thing also arrived via the CIA. Each confirmed the contents of the other. The President realized he had been lied to. He had in any case long denounced the treaty which had caused the US to relax the financial penalties imposed on Iran in exchange for a cessation of nuclear research, let alone uranium purification. He tore up the treaty and reimposed the ruinous economic sanctions.

At about that hour, Sir Adrian received a letter at his Admiralty Arch apartment. It intrigued him. Very few people knew that address, and the envelope had been hand-delivered. The contents were brief and courteous. The writer suggested that a meeting might be mutually valuable and invited Sir Adrian to visit him for a discussion. The letterhead was that of the Israeli embassy. The signature was of Avigdor Hirsch, a name he did not know.

In his time with MI6, Sir Adrian had been a specialist on Russia, the USSR and the Soviet empire's East European satellites. The Middle East had not been his terrain and over a decade had now passed since his retirement. Others had also retired, and there had been promotions, postings, departures – some voluntary, some encouraged. But he still had contacts, and one was the man who had 'run' the Middle East and who, being younger, was still in post at Vauxhall Cross. Name of Christopher.

'Avi Hirsch? Of course I know him,' said the voice on the secure line. 'Been here three years, head of station for Mossad. Very bright.'

'Anything more?'

'Well, he started as a lawyer after national service in their Special Forces. Qualified in three jurisdictions – his own, ours and the USA. Got his degree at Trinity College, Cambridge. Absolutely not a horny-handed kibbutznik. We regard him as a rather good egg. What does he want?'

'I don't know yet,' said Sir Adrian.

'You've heard about the disaster at Fordow?'

'Of course. And the US response.'

'Well, my department is working round the clock. Good luck with Avi.'

The Israeli embassy in London has extreme security. It needs it. There have been attempts at attack and numerous placard-waving demonstrations outside. Sir Adrian's car drew up at the wrought-iron gates and his identification was minutely examined. Calls were made from the gatehouse. Then he was waved inside. Another security officer pointed to a parking place and when his driver had parked he was escorted into the building.

There was no intrusive checking, as at an airport, but he knew that hidden scanners would have examined every inch of him. He carried no luggage, not even a briefcase. The chosen meeting room was in the basement, certainly a conference space scanned and sterilized to be totally secure.

Weston having been forewarned, Avi Hirsch was as he expected: mid-forties, athletic, tanned, urbane and very fluent in the language of Shakespeare. Coffee was offered, and declined. Then they were alone. Sir Adrian knew that this conversation would not be taking place without extensive briefing from Mossad high command at their HQ on the northern outskirts of Tel Aviv.

'I am instructed to tell you that my government and my country are very grateful,' said the Mossad bureau chief. Both knew he was referring to the donation of the access codes to the master computer at Fordow.

This was praise indeed. In the spook world, and especially in the now-integrated cyber-world, the state of Israel stands head and shoulders above the rest. Mossad has agents worldwide and, in the Middle East, it is unmatchable. Buried beneath the Negev Desert outside Beer Sheva is a think tank known as Shmone Matayim, or Unit 8200. There are grouped the finest cyber-brains of the republic, cracking codes, creating fresh ones, penetrating hostile databases and monitoring a tidal wave of coded exchanges that flit between the agencies of its enemies – and its friends, for that matter. Unit 8200 never rests.

Sir Adrian's career had largely preceded all this. He was a veteran in a world of youngsters. But some things do not change. There are friends, there are enemies, there are traitors, there are fools who talk too much. The days of brush passes in the cobbled alleys of Soviet-occupied Bratislava might seem a thing of the past, but the right piece of information in the right place at the right time could still alter history.

More to the point, a knife between the ribs or a hidden bomb beneath a car could still end a human life. And Sir

Adrian knew perfectly well that the urbane bureau chief across the table represented an agency that had in no way abandoned these old ways when their use was thought necessary.

Backing the intelligence-harvesting of the Mossad is a range of Special Forces units that match the Special Air Service, Special Boat Service and Special Reconnaissance Regiment of the British, or the USA's Delta Boys, Navy SEALs and Special Activities Division of the CIA. The Sayeret Matkal specialist commandos, the Kidon ('Bayonet' or 'Speartip'), who carry out overseas assassinations, and the even more mysterious Duvdevan, whose particular skill is to be so fluent in the languages and communities of the Middle East that they can infiltrate enemy countries, pass for a native and 'sleep' for years before going active.

All this Sir Adrian knew because, although the Middle East was never his area, it is common knowledge in espionage circles. So he was aware that Iran had to be impregnated with Israeli sleepers, some, no doubt, in high places. He sat quietly and waited for Avi Hirsch to start the ball rolling.

'Let me be perfectly frank,' said the Israeli, meaning the opposite. 'It is clear that the source of the extraordinary information you gave us – the access codes to Fordow – must have come from some kind of cybergenius. We have some very good code-crackers in Unit 8200, but your boy was ahead of them. He crossed the air gap, which is deemed impossible. That makes him very valuable, but also very vulnerable.'

'Vulnerable?'

'To revenge. With hindsight, the circumstances surrounding the disaster that struck the *Admiral Nakhimov* are becoming a little clearer. It looks as if someone took over the controls of that vessel.'

Sir Adrian replied in full. He said: 'Ah.'

'I can tell you that, just over a week after the Fordow burn-out, the Russian ambassador had a private meeting with the Ayatollah Khamenei. Any ideas?'

Sir Adrian said, 'Ah,' again.

'You see, Sir Adrian, it has occurred to us that Moscow may now have informed Iran of the identity of this remarkable person you seem to have under wraps. And possibly of his location – that is, if they know it. If the Iranians have this information, they might consider revenge. Just a piece of friendly counsel. From a grateful agency. It might be wise to move him. Without delay. Iran also has killer units.'

'Very kind of you,' said Sir Adrian. 'Most grateful. Certainly worth considering at the highest level.'

He knew what Avi Hirsch did not know. Moving Luke Jennings to a new and strange environment was easier said than done. Such was the youth's mental state, so obsessional his attachment to his immediate surroundings, to the placing of every ornament in his living area, although above all to the arrangement of the algorithms in his computer, that a sudden uprooting and transfer to somewhere miles away could provoke a breakdown.

But it was a timely warning. Iran had suicide bombers, fanatics and professional killers at its disposal. Within the

Islamic Revolutionary Guard Corps, the Pasdaran, was the inner kernel, the Al-Quds Brigade, which had killed generally and selectively all over the Middle East. Was Chandler's Court out of reach? Would the Prime Minister permit another shoot-out on the peaceful green grass of Warwickshire?

He doubted it. To avenge the naked attack with the Novichok nerve agent on the streets of Salisbury by grounding the *Admiral Nakhimov* had been retributive justice and, to the world, unprovable. To assist Israel in unmasking the nuclear treachery of Iran to the American President was one thing. To provoke revenge attacks by Middle East maniacs in the English countryside was another.

'Tell me, Avi, if there were one other highly secret Iranian organization the contents of whose database your masters would value more than any other, which would it be? VAJA or FEDAT?'

The Israeli agent struggled to keep his composure. He was surprised that this elderly retired Kremlinologist knew of either of them. But Sir Adrian had been reading up. He knew that VAJA is the Iranian Secret Intelligence Agency and employs its own killers, at home but mainly abroad, and that FEDAT is the extremely secret nuclear weapons research and development HQ, operating under the Defence Ministry. It works from a modern complex of office blocks in central Tehran, right opposite Malek Ashtar University.

As he was driven away from the wrought-iron gates of the Israeli embassy Sir Adrian mused upon the chances that his latest ruse – doing the Israelis a second favour – would also work. Helping them wreck the centrifuges at Fordow had been helpful to world security. What he had in mind now was closer to home.

He needed a favour and, in his world, and that of Avi Hirsch, favours were purchased with favours.

Privately, Sir Adrian surmised that, whichever Tel Aviv chose, the other one would probably have been penetrated already by Unit 8200, tapping away at their keys under the Negev Desert outside Beer Sheva. Three days later he had his reply: FEDAT.

Chapter Thirteen

W HEN A NATION decides to try to become a nuclear power, vast amounts of records are generated. Iran made the decision many years ago, just after the ayatollahs took over and created their ruthless theocracy. The statement by Ayatollah Rafsanjani that Israel should be wiped from the face of the Earth was like a declaration of war – an undercover war, but still a war, to be fought out of sight and with no regard to the Geneva Convention or any accepted rules.

In declaring an existential war on the small and encircled country across the Arabian Peninsula, Iran was taking on the most formidable opponent for 2,000 miles around Tehran. Israel was born out of covert operations, first against the war-weary British of 1945 but since 1948 against the surrounding array of angry and vengeful Palestinian and Arab entities.

The Arabs were able to bring to their arsenal huge numbers, enormous space and limitless funds. The Israelis had none of these, but their weapons and skills were better.

These included years of experience of undercover planning, plotting and executing. Add to that fanatical patriotism, the sure knowledge that to fail would be to die, a worldwide network of fellow Jews prepared to help in any way they could and upon first call, and the chameleon-like ability to pass for anything except an Israeli or a Jew.

Further elements were exceptional levels of technology. Faced with obliteration if it failed, Israel had no scruple about accepting help from white South Africa, another embattled minority, in acquiring the necessary quantities of refined uranium to become a nuclear power, setting up its own bomb factory at Dimona in the Negev Desert.

The payback was helping South Africa to rebuild its own six atomic bombs, dismantled before the African National Congress took over under the Rainbow Coalition.

The undercover war raged for six decades, and still rages. Occasionally, the public see a tiny trace of it – a dead body here, a destroyed facility there. The old Mossad LeAliyah Bet, set up to smuggle European Jews who had survived Hitler's Holocaust out of the camps and into the Promised Land, was transformed into the Mossad and it became probably the most formidable secret intelligence service on earth.

The American CIA has its Special Activities Division, which will go to war and kill if so ordered. The British MI6 (or SIS) prefers to keep its hands as clean as possible and relies on the Special Forces regiments to do what has to be done. Israel also has its Special Forces, but the Mossad will unhesitatingly carry out 'terminations' at home or abroad when required. Hence the litany of selective assassinations of enemies across the world, either on the grounds of future danger to Israel or, as with those who slaughtered the Israeli athletes at the Munich Olympic Games in 1972, for retribution.

Under the Shah, Israel had little to fear from Iran, but after the arrival of the ayatollahs all that changed, and even more so after the Iranian mission to build its own nuclear bomb got under way. Iran armed herself with the Pasdaran, and its inner Al-Quds Brigade, tasked to execute acts of terrorism and murder both inside and outside that country. To that can be added the VAJA, the Secret Intelligence Agency, and the SAVAMA, the secret police, with its chain of hideous prisons and torture facilities.

The body charged with creating that elusive nuclear bomb was and remains FEDAT, guardian of the vast archive of activities undertaken, purchases made, scientists suborned, location of stocks of fissionable materials and details of progress so far. For years, Iran perpetrated a cunning deception regarding all these records. As the world moved from paper records to computerized databases, Iran kept many of her secret records still in paper form. On the theory of 'hidden in plain sight', they were stored in an enormous but shabby warehouse in south Tehran, at a place called Shorabad.

Then they were stolen, the whole half-ton of them. It was the Mossad that accomplished the coup, although exactly how remains a mystery, save to its leadership in its equally anonymous office block north of Tel Aviv. Its agents seem to have gained access to the Shorabad ware-house and then, amazingly, shifted the whole cargo either to a helicopter landing pad or direct to a ship waiting off-shore in the Gulf. And thence to Israel – round the Saudi peninsula and up the Red Sea.

But that harvest was not the whole story. The rest was still locked into the database of FEDAT, and that had not been penetrated. Yet. This penetration was Sir Adrian's part of the deal he had struck with Avi Hirsch, who had clearly secured the go-ahead during a blitz visit to Tel Aviv, travelling incognito on El Al.

The Israeli executive jet was a Gulfstream VI and it landed at RAF Brize Norton in Oxfordshire. It belonged to an Israeli multimillionaire and was in the livery of his IT com-pany. He was one of the Sayanim, the Helpers, a worldwide network of Jews who cannot be traced to Mossad but who will 'lend a hand' when asked. The executive jet was based not at Ben Gurion Airport, Tel Aviv, but at the military air-base of Sde Dov to the north. The British group had been waiting out of sight. They emerged after refuelling and were led by a senior NCO from ground-handling to the steps of the Gulfstream. The reception committee, who would accompany them to Israel, did not leave the aircraft.

The British party included a handsome blonde woman who was clearly very protective of a nervous, painfully shy and evidently unwilling teenage boy and his kid brother. Also in the group were three cyber-technicians who lived with him and his mother.

On board were the two-man crew and the stewardess, all in company uniforms. And there were four from Mossad, who only ever gave their forenames – Yeuval, Moshe, Mordechai, known as Motti, and Avram – and these were not their real names. Photography was forbidden – not that anyone wanted to produce a camera anyway.

The not-so-good news was that one of them was a traitor. Iranian-born and raised, he had been approached by VAJA and offered a very large sum if he would spy for them. Desirous one day of emigrating to the USA as a very rich man, he had succumbed.

The better news was that the Director of Mossad, Meyer Ben-Avi (codename Cufflinks), knew about this and was using him to transmit a torrent of disinformation to Tehran. Still, there were limits and, one day, not long in the future, there would be a pre-dawn arrest, a secret trial and a very long sentence in a below-ground cellar, or, more likely, a terminal car crash. After that a secret bank account which was not entirely secret would be seized and its contents donated to the widows and orphans fund.

It was an uneventful flight, and they landed at the old Ovda airport to be met by three limousines that would take them to the newly equipped villa on the outskirts of Eilat, well away from any tourist gaze but close enough to the water to permit daily bathing in the warm blue sea. The cove and bar that had been established by Rafi Nelson were just along the shore.

★

With the British party installed in their villa beside the waters of the Gulf of Eilat, the four escorting Mossad agents were released and flown back to Tel Aviv. One of them, the one known as Motti, had a major problem. He needed to report all he had learned to his paymasters in Tehran.

The disaster that had befallen the uranium purification plant at Fordow was by now common knowledge. But Motti also knew that, bizarre though it might seem, the computer genius who had obtained the access codes to the master computer at Fordow had been sitting a few feet away from him during the six-hour flight from Brize Norton to Eilat.

The British party did not speak a word of Hebrew and had conversed solely in English, but Motti was fluent in that also. The anxious teenager had sat at the rear of the Gulfstream with the blinds drawn over the portholes, refusing to look out and down at the seas and landmasses passing beneath the wing. He had buried himself in technical magazines which, for Motti, with his workaday grasp of normal computer systems, would have been impenetrable. He accepted only lemonade from the stewardess, smiling shyly when she addressed him. But it became clear that his was the mind that had cracked the codes of Fordow. Now, from his small flat outside Tel Aviv, Motti had to get that information a thousand miles east to Tehran.

He had been born and raised in Isfahan, the scion of a family from the tiny 30,000-strong Jewish community that still lived in Iran. In his late teens he had slipped away, crossing the border in the tumult as the Shah fell from power, and took advantage of the Law of Return to emigrate into Israel.

He could of course pass for an Iranian, speaking accentless Farsi. He volunteered for the Duvdevan, but it was judged that it would be too risky to return to Iran on secret missions with the country under the newly installed ayatollahs. Anyone from his past would be able to recognize and denounce him, even if by accident. Instead, he was inducted into Mossad itself.

Someone in Isfahan must have blabbed. He was approached in Old Jerusalem and offered a deal. For a large fee, to be repeated for future information, he should switch sides and work for VAJA. Thinking ahead to that rich retirement, he agreed.

His exposure as a 'double' was not long delayed. It is rare for an Israeli to change sides and work for Iran or any other Middle East dictatorship, but the reverse is not the case. In Iran, a population of many millions is held in subjection by the feared Pasdaran, and there are many prepared to work against it and who long for root-and-branch reform.

Meyer Ben-Avi ran a string of agents in Iran, including two inside VAJA, and the acquisition of Motti as a new recruit was rapid. It would have been simple to arrest Motti and break his resistance in a certain subterranean complex beneath the sands of the Negev, but Ben-Avi chose another way. Though it was expensive in manpower terms, he put the renegade under surveillance, eavesdropped on every syllable he uttered in voice or print and noted to whom he talked.

In espionage, deliberate disinformation is a powerful weapon and to have a 'feed' direct into the highest counsels of the enemy is very desirable. This was the role that Motti now unwittingly played.

The coming of completely digitized message-passing has made life much easier in every legitimate and legal activity. It has also made interception child's play. Faced with this, there has been a trend to go back to the old ways.

For years, Iran had managed to get away with storing its nuclear records on paper in the Shorabad warehouse, far away from any checks by the International Atomic Energy Agency in Vienna. Faced with a blizzard of cyber-detection, secret agents have also resorted to the ways of yesteryear. Among these are the brush pass and the dead-letter box.

The former is simple but relies on split-second timing. The spy carries hundreds of classified documents miniaturized to microfilm in a canister no larger than a matchbox. This receptacle must pass absolutely unseen into the possession of his handler. But the spy is already suspected and is being tailed down the street by members of the secret police.

Without warning, he swerves off the pavement into the door of a bar or restaurant. Inside, the handler has left the bar and is walking towards the door. For half a second the two men brush past each other. The switch takes place. The police agents turn into the doorway. The handler politely steps aside to let them pass. Then he leaves with his cargo. The spy is now completely 'clean'.

The dead-letter box, or 'drop', is simply a hole some-where. It could be behind a loose brick in a wall, or in the trunk of a tree in a park. It is known only to the spy and their handler. The spy visits the drop, ensures he is not being watched and deposits the package, which passes out of sight. Later, a chalk mark appears in a pre-agreed place. The spy and the handler need never come within miles of each other. Alerted by the chalk mark, which he checks for regularly, that the drop contains a package, the handler visits and retrieves it. Motti had a drop behind an Arab coffee shop in Old (East) Jerusalem.

He wrote his report in careful Farsi on a single sheet of very ordinary store-bought stationery, wiped it clean with a bleach-damp sponge and inserted it, folded many times, into a matchbox, also wiped free of prints. The box went into a cotton bag and would never again be touched by his fingertips. Then he took the Egged bus to Jerusalem.

He got off in the western half and joined the columns of tourists meandering through the Mandelbaum Gate into the warren of historic alleys and bazaars that make up the Old City. An hour later, the matchbox was in its hole behind the loose brick and a chalk mark had been placed on the stonework of a bridge support not a hundred yards from the Via Dolorosa. Neither city-dweller nor tourist noticed a thing.

His precautions were meticulous; he took no risks. But high in a garret window overlooking the latrines of the coffee shop, a young Mossad probationer had the boring chore of keeping the dead-letter drop under observation. He saw Motti make his drop and reported in. Hours later, he saw the swarthy collector slip past the latrines, turn the corner into the deserted alley and make the pick-up. He reported back again.

By nightfall, the swarthy man had crossed the Allenby Bridge back into Jordan, the matchbox was on its way to Tehran and into the possession of Hossein Taeb, head of intelligence for the Pasdaran. Outside Tel Aviv, Ben-Avi, indulging his taste for very old Scotch whisky, was sipping a Chivas Regal as he watched the last glimmer of a dying sun across the darkling Mediterranean.

He had done what he could. Now he could only wait. In espionage, there is an awful lot of waiting.

Chapter Fourteen

HOSSEIN TAEB, ALTHOUGH appointed Pasdaran head of intelligence, was neither a soldier nor an intelligence officer, nor had he ever been. He was a cleric, steeped in the theology of the Shia branch of Islam and utterly devoted to the Supreme Leader, Ayatollah Khamenei, and the revolution that had governed Iran since the fall of the Shah. The report from one of his only two sources inside the Israeli intelligence machine caused him to be consumed with rage.

He knew exactly what had been done to the great facility at Fordow and who had done it. He had been present at the extremely restricted briefing at which Iran's top nuclear physicists had explained how many years it would take, and how many resources, even to approach the level of what had been lost at Fordow and the stored weapons-grade uranium that was no more.

He knew that years earlier, Israel, impressed by the skills and wealth creation of California's Silicon Valley, had decided to create her own equivalent. His department

had watched the creation of the cyber-city that transformed the once dusty desert township of Beer Sheva into
an enclave of gleaming tower blocks. His experts had
informed him of the steady recruitment of the finest young
brains of his enemy, Israel, to live and work either above
ground or below, in Unit 8200 – the best ultra-secret
cyber-spy agency his side of Cheltenham or Fort Meade.
And he knew Iran had nothing to match it.

But he also knew that it was not the teams of brilliant
young Jews at Beer Sheva who were responsible for the
destruction of Fordow. Yes, they had penetrated the master
computer and primed it with those lethal instructions. But
someone else had given them the access codes which they
had tried for so long to discover – and had failed to do so.
Now Moscow had kindly informed the Supreme Leader of
the identity of the person who really had achieved the
impossible – a youth from England who must surely rank
as the most dangerous cyber-hacker on earth. And he had
come to Israel to be rewarded with a free holiday by the
waters of the Gulf of Eilat. The cleric summoned his head
of operations.

Colonel Mohammed Khalq was not a cleric; he was a
born and lifelong soldier and killer. As a youth he had
joined the Basij, the Pasdaran reserve of eager volunteers
who, in the Iran–Iraq war against Saddam Hussein had
hurled themselves in suicidal droves on to the Iraqi mine-
fields along the border to die for Allah and Iran.

His dedication and courage had attracted attention. He
moved from the Basij into the Pasdaran regular forces,

rising through the ranks in operation after operation, serving in South Lebanon with the Iranian-trained Hezbollah and more recently with Assad's forces in Syria. He read the report from the Mossad renegade and his gaze met Hossein Taeb's.

'He must die,' said the cleric.

'Of course,' said the soldier.

'I wish you to take personal command,' said Taeb. 'I will secure all the necessary clearances. But do not delay. The English party will not be there for long.'

Colonel Khalq knew at once the kill operation would have to be mounted from the sea and that he had an enormous range of sea-going options. The Pasdaran is not only an army within an army, a cohort of secret police, a national enforcer, a purveyor of terror and a guarantor of national obedience. It also has its own air force and navy, its own widespread industrial and commercial empire and its own merchant fleet. Khalq left his superior and went to confer with the general commanding all Pasdaran ships, military and commercial.

The selected vessel was the SS *Mercator*, formerly bearing an Iranian name, now retitled and flagged out of Valletta, Malta. That tiny republic inside the European Union appreciates the fees it can charge for registering merchant vessels whose cargoes it never needs to examine.

The selection was aided by the fact the *Mercator* was only a 2,000-ton tramp steamer, scruffy and rust-streaked, unlikely to draw attention to herself as she chugged from port to port with her small cargoes. More, she was currently lying empty in Bandar Abbas, in the deep south of Iran.

The first task was to replace her skipper and entire crew with a team of combat-experienced fighting seamen drawn from the aggressive torpedo boats that regularly harass Western shipping in the Persian Gulf. This was achieved by Ali Fadavi, head of the Pasdaran Navy, within twenty-four hours. The *Mercator* was then loaded with a cargo of planks, poles and beams, with papers showing they had been ordered by a construction company in Aqaba, Jordan, a thriving port a few miles across the bay from Eilat in Israel.

To cover the last five miles from Aqaba to Eilat the colonel commandeered two of the fastest speedboats in the world, Bradstone Challengers, of which Iran had recently acquired a dozen for no explained purpose. Hammering at over fifty knots across flat water, they are normally the playthings of the rich and self-indulgent. Colonel Khalq had two driven south to be hoisted on to the *Mercator* with their crews. The racers were hidden beneath tarpaulins on the deck-covers.

Now, he needed his men. He chose twelve marine commandos; all experienced in shore-landings and skilled with small arms at close quarters. The entire party went south by helicopter to meet the *Mercator*, already at sea, twenty miles offshore, in the Strait of Hormuz. Led by Colonel Khalq, the attack party rappelled from the choppers on to the foredeck of the *Mercator* and were shown to their cramped quarters among the timbers of the cargo. It would be a five-day run with labouring engine to the Gulf of Aqaba.

Motti in his report had related that security around the villa was assigned to the Eilat police, which had allocated a rotating force of two officers in order not to cramp the holiday of their country's guests. That was what Motti had been told as the Mossad team flew north. It was not quite true. Meyer Ben-Avi had in fact assigned twenty men from the very special Special Forces unit called the Sayeret Matkal.

The Matkal usually operate outside the borders of the republic and are skilled in penetrating unseen and unheard anywhere in the Middle East and remaining there until they go operational. Their speciality is invisibility, but when they choose to become visible they can be very lethal indeed.

The *Mercator* had passed the port of Aden and entered the narrows of the Bab-al-Mandab when she was finally identified. For the Israeli aircraft overhead it was a question of elimination. She was the right size, her Maltese flag fooled no one and her wake showed she was churning along as fast as she could. A quick check in the office of the harbourmaster of Aqaba revealed that this was her destination. There were canvas-shrouded humps on her deck and the Jordanian constructor which had supposedly ordered a cargo of timber had gone into receivership several months earlier. Hossein Taeb's intelligence unit was seemingly long on motive but a tad short on detail. After

Jeddah, the SS *Mercator* was monitored all the way to Aqaba.

When the ship reached her destination she did not berth in the inner harbour but moored in the roads. Using the *Mercator*'s davits, the two speedboats were lowered into the water and tethered beside her. Fully fuelled, they could cross the five miles to the Gulf of Eilat in minutes, then race south to make rendezvous with the much larger and more heavily armed Pasdaran warship steaming north.

Before leaving Iran, Colonel Khalq had instructed the agent who had serviced Motti's dead-letter box, now in Jordan and posing as a tourist, to cross the land border into Israel. Thence, still a harmless tourist, he would head south to Eilat and reconnoitre the villa described by Motti, south of the resort and close to the bar that had once been run by Rafi Nelson.

Watching through field glasses from the shore, the agent saw the *Mercator* arrive and, in a rented boat, went out to confer with his commander.

In the captain's cabin he was able to describe the target villa minutely. He had seen the two Eilat policemen on guard at the gate. He had not seen the Sayeret Matkal hidden inside the villa or in the surrounding landscape.

He had noted the English party of six: three men, the mother and her two sons, one of whom, shy and nervous, had to be encouraged into the warm blue water. He had not produced a camera near the villa but was able to create accurate sketches, which he now passed to Colonel Khalq. The colonel planned his attack for the following night.

It was two in the morning, the hour of the night assassin, when the two speedboats slipped their moorings and eased out into the gulf. There was no need for speed – that blistering pace would be needed for the escape down the gulf to the Red Sea. Since darkness had fallen at nine the previous evening, the lights of the tourist magnet of Eilat city had blazed to the west and the music from a hundred bars, restaurants, clubs and parties could be heard across the silent sea. Behind them, the industrial port of Aqaba, once liberated from the Turks by Lawrence and the Hashemites, was quieter and, by 2 a.m., asleep. The powerful but muzzled engines of the two Challengers made little more than a burble and they drove the speedboats westwards at under ten knots.

The scattered lights of the out-of-town villas came into sight south of the town, set in their own grounds. Earlier, in daylight, crouching in the rigid inflatable that served as the *Mercator*'s lifeboat, should its crew ever have to abandon ship, the colonel had mingled with holidaymakers and cruised off the beach, noting the location of the target house. A lone beach bar acted as a marker. They would make landfall a dozen yards to one side of it, with a clear hundred-yard run to the target.

Each Challenger had a crew of two. In each speedboat, with them were six armed commandos. There was room for more, but Colonel Khalq wanted no colliding as they leapt into the knee-deep water and raced up the beach. The firepower of twelve experienced shooters would be more than enough to eliminate the targets.

He did not know that other eyes, aided by powerful night-vision lenses, had noted the speedboats emerging from the blackness of the sea and heading for the beach. Quiet orders were issued inland, not in Farsi but in Hebrew.

The colonel's men made perfect landfall and were almost in line abreast as they began their race across the sand. They could have been dropped by the snipers much earlier, but the Matkal also had their orders. There was no one in the villa but the dummies, curled up, seemingly asleep, in their beds. The Pasdaran reached the villa, with its open doors and windows, raced inside and ran upstairs. Then the firing started, shattering the quiet of the night, causing others a hundred yards away to jerk from their slumber with yells of alarm.

The other tourists, waking in their villas up and down the beach, dived for cover. The last two drinkers at the beach bar swore and went for the floor, joining the barman.

Inside the target villa there was no resistance. Every bedroom was invaded, the sleeping figures sprayed with bullets. The youngest commando ran into a bedroom as Colonel Khalq rushed out. By the watery-green half-light of his night-vision goggles, he clearly saw the form of a blond youth in white cotton pyjamas, soaked in blood from chin to waist, sprawled across the dripping sheets. He turned and followed his colonel. Job done. Mission accomplished.

The dozen assassins ran back out of the villa the way

they had come – through the front doors and windows. The silenced rifles of the snipers made no sound. The panicking tourists heard nothing. Colonel Khalq wondered just before he died why the two Eilati policemen had not been where he had seen them during the afternoon cruise offshore. His query was never answered.

Like the Special Forces men at Chandler's Court, the Matkal were using hollow-point ordnance. Each round penetrated the running body and then expanded to leave an exit hole the size of a saucer. All but two died. The orders had been quite clear. One, maybe two, had to make the shoreline and scramble aboard the boats. The other ten made no more than fifty of the needed hundred yards.

The young one who had been with the colonel in the boy's bedroom was a survivor. He realized his comrades were dropping around him but thought for a few seconds they were merely stumbling and wondered why. Then he was knee-deep in seawater, reaching for the hands stretching towards him. The two Challengers, engines roaring, swerved away from the beach and raced for the darkness. No bullets pursued them.

From a bunker above and behind the target villa Avi Hirsch watched the cream smudges of the two wakes fade into the darkness. He had been allowed to leave his number two in command of the station in London so that he could fly home and control the Eilat operation. After all, he had reasoned to Meyer Ben-Avi, the idea had resulted from a talk in a bug-proof room off Palace Walk between himself and a wily old knight who had spent his career with MI6 and with whom Mossad had done joint operations before.

It took the two Challengers an hour, racing flat out down the Gulf of Aqaba, to rendezvous with the Pasdaran warship. The speedboats, short on fuel, were craned aboard for the cruise home; out of the Red Sea, along the coast of Oman and back to the Strait of Hormuz. But radio waves are faster.

What the debriefed commandos had to report, eavesdropped by the young listeners of Unit 8200 under Beer Sheva, reached Hossein Taeb within an hour. He in turn reported to the Supreme Leader in his frugal apartment on Pasteur Street. There had been heavy loss of life among the commandos when the infidel Jews woke up and fired back. But they had been too late. The English boy was dead – there had been eyes-on identification by one of the Pasdaran survivors.

This fiction was maintained in Israel. Jubilation would have leaked sooner or later. For the media based in Eilat, it was a big story – a clash between two rival criminal gangs on a beach outside the town in the middle of the night. Tourists were reassured. The gangsters had all been caught by the police, who had been tipped off and were waiting for them. Like most media stories, it lived and then it died. Tourists have the delightful habit of going home when their holiday is over. No one had even seen a body – they had all vanished before dawn.

The warmest congratulations were offered to the six

actors from the Israeli Film School, especially the look-alike youngster with his blond-dyed locks who had mastered his role as Luke Jennings. And also to the technical department of Spiro Films, who had created the six dummies which, when shot full of bullets, exploded into buckets of very real-looking blood.

The former were also praised for maintaining their fluent English on the flight from Brize Norton to Ovda airport and to the villa. Even Motti had been convinced.

There were celebrations in Tehran, which remained convinced that the destroyer of the Fordow centrifuges was at last rotting in the hell of infidels.

In Moscow the Iranian ambassador asked for a personal reception with the Vozhd. He intimated that he had significant information to impart and that it should be directly to the ears of the master of the Kremlin. When they met it was the Russian who was initially sceptical. His mood turned to congratulations and pleasure when the Iranian diplomat disclosed that, during a putative holiday visit to Israel, the cyber-genius Luke Jennings had been assassinated by a group of Iranian commandos.

When the ambassador had left, after politely declining a toast in vodka, the Russian put in a personal call to his spy chief at Yazenevo. Yevgeni Krilov accepted the congratulations with pleasure. But when the call ended he demanded some files from the archive. It is a simple fact that espionage centres the world over keep tabs on their known friends but far more detailed files on their enemies. The archives at Yazenevo contained copious information on known staffers with the CIA, the FBI and other American agencies. It was matched by the information on those in Britain's MI5 and, even more so, in MI6. And they went back many years.

Sir Adrian Weston had come to attention when he was promoted to head the Eastern Europe department during the Cold War. That might have ended, officially at least, but interest in him had not. His elevation to deputy chief of MI6 was also very much on file. This was the file Yevgeni Krilov called for. When it arrived, he studied it for an hour.

It reported that the then Mr Weston had been quietly but spectacularly successful against the USSR and later against the Russian Federation. It was known that he had recruited two major Soviet and Russian traitors, and the recruitment of others was suspected. It seemed his speciality was deception: misleading, diverting attention, trickery. There was even a reference to a possibility that, after retirement, he had been quietly recalled as adviser to the new British premier.

Was he back in harness? Everything that had recently gone wrong for Russia and her allies bore the hallmark of the man whose file in front of Krilov was an inch thick. And there was a photo, another shot snatched through a buttonhole camera at a diplomatic reception years earlier. His suspicion hardened into near-certainty. It had been Adrian Weston who had visited Fritsch at the Vaduz Bank – he had been photographed crossing the lobby, and the photo in the file was obviously of the same man. But he had clearly not swallowed the bait. Disaster had followed disaster. Krilov stared at the photo and began to have doubts about the Gulf of Eilat massacre.

Sue Jennings had enjoyed the stay of the six visitors from Israel. She did not know why it was necessary that they be there, but she trusted Sir Adrian enough to believe him when he told her he had in mind a plan to safeguard her and her children.

She noted the resemblance between herself and the blonde woman and between her sons and the young curly-headed boys. She was not foolish enough to believe that there was no point to this. There had to be some form of impersonation in the offing, but she did not know why. Nor did she need to know. That is how it is in the world of smoke and mirrors.

But she had enjoyed their stay. It made a change from the monotonous routine. They had stayed only a couple of days, observing her and her sons closely throughout that time, then they were gone.

That apart, in the embrace of the SAS captain Harry Williams she was enjoying love-making she had never experienced nor even imagined in her previous life. Her second son, Marcus, was perfectly content at his new school. He had been named captain of the Colts XI cricket team, and that had brought him the attentions of his first girlfriend.

What Sue did not know was exactly what was happening in the computer wing, where her elder son, Luke,

as self-contained at a screen as ever, spent hours tapping away, in a world where it seemed no one, not even
Dr Hendricks, could follow him.

It was that same Dr Hendricks who, on a supremely hot
day at the beginning of August, withdrew to his own private office and dialled the phone number of Sir Adrian.

'He's done it,' he blurted when the connection was
made. 'He's bloody well done it. He's gone through the
lot . . . firewalls, air gap, the bloody lot. It has defeated
everyone for years, but we have them. And Tehran has not
even noticed the penetration.'

Sir Adrian could have told Avi Hirsch, now back in
post, but he was a modest man and gave the present to Mrs
Marjory Graham. The Prime Minister secured a very private line to the Israeli ambassador instead and alerted him,
in the knowledge that Israel's Prime Minister would not
be displeased. Then she ordered that the access codes to
the main computerized database of FEDAT be passed to
Jerusalem and to Washington.

The harvest that these codes permitted to emerge from
the Iranian nuclear research department in Tehran proved
that both presidents, Israeli and American, had been right.
Iran had consistently been lying to the International
Atomic Energy Agency and thus the world. Nuclear
research had never ceased, not even slowed. In the light of
the FEDAT harvest, the yield from the archive raid on
Shorabad paled to a fraction of what had been concealed.
It caused uproar.

The US had pulled out of the international treaty abrogating the economic sanctions against Iran. Most of the other parties to the treaty had objected to this. But they had not seen the contents of the FEDAT archive.

In Jerusalem, a dead-letter drop in a wall behind a coffee shop was closed down, and in Tel Aviv a quiet arrest was made.

Chapter Fifteen

IT WAS A very private consultation and it took place over a lunch on the sunlit terrace of Chequers, the British Prime Minister's official country mansion outside London. The staff, as ever, were drawn from the catering arm of the RAF. The PM's husband, Colin, put his head through the patio doors, nodded, beamed and withdrew to watch the cricket match between England and Australia.

Marjory Graham was not a great drinker but she enjoyed the occasional glass of Prosecco before Sunday lunch. Sir Adrian took the same. When the waitress withdrew, Mrs Graham turned to her guest.

'This North Korean business. What do you make of it, Adrian?'

'You have already received a full briefing from the Foreign Office?'

'Your former masters. Of course. But I would appreciate your take on it.'

'What was the official view?'

'Conventional, of course. Conformist. We should follow

the American lead. Agree with the State Department and the White House. And you?'

Sir Adrian sipped and stared across the rolling lawns.

'I have on occasion participated in a few deception operations. Even run one or two. They can be exceptionally damaging to the opponent and beneficial to oneself. They can cause the enemy months, even years, of error. Time, money, effort, sweat, toil and tears. And all for nothing. Even for a lot less than nothing. For error. But the worst variant is self-delusion. I fear that is the ocean the Americans have chosen to swim in.'

'The complete denuclearization of North Korea. Not feasible after all?' she asked.

'It is a scam, Prime Minister. A lie, a confidence trick. But skilfully offered, as ever. And I fear the White House is falling for it. Again.'

'Why? They have some very fine brains.'

'Too many have been fired. And the man who lives there lusts to be awarded the Nobel Peace Prize. So the desire to believe is triumphant. Always the precursor of a successful confidence trick.'

'So you think Pyongyang is lying?'

'I am sure of it.'

'How do they get away with it? Time after time?'

'North Korea is an enigma, Prime Minister. On the face of it, she has nothing. Or very, very little. In world terms, the country is small, barren, devoid of raw materials, hideously governed, bankrupt and very close to starving. The two grain crops – rice and wheat – have failed again. And yet North Korea bestrides the world like a conqueror.'

'And how does the regime manage this, Adrian?'

'Because it is allowed to. The logical are always frightened of the insane.'

'And because they have nuclear bombs.'

'Yes, both types. Atomic and thermonuclear. Uranium and polonium. North Korea has ample stocks of both and, though the Kim regime may seem to be handing some over for destruction by the International Atomic Energy Agency, I am convinced it will retain others in secret places. It depends on whether the outside world will believe the lies.'

'But if North Korea publicly destroys its weapons-testing site – what is it called?'

'Punggye-ri, Prime Minister.'

'With that destroyed, how can they go on?'

'Firstly, because Punggye-ri, which is or was a mountain, is already destroyed. And by them, in error. For thirty years at least, three successive regimes, all dominated by the Kim dynasty – grandfather, son and now grandson – have laboured night and day to create and own an entire armoury of nuclear bombs.

'Years ago, they chose the mountain of Punggye-ri and began to bore into the side of it. They dug and dug until they reached the heart. Machines were used, but also slave labourers. Many thousands died of malnutrition and overwork. Enough spoil was dug out of the mountain to create two more; it was trucked far away so as not to be seen from the air.

'When they reached the core they went on digging. More tunnels, galleries, testing chambers, over 180 miles in all. That is a motorway-sized tunnel from London to the Hook of Holland. Then Mother Nature took over. The mountain could take no more. It began to fracture, to collapse inwards.

'Still they would not stop. Then they tested their biggest H-bomb deep underground. They triggered an earthquake measured at over six on the Richter scale. That completed the implosion of the mountain of Punggye-ri.

'Simultaneously, the North Korean economy began to collapse, like the mountain, due to the economic sanctions imposed by the outside world after they expelled the inspectors from the International Atomic Energy Agency. That is when, last year, they hit upon the ruse: we will publicly destroy Punggye-ri if you will ship us the grain and oil we need. And the West has fallen for it.'

At this point the Prime Minister interjected:

'How do you know all this?'

'It is all in the public domain, if you know where to look. There are men and women in the Royal United Services Institute for Defence and Strategic Studies, RUSI for short, who spend their lives studying every detail of the strategic dangers, worldwide. It pays to consult them.'

'Then why has the West fallen for a scam?'

'Actually, Prime Minister, it is the USA in the form of the State Department and the White House that has fallen for it.'

'I repeat, why have they fallen for it?'

'Because, Prime Minister, they have chosen to.'

Sir Adrian had spent his working career as a civil servant in one of the most rigorous disciplines that exists in secret intelligence. He was convinced that most politicians and far too many senior civil servants possessed personal egos of Himalayan proportions. Such vanity could permit self-delusion with little harm done other than the expenditure of huge sums of taxpayers' money to no purpose. Government waste is a fact of life. But if you indulge in self-delusion on a covert mission in the heart of an enemy dictatorship, you can end up very dead. The reason he was prepared to work for Marjory Graham was because he knew she was a rare exception to the rule of ego.

'Oh dear, do you really think so little of us, Adrian?'

'In 1938, I was not even born. I was a 1948 baby.'

'And I ten years later, in 1958. Your point?'

'In 1938, we had MI6. The Americans had not yet founded the CIA. And the USA was plunged in isolationism. But our agents were active in Nazi Germany. They knew about the first concentration camps – Dachau, Sachsenhausen, Buchenwald. We discovered what they were, where they were, what went on inside them. We reported back. No one wanted to know.

'We reported that Hitler was laying down the keels for warships that a peace-loving Germany would never need. Again, no one in London wanted to know. We discovered new Messerschmitt fighters were rolling out at two a day. We reported this. Downing Street once again turned its back.

'A gullible Prime Minister listened only to the appeasement-fanatical Foreign Office. Hitler, he allowed himself to be convinced, was an honourable gentleman who, once he had given his word, would abide by it. But day by day the Führer was breaking every term of the Versailles Treaty of 1918, every pledge he had ever made. And it was all provable.'

'Adrian, that was then, this is now. What is your point?'

'That it is happening again. The world's leading Western power has decided to delude herself that an oriental monster of proven savagery will convert into a peace-loving partner in exchange for a bit of rice. It is another triumph of self-delusion.'

Mrs Graham replaced her coffee cup and gazed across the green fields of England, so far from the gutted mountains of North Korea.

'And this mountain . . .'

'Punggye-ri.'

'Whatever. It really has no value?'

'None at all. It is no longer a testing site. What they will be dynamiting in front of the applauding world is already little more than rubble. The site is no longer fit for purpose. But, they have others. And, in any case, at the moment, they do not need to do any more tests. They have stocks enough to threaten the civilized world.

'Destroying Punggye-ri is not a problem. But they do have two other problems. There is not much point in having nuclear bombs if you cannot deliver them on target many miles away, even thousands of miles away.

Their biggest intercontinental ballistic missile is still not strong enough to deliver their smallest thermonuclear warhead. They are seeking to miniaturize the warhead and increase the ICBM. Eventually, they will succeed.

'The Hwasong-15 missile will be improved to carry their thermonuclear warhead, making it capable of reaching not the American island of Guam but any point on the entire US mainland. When that is done, they will not need to ask for favours; they will demand them. Or else.'

'So, if the public destruction of an already-destroyed mountain is nothing but a sideshow, what do they really want?'

'A sort of bridging loan, Prime Minister. Many millions of tons of grain, billions of gallons of fuel oil. Except that a loan should be repaid. This would never be repaid. So it would be . . . a gift, to be set against good behaviour. So long as it lasts, meaning so long as it suits. For years, China has been North Korea's saviour. But President Xi is running out of patience. Hence the desperate wooing of the White House.'

'And if the North Korean dictator does not get this "bridging loan"?'

'Then Kim Jong-un runs into problem number two. Unlike our Foreign Office, I take the view that pudgy little Kim is much weaker than he seems. All we ever see are vast squadrons of strutting, goose-stepping, ultra-trained and ultra-fanatical loyalists in Pyongyang. But only the million privileged loyalists are allowed to live in the capital – well housed, well fed, well employed. Only these, carefully selected, are allowed to appear before Western cameras. Plus, the 200,000-strong ultra-loyal army, the praetorian guards, who would die for him and his regime.

'But outside the capital are twenty million country-dwellers and a million more soldiers. They stand on the threshold of mass starvation. Not the soldiers – they are fed. But they have mothers, fathers, brothers, sisters, withered by malnutrition, clinging to life, producing undersized, dwarfish children. I wonder, Prime Minister, do you recall Nicolae Ceauşescu?'

'He came here once, did he not?'

'He did indeed. We very foolishly made him an honorary knight of the realm for supposedly standing up to Moscow. Another Foreign Office idea. King Charles Street seems to have an appetite for dictators. Later, we stripped him of it. When he was dead. A bit late.'

'So what has he to do with all this?'

'Before he died, Kim Jong-un's father, Kim Jong-il, admitted to Condoleezza Rice that his secret fear was what he called his "Ceauşescu moment".'

'And that was?'

'Like the Kims, Ceauşescu was a ruthless Communist tyrant. He ruled Romania with a rod of iron. Like the Kims, he was cruel, self-enriching and corrupt. And, like the Kims, he drenched his people with unrelenting propaganda to persuade them to worship him.

'One day, making a speech at the provincial town of Timişoara, he heard a sound he had never heard in his life.

It is all on camera. He could not believe what his ears were telling him. He tried to go on, then lost his thread. Finally, he fled the podium, ran to the roof and was taken away by helicopter. The people were booing him.'

'He didn't like that?'

'Worse, Prime Minister. Within three days, his own army had arrested him, tried and convicted him and shot him, along with his ghastly wife. That was Kim Jong-il's dreaded moment: when the people eventually turned and the army acted to save themselves.'

'That could happen to the Pudding?'

'Who knows how much starvation the North Korean people can take? Unless, of course, the West capitulates and bails him out.'

'In which case, Adrian?'

'He will have enough time to complete the increase in payload of the Hwasong-15 missile and the reduction of the thermonuclear warhead to portable size. Then he can blackmail the world. No more concessions by blowing up useless mountains.'

'So the grain shipments are his real Achilles heel?'

'In part. The real key is not the A-bombs or the H-bombs but the missiles. He must perfect his launch systems. I suspect it will take two years, maybe three, with several more test launches. At the moment, the Hwasongs are waiting in their silos.'

'Self-delusion or not, Adrian, I cannot start a war of words with the White House. Short of that, is there anything we can do?'

'I believe the Hwasongs are all controlled by super-computers, which are heavily protected but contain the proof of the North Korean nuclear ambition. Like the FEDAT archives in Tehran, which at last convinced the White House it was being lied to. If we could prove that the Pudding is lying . . .'

'Well, can we?'

'We have one bizarre weapon. An anxious boy with spectacular gifts. I would like to direct him at North Korea.'

'All right. Permission granted. But keep it very quiet indeed. Keep me posted. And try not to start a war. There is a man across the Pond who wants the Nobel Peace Prize.'

In her inner circle, Marjory Graham was known for her sardonic sense of humour.

Chapter Sixteen

THE YELLOW SEA is not yellow. It is grey, cold and hostile and the four men crouched in the broken-down fishing skiff were shivering. It was a bleak dawn but neither the chill nor the covered sky blotting out the sun rising over Korea to the east had caused their misery. It was fear.

To defect from North Korea, whose coast was still visible through the morning mist, is extremely hazardous. It was not the tossing sea that made them shiver but the knowledge that, if caught by one of the numerous North Korean patrol launches, they would face a life sentence in a slave labour camp or execution by the more merciful firing squad.

Three of the men were fishermen, accustomed to the waters of Korea Bay, the northern part of the Yellow Sea. They had been massively bribed by the fourth man to attempt to avoid the patrols, to dump him on the coast of South Korea then sneak home before daylight came. And they had failed. Halfway through their southward journey their clapped-out old engine had broken down. Though they had paddled furiously for hours, wind and wave had been from the south, holding them motionless off the coast of the fearful North Korean peninsula.

They heard the sound of the engine before they could make out the smudge of grey on the horizon or discern any flag or pennant to ascertain its identity. But the engine rumble came closer and closer. They hoped that the rolling waves might disguise their tiny hull, draped with their nets as an optimistic camouflage. But the patrol boat would have radar and it must have spotted something. It kept on coming. Five minutes later it hovered over them and a loudhailer ordered them to heave to.

Abeam was another smudge, emerging from the strengthening light. They hoped and prayed it might be Kaul-li island with its tiny port of Mudu; a dot on the ocean, but within South Korea. The voice behind the bullhorn called again and one of the fishermen looked up, his face suffused with hope.

The language, of course, was Korean, but that accent did not come from the coast behind the dawn. It came from much further south. The fisherman peered out from under his nets and now saw the pennant flying from the stern: the twin-teardrop emblem of South Korea. They would not see their wives again, but they would not face a firing squad. They had made it, against the odds. They would be offered asylum. The North's secret police would not have them after all.

The South Korean navy boat, one of the new Chamsuris,

took them on board, and two seamen offered blankets. A third tied their waterlogged skiff to the stern. The helmsman powered up the engine and turned the prow south, towards Kaul-li. The young captain with the southern accent keyed in his radio and spoke to base. This was an incident; there would be an inquiry. Successful defections were impossible overland, extremely rare by sea. He needed to cover his back. No delay in checking in. He asked for names.

The older man, the one who had bribed the fishermen to bring him south despite the risks, sat under his blanket, still shivering. The chill? Fear? More like the relief that replaces the certainty of interrogation and death. The crew had established that three of their refugees were penniless fishermen. One of the navy men approached the man under the blanket.

'What is your name?' he asked, clipboard in hand.

The fourth man looked up. 'My name,' he said, 'is Li Song-Rhee.' The blanket slipped. The shoulder boards of his uniform, the dress that had secured him passage through the checkpoints on the road from Pyongyang to the coast, gleamed in the weak sun. This was not a frantic corporal looking for a better life in South Korea. This was a four-star general of the army of the DPRK, the Democratic People's Republic of Korea, one of the ultra-elite of Kim's dictatorship.

The captain listened to his crewman and checked the shoulder boards of the sea-stained uniform. Then he returned to his radio. They would not bypass Kaul-li island. It has a heliport. A chopper would be coming up from navy HQ at Incheon. The history of the peninsula of the two Koreas was about to change.

Nine hours and the same number of time zones to the west, it was also dawn when a phone rang in a modest apartment off Admiralty Arch. Sir Adrian picked it up.

'Yes, Prime Minister.'

'There has been a development. You recall what we were talking about a couple of weeks ago? Well, it seems a four-star general of North Korea has defected to South Korea. Something to do with Kim's missile programme.'

From his years with SIS, Sir Adrian knew there was a procedure whereby matters considered of sufficient import-ance could be sent to Downing Street ahead of the usual morning briefing, the 'flimsies' which prime ministers read over breakfast. If the incoming news was pressing enough, the PM could be woken at any hour, not that it seemed to make any difference with this one. Her staff wondered when she ever slept anyway.

'I'll ask our people over there to keep on top of it,' she said.

'Very wise, Prime Minister.'

The phone went down. Sir Adrian sighed and replaced the receiver. He knew she meant the head of station of the British SIS team in the embassy in Seoul, South Korea. He rose, pulled on a robe and went to make himself buttered toast. And coffee. Of course coffee, his favourite strong black arabica.

There was no point in telling even the PM how many hours he had spent with the best brains on North Korea that the Royal United Services Institute could furnish. He had listened to hours of briefings before settling on General Li Song-Rhee. Even then, it had been a long shot that the mastermind of the missile programme would receive the phoney email, let alone believe it. Still, as they say, nothing ventured . . .

It was Luke Jennings who, once again bewilderingly, had secured the access codes to the North Korean mobile-phone database. They were very obscure and heavily guarded and, when it came to cyberspace, the North Koreans were no beginners. Indeed, they were brilliant, constantly attacking the West with malware, Trojan horses and every trick in the book. But they were not an eighteen-year-old with Asperger's syndrome.

In this paranoid dictatorship, there are only 1.8 million landlines, and these are confined to the topmost layers of government and administration. Phones may be the source of plots, conspiracies; they are not for the masses. Even the trusted must fill out many forms to secure one, and all are permanently bugged. Checks on ownership of mobile phones are even more stringent.

The nationalized service is Koryolink, a partner with Egyptian-owned Orascom. An estimated 400,000 people are allowed a mobile phone, and these 400,000 consist almost entirely of the privileged living in the capital. Among the really elite there is an even smaller service. This was what Luke Jennings, after weeks of work, had penetrated. Then the fluent Korean-speakers of RUSI, the Foreign Office and SIS had taken over, prowling the database to discover the personal phone number of General Li Song-Rhee.

It was a North Korean defector, sequestered in a safe house under guard, who had composed the message. In 2013, Kim had ordered the arrest and execution of his uncle and mentor Jang Song Thaek, possibly the most powerful man in the state after himself, on trumped-up charges of treason. The mandarin was torn apart by heavy machine-gun fire. The message to General Li, anonymous but evidently from a friend inside the elite, warned him that this fate was planned and pending for him too.

No, there was no need as yet to tell the PM all this, mused Weston as he sipped his arabica. Need to know, and all that. The Americans would take Li, of course. He would be crazy to stay in South Korea. A safe house close to the CIA at McLean would be safer and just as comfortable. Hours and hours of careful debriefing in the Korean language.

What would General Li reveal? And would the Americans let a Britisher sit in? It had been so long, many of his best friends in the Company were, like him, retired. Or supposed to be. But some of the old alliances, forged behind the Iron Curtain, 'back in the day', as the expression has it, still ran deep. Hazards shared, toasts drunk. As the veterans said at the bar of the SF Club, we had some fun. He would have a word with a few.

★

Sir Adrian's instincts turned out to be accurate. From the South Korean navy base at Incheon, the defector was rapidly flown the short distance to the capital, Seoul. No local commander wanted to be in charge of this potential grenade for any longer than necessary.

The same applied to the South Korean government. This was supposed to be a time of détente between North and South, massively publicized and lauded worldwide, and now the government of the South had found itself in possession of a diplomatic bomb that could blow the whole process from détente back to open war.

The loss of face in Pyongyang would be staggering, and the Northern government learned of its loss in the late morning. The demand that General Li be returned to the North was immediate. Far from being affronted, the South Korean regime was relieved when the CIA moved in, and in strength, from the US embassy in Seoul. Still in his salt-stained uniform, the general agreed with the Americans that he did indeed wish to be transferred to America.

The transfer, in a US Air Force jetliner, took place that very evening. Within an hour, while General Li was still airborne and, as it happened, fast asleep, Seoul was putting it about that the entire operation had been organized by the CIA. The Agency showed zero energy in denying this. Were it true, it would have been a masterstroke.

On his second private prediction the British veteran also turned out to be prescient. Within hours of landing, General Li Song-Rhee was lodged in very comfortable quarters, and heavily guarded by SAD hard men within the huge agency complex at Langley, Virginia.

Experts in North Korea, in its government, its weapons programme, its culture and language, culled from the Agency, the Pentagon, the State Department and academia, were hastily assembled to form the core interrogation team and its attendant body of observers. The general did not need to be advised, even delicately, that full cooperation would be the fee for his salvation and protection. He was no fool.

The White House demanded no delay. Whatever the man at the very heart of the North Korean power and armaments machine had to reveal, the POTUS wanted it, and now.

The diplomatic and media worlds were in torment. It was soon impossible for the USA to plan for any more head-of-state-level summits. The palaver that had attended the meeting between the President and the Korean dictator on a small island off Singapore began to fade. Of more concern than another showbiz spectacular was the curiosity as to what the defecting general would have to say.

Menacingly, the government of North Korea went silent. The hermit state, after a single denunciation of the West and all its tricks, and a lame attempt to claim the defector was a phoney, lapsed into an enraged shutdown. Clearly, as Western media analysts told the world, the primary concern of Pyongyang was that the North Korean people not learn of the disaster. It worked for a while but, slowly, word spread.

*

The actual interrogation of General Li, politely referred to as a debriefing, began at the CIA base in a rigorously sealed environment guarded by SAD security forces two days later.

The general was in a made-to-measure dark suit with shirt and tie – his choice – and his questioners had chosen the same. There were four of them, and two interpreters: an American scholar bilingual in Korean and a Korea-born earlier defector and thirty-years US citizen. Another twenty observers watched the meeting on CCTV screens.

The intention was to put General Li in a relaxed, comfortable, no-stress environment, five professional men having a friendly chat, as it were. The lead questioner was a professor of Korean studies who was fluent in the language after a lifetime steeped in his chosen subject. He had been briefed extensively on what the military needed urgently to know.

As it happened, General Li was one of that infinitesimally small percentage of North Koreans who spoke fluent English. The two interpreters checked for accuracy and occasionally helped with technicalities. All, including those outside the room, were security-cleared to a high level. One of them was an elderly Englishman who sat at the back and remained silent – his favoured position.

Even if, among politicians and the senior job-holders who could be ousted within the hour for a disagreement with the President, the mood for self-delusion reigned, the CIA still retained its core of full-time, long-haul professional realists. It was among these that the British counterparts from MI6 had very good contacts. It was they who had prevailed on their American colleagues to include the retired Brit on the very small guest list.

The moving force behind this was the Director of the CIA, who was informed in total confidence that, but for a teenager now tinkering with his computer in the heart of Warwickshire, General Li Song-Rhee would still be in Pyongyang. No one else in Washington had a clue that the cellphone message that had brought the North Korean to defect was a confidence trick, and that included the general himself.

These debriefings do not confine themselves to a single session, even a long one. They last for days. It was on the second day that General Li was allowed to lapse into his area of true expertise – Kim's missile programme, of which he had had overall charge. That was when he dropped his bombshell, possibly without knowing what it was. He was unsure how much the Western allies really knew, and unaware they knew less than they thought they did.

On the first day he had confirmed what Sir Adrian, at least, had warned of: the destruction of the nuclear testing site of Punggye-ri had been a ruse. It had certainly fooled the world media, who had announced with delight to their readers, listeners and viewers a major concession by North Korea.

In fact, the testing base was already a ruin, the general averred. A victim of over-drilling, bomb-testing and an earthquake, it was a collection of collapsed tunnels, caverns and galleries. Behind the access entrances sealed by explosive charges were mere piles of rubble and roof-fall.

He also confirmed that the much-hyped Hwasong-15 intercontinental ballistic missile was far too weak to carry the thermonuclear warhead that would make North Korea a true nuclear power.

It was on the second day that he revealed two things the West truly did not know. The first was that the dictator Kim Jong-un was weaker than they all suspected. General Li swore he was a front man, held in place by the so-called 'selectorate' of about 2,000 generals and senior bureaucrats. These were the ones who owned and ran the country, living in extreme luxury as the people starved. This allowed Kim to do what he did best – posture for the media, wave at the adoration of the proletariat and eat.

His second revelation was that the inadequacy of Hwasong-15 was not the end of the line for the Korean nuclear programme. Deep beneath a secret mountain, unspotted by the outside world, was another cavern, where, even as he spoke, its mighty successor, Hwasong-20, was being prepared. It would certainly carry their heaviest thermonuclear warhead to any destination on the surface of the world. All it lacked were the multistage engines, and these were due to be working and available at any time.

By the end of the first day of interrogation a second announced meeting between Kim and the American

President had been cancelled by Washington, alleging bad faith.

On the evening of the second day Sir Adrian flew back to the United Kingdom. He had a lady to report to but, first, a little more research.

Chapter Seventeen

Every major city has its libraries where scholars may pore over records and ancient texts, but London is a researcher's dream. Somewhere in that sprawling metropolis are archives covering everything man has ever thought, written or done since the first troglodyte emerged from his cave.

Some are in bright new libraries of steel, concrete and plate glass. Others are ancient cellars where the skulls of those who died in long-ago plagues stare back at the living as if to say: 'We were here once. We lived, loved, fought, suffered, died. We are your history. Discover us, remember us.'

Sir Adrian settled upon the Royal United Services Institute, tucked away off Whitehall, close to the rolling Thames. The man he sought after diligent enquiries was, he thought, remarkably young. But then, again, they always were nowadays. Advancing age is merciless. Professor Martin Dixon was forty and had been studying missiles since he became obsessed by them in his early teens. That led to a study of both Koreas.

'The North Korean regime's appetite for nuclear weapons and missiles to carry them began over fifty years ago with the founding father, Kim Il-sung,' he said. 'After 1945, as a defeated Japan withdrew from the Korean peninsula, it was Joseph Stalin who personally selected the first Kim to create the communist state of North Korea and invade the South. Three years later, the Korean stalemate led to the permanent division of the peninsula.

'By the time Kim Il-sung died in 1994, he had created the world's first communist dynasty and was able to hand over to his son, Kim Jong-il. He had also established a code of absolute worship of him and his family among a people propagandized, brainwashed and trained like puppets to adore him and never, ever, question his near-divinity. To do that he had sealed North Korea from all external influences, creating today's hermit state.

'In the process he had realized that a small, almost barren state of twenty-three million people unable to be self-sufficient even in food could never be a world-feared power unless it had nuclear weapons and the missiles to launch them worldwide. That became the abiding obsession and remains so under his grandson. Everything – absolutely everything that North Korea is or could have been – has been sacrificed to that lust to threaten the world.'

'And the missiles?'

'First came the bomb, Sir Adrian,' said the young scholar. 'The Koreans, North and South, are extremely intelligent people. The North cracked technical problem after problem, refining enough uranium-235 and then

216

plutonium to create their own atomic and now thermo-nuclear weapons to have today reserves of both. Every penny of foreign exchange resources went on that quest.

'But it became plain that having an atomic bomb serves no purpose if you can only detonate it under your own backside. To be truly threatening, and thus to be kow-towed to, you have to be able to deliver and detonate it many miles away. They imported rocket technology at first and built a range of missiles they called Musudan. These could carry modest-sized bombs in their warheads, but only across limited distances.

'In the West, we watched them test the atom-bomb programme over and over again, always underground, until they had blasted huge holes all over the country. In parallel, the missile programme progressed from the Musudans to a new type of missile – much bigger payload, much longer range. As you know, these are called Hwasong.'

'How far exactly have they got?'

'Kim Jong-il carried on his father's policies. The scientists pushed ahead with the Hwasong missile programme until the second Kim died, in 2011. There was a brief power struggle, but the dead dictator's favoured son won by a mile. Fat, ugly, insisting on a bizarre haircut – it doesn't matter. His ruthlessness is total, his obsession with himself absolute.

'Since he came to power he has pushed ahead with both bomb and missile programmes with increased speed and urgency. Test after test, launch after launch. They were incredibly expensive and many of them failures, and his behaviour has become more and more weird. It does not seem to matter. Trade sanctions are imposed, then relaxed. The fact is, the world is frightened of him.

'The USA could snuff out him and his regime by a first-strike onslaught, and so could his vast neighbour and patron, China. But both fear he would detonate enough thermonuclear devices to devastate the entire peninsula and much of north-eastern China. So . . . the constant indulgences, the elevation to world-class statesman.

'As for the missile programme, that is my particular study. The latest, with the biggest range and payload, is the Hwasong-15. It is huge, but not quite big enough to carry the thermonuclear warhead Kim Jong-un wants to install on it to any part of the world – and, in particular, Washington. You know about the defection of General Li Song-Rhee?'

'I was in some small way involved,' admitted Sir Adrian.

'Well, I understand General Li has admitted that North Korea is going for one last throw of the dice. All or nothing. The Hwasong-20. Under construction now.'

'That is exactly what he said. I was there.'

'Lucky you, Sir Adrian. I hope I may have access to the general later. The Americans are first. But the Hwasong-20 will have to be quite different to its predecessor.'

'In what way?'

'Missiles that large are usually stored in underground silos and fired from them. The silo cover disguises the missile from prying eyes in the sky until it is removed for firing. Then the missile emerges vertically, riding a huge fireball that launches it into space. When clear of the earth it tilts on to its new trajectory, which will carry it to its target, where the warhead separates, drops and explodes.

'But Hwasong-15 is carried on the back of a 32-axle vehicle. The two weigh a hundred tons. In North Korea, only a few specially prepared roads can begin to accept such a load. But it doesn't matter. It only needs one to be successfully hidden in a cavern with a few miles of disguised highway for it to emerge and fire.

'However, Hwasong-20 will have to be silo-based, built and hidden in some underground complex we do not yet know about.'

'That is also my information,' said Sir Adrian. 'And that is where General Li comes in. He does know.'

'That is bad for Kim. But not the last of his problems. That honour goes to the missile's engine. North Korea has never been able to build missile power units big enough for the Hwasongs.'

'So where does she get them? China?'

'No, Russia. The missile potential of North Korea has increased rapidly since Kim Jong-un came to power. The reason is that he switched power units. There used to be two factories in the old USSR that built the Soviet engines. One was in Ukraine, the other just outside Moscow. Then came the break-up of the USSR, and out went the Ukrainian one. The Russian plant went on making the RD250 rocket engine. That was what was used to power the Hwasong-12, 14 and 15, and it accounts for the sudden increase in North Korean threat-level under the Fat Boy.

'Then came disaster. In Moscow, the government began a trillion-ruble rearmament programme and switched to a new missile engine. The manufacturer of the RD250 lost the contract. Their name is Energomash. They found themselves with spare RD250s, but no orders. In steps Kim Jong-un. My information is that Energomash is rapidly upgrading some of its RD250 engines for shipment to Pyongyang to form the power unit of the Hwasong-20. If Energomash would stop doing that, Kim would be virtually finished. They would have the bombs, but no missiles to launch them.'

'The government in Moscow will not prevent that,' said Sir Adrian. 'Not in their present mood. Russia is now as aggressive to the West as she was during the Cold War. So, no help there. When Energomash is finished and wishes to make delivery, how would they do that?'

Professor Dixon thought it over.

'It will be a big bastard,' he said. 'A liquid-propellant engine, but only a single-stage one. And enormous quantities of hypergolic fuel, which is extremely toxic and unstable. I doubt it could be carried in an airplane. More likely on a sealed train. Across Siberia, north of the Chinese and Mongolian borders, down the isthmus to the tiny crossing point from Russian territory into North Korea.'

'You said it was unstable. Could anything go wrong?'

'Only if it were made to.'

Sir Adrian thanked him and left.

*

The summer sun was still shining and the terrace at Chequers still a pleasant place to lunch when the premier and Sir Adrian met again. When they were alone she asked:

'So, your Korean defector. How was he?'

'Very smart and very angry. Of course, the concept of "face" demanded that he hide it.'

'Is that good?'

'Very much so, Prime Minister. When a man is convinced he has been treated unjustly, he seethes with rage and therefore holds nothing back. General Li will tell everything he knows, and it will be a lot.'

'Does he know why he was destined for arrest?'

'No, he does not. He was utterly loyal to the Kim regime.'

'Or who tipped him off in time to flee?'

Sir Adrian remained silent as he thought about his reply.

'He has no idea, does he?'

'Fortunately, no. Neither does the North Korean government. The denunciation and the tip-off remain a mystery to both.'

'It was you, wasn't it, Adrian?'

'One does one's best, Prime Minister.'

Marjory Graham took a long and thoughtful drink of her wine in order to keep a straight face.

'Was there a fox involved?'

'I fear you may be right, Prime Minister.'

'And the General's news?'

'The principal nugget is that there is no way the Kim regime ever intended to denuclearize North Korea in exchange for trade concessions – even vital ones. The Americans are not best pleased at having been nearly fooled.'

'Hence the cancellation of those concessions, and no further summits?'

'Precisely.'

'Winter is coming. Without huge imports, which they cannot pay for, the North Korean people will starve again.'

'The Kim regime does not care, Prime Minister.'

'So, his next stage?'

'It seems – or so General Li claimed, and I have further information to back this up – that a truly massive new missile is being built under his direction in a secret cavern which American over-flights have not yet spotted.'

'Could our young cyber-hacker out at Chandler's Court find it?'

'We could always try, Prime Minister.'

'Yes, Adrian, so please do. Coffee?'

Sir Adrian found Dr Hendricks in his office in the computer wing of the old manor house, next to the operations hall, with its state-of-the art banks of computers humming gently. He laid a single sheet of paper in front of the scientist's nose.

'There is a factory in Russia called Energomash,' he said. 'Is there any mention of it in the public domain?'

Jeremy Hendricks pulled his computer towards him, logged on and began to tap in his question.

'It's there all right,' he said. 'Publicly listed: manufactures equipment and component parts for the space industry.'

'That's one way of putting it.'

'Board of directors, share issue, a reference to government and defence contracts. A lot of subject headings are classified, meaning covert. So the chances are most enquiries will be rebuffed on security grounds. We would do the same. It seems they build missile parts.'

'Never mind the corporate structure. Can we learn anything about their technical side?'

'Not in here. We'll have to go next door and consult our own classified intel on these people. Not for public consumption.'

In the main hall Dr Hendricks crouched over a different computer and tapped in his questions.

'Their safety mechanisms are rigorous at every stage and, yes, they are computer-controlled. With ultra-complicated firewalls to protect them from examination, let alone interference.'

'But if one could get through the firewalls, cross the air gap – even though supposedly impossible – could one insert a tiny malware and withdraw unnoticed?'

'There is only one computer hacker in the world who might be able to do it, and we both know who that is.'

Luke Jennings came from the residential wing with his mother. He was, as ever, pathologically shy in company, unwilling to shake hands or make eye contact, despite his mother's promptings. Sir Adrian did not insist.

Inside the computer hall, having checked that everything was in its exact place, he relaxed visibly. The mere hum of the computer banks acted almost like a sedative on him. Dr Hendricks showed him a piece of paper with line after line of figures and hieroglyphs on it. They were the firewalls of a super-computer far away in Russia.

Sir Adrian again noticed a change in the relationship between the boy and the older man. The two seemed to have grown still closer. He spotted what he thought it could be. For the first time in his life, Luke Jennings had a colleague. All his young life, tapping away in the attic in Luton, he had been alone. At Chandler's Court, at first, they had all been strangers. It seemed that, at last, one other human being had entered the boy's closed world and been allowed to remain there. But, for all his knowledge of the cyber-world, for all his years at GCHQ, for all his weeks of observing Luke over his shoulder, Jeremy Hendricks could still not comprehend, let alone emulate, whatever it was the boy did to achieve the impossible.

'These people are being very dangerous to our country, Luke,' said Hendricks. 'Do you think we might find out what they are up to?'

The boy's eyes lit up. He studied the figures in his hand. Another challenge. When he heard the admonishment 'I suppose it cannot be done,' he came alive. It was what he lived for.

Sir Adrian spent the night at a local hostelry: ancient brickwork, age-blackened timber beams, locally raised game pie. Over coffee and Calvados he found a discarded *Daily Telegraph* and tested himself on the Toughie crossword, completing two-thirds of it before conceding that was as far as his brain could take him. He knew that, in semi-darkness, the Fox would work through the night.

He returned to the manor at 8 a.m. Somewhere inside, the teenager who was baffling the world's superpowers was asleep. In the surrounding woodland the close-protection soldiers were changing shift. The night team had not slept – just in case. Dr Hendricks was still up, waiting.

'I watched every move he made,' he told Sir Adrian, 'and I just don't understand how he did it.' He held out another sheet of paper. 'These are the access codes to the master computer of Energomash. That computer controls the manufacture and fitting sequences for the RD250 missile engine, latest model.

'The Achilles heel lies in the fitting procedure. With all that hypergolic fuel sloshing about, one single tiny spark . . . In any case, Luke has got the codes, and no one over there seems to have noticed a thing.'

On the drive back to London Sir Adrian had cause to thank Ciaran Martin at the National Cyber Security Centre for allowing him to snitch Jeremy Hendricks from his staff. The man had turned out to be exactly the one to bridge the gap between the vulnerable eighteen-year-old who understood everything about the cyber-world and little about the real world and the much older spymaster who had seen and sometimes practised the tricks and deceptions of the secret world but could no more fly through cyberspace than to the moon.

But Weston was worried about one thing more than any other. There would have to be an end to the clandestine unit at Chandler's Court. As Alexander the Great wept when there were no more worlds to conquer, there would come a day when there were no more puzzles to crack – or at least not at government command.

To crooks, Luke Jennings would be priceless – he could break into banks. But that must never happen. He could not be signed up to work in an office block with a hundred other colleagues – he was too fragile. Jeremy Hendricks might wish to remain his mentor, his professional adoptive father, but Operation Troy would end. What then for Luke? Weston was still consumed with worry on that score when he arrived back at Admiralty Arch.

Chapter Eighteen

IT IS OFTEN thought that, because North Korea announces itself as a communist state, it can have no religion and must indeed be dedicated to atheism. Not so. The Democratic People's Republic is profoundly religious and the devotion of all its citizens is compulsory.

The break with convention is that every North Korean is obliged by law to worship three mortal gods – one alive and two deceased. These are the three Kims – grandfather, father and son. Portraits of the dead two, Kim Il-sung and Kim Jong-il, are mandatory in every home. They are on the wall as would be the crucifix in a devout Catholic house. Regular checks are made to ensure they are mounted, displayed and worshipped.

Lapel badges of the living god, Kim Jong-un, are also pandemic. Any reference to him without the title 'The Marshal' is punishable. Every personal benefit derives from him.

As with all religions, legends have been concocted to underpin the national faith. In the case of North Korea, one of these is the sanctification of a mountain where the middle Kim, son of the Founder, is said to have been born. This is holy ground. The mountain is called Paektu.

It is a dormant volcano situated in the extreme north-west of the country, north of the Yellow Sea and Korea Bay, up against the Chinese frontier. This was where the regime chose to construct its ultra-secret rocket silo to house the in-development Hwasong-20.

Just below the lip of the caldera is a humble timber shack, the putative birthplace of Kim Number Two. The idea behind the legend is to 'prove' that this Kim was born to humble but holy origins on Korean territory and rose by his own merits and therefore is well worthy of being worshipped as a living god. Of course, it is all nonsense.

The second Kim was in fact born in Siberia, safely under the protection of Stalin, where his father com-manded a military unit of Chinese and Korean exiles. His boyhood and upbringing were perfectly comfortable. It was the genocidal Stalin who, after the defeat of Japan in 1945, virtually created North Korea and imposed Kim Il-sung upon it as communist dictator. It was he who, with Soviet support, launched the Korean War.

Being a holy mountain, Mount Paektu remains forbid-den to the North Korean people and is wholly army-occupied: this enabled the excavations to be carried out in secret. Many of them were hand-dug with the use of thousands of slave labourers from the numerous concentration camps. No one knows how many died of overwork, malnutrition, disease and exposure in the bitter sub-zero winters that clothe the summit for five months a year.

General Li had revealed all this to the Americans, but no condign action was taken. Attempts to engage in a constructive dialogue with the third Kim persisted, the elusive prize being the voluntary denuclearization of North Korea in exchange for trade concessions in the form of Western donations of food and oil. In parallel, the manufacture of the Hwasong-20 continued until it lacked only those crucial engines from Russia.

The chill of winter came early to Moscow, with the telltale sign – the biting winds off the Eastern Steppes – warning of the freeze to come while most of Europe still enjoyed late-summer sunshine.

In an isolated siding behind the Yaroslavl railway station a very secret train was being prepared. The Trans-Siberian is a famous railway, but only one of its several variants makes an unbroken journey from Moscow to Pyongyang without ever entering Mongolian or Chinese territory. This is run by the North Koreans themselves. Such a vehicle was the secret train in the siding.

The scene was reminiscent of something out of Tolstoy. The huge engine was wreathed in plumes of smoke. On the longest rail network in the world, nearly 4,000 miles, over seven time zones, there are long sequences where there are no engines powered by diesel or cables. Coal-fired steam trains are still used.

To cope with some of the slopes, and in case of a remote

breakdown, there were two massive locos decorated with the crossed flags of Russia and North Korea. The crew was made up of Koreans. Behind the locomotives and their coal bunkers were three sealed freight wagons. These contained, in component parts still unassembled, the new RD250 missile engines from Energomash. Russian and North Korean security guards ringed the train to prevent any unauthorized person even attempting to approach it.

Finally, the last bureaucracy was satisfied, the last official pacified and permission given to roll. The iron wheels screamed and began to turn, the steam-spewing monster eased out of the siding, past the passenger trains with their scurrying human cargoes, and turned towards the east.

Those who have ridden the Trans-Siberian will testify it is not the most comfortable train in the world. Only devotees of rail travel try it.

For seemingly limitless tracts it passes through Russia's all-embracing forests of pine, larch and spruce. This is the vista, hour after hour, day after day, for those who choose to stare out of the window. The killer is the boredom. The only humans on this train were the security guards: docile, impassive, obedient, devoid of reading matter but apparently immune to tedium.

In the guard coach there were bunks where many simply dozed through the journey. There was basic, tasteless food, but at least there was enough of it, a blessing in itself. And the tea – endless mugs of tea from the inexhaustible samovar. Whether they knew what awesome power they were guarding or how unstable the huge canisters of hypergolic rocket fuel were will never be known. But probably not. They had no idea. They just had their orders and a job to do.

Night became day and then night again. They rolled out of European Russia, through the Urals and into their native Asia. They steamed slowly through dimly lit towns wreathed in pollution clouds, and on to Yekaterinburg, where, in 1918, the last Tsar and his family were slaughtered in a cellar, and neither knew nor cared.

The days dragged by, and the nights, as the Siberian cold gripped the fathomless forests. The coal was shovelled in the engine cab, the engine roared, the water boiled, the pistons turned and the wheels rolled.

They passed through cities with names the Korean guards could neither read nor pronounce: Novosibirsk, Krasnoyarsk and Irkutsk, where US pilot Gary Powers was shot down in his U-2 spy plane in 1960. Out of the windows here the guards saw a huge lake. It was Baikal, the deepest in the world. They did not know that.

To the south lay Mongolia, but they didn't cross the border. This cargo was not to risk possible impoundment, or even examination. Then the country to their south became China, but the track stayed inside Russia. Khabarovsk came and went and they turned south at last for the border with their home. Vladivostok slid past and, finally, the train stopped.

But it was only Tumangang, the Russian–Korean border halt. The train crews, though they had 'spelled' each other for seven days and six nights, were exhausted. Fresh teams came on board. Had the vehicle been a passenger train carrying those very few Western tourists who make the journey it would have rolled on the last few hundred miles to the capital.

But this was a special cargo for a special destination. Mount Paektu was many miles away from the main line Pyongyang to Moscow. The train would be diverted and its cargo disembarked for reloading on to a branch line. The border station teemed with agents of the NIS secret police.

Under new command it rolled across the estuary of the Tumen River then turned towards the west and the hinterland which housed the sacred mountain and the secret silo keeping the Hwasong-20 from prying eyes.

The Marshal took the news in his palace in Pyongyang and beamed with pleasure. His duplicity had worked. Eager for détente, President Moon to his south was sending relief aid of corn, wheat and rice. South Korea had had a good harvest, with ample surpluses to donate. He, the Dear Leader, was within a week of becoming a truly global thermonuclear power.

Sir Adrian had the habit of subscribing to several small-circulation technical magazines on foreign affairs and intelligence analyses. It was in one of them that he read of a man called Song Ji-wei, of whom he had never heard. The visitor was going to give a talk about Korea. A small attendance was expected. Nevertheless, the retired spymaster decided to meet him.

Mr Song had had an extraordinary life. He had been born North Korean fifty years earlier and when he was just ten his parents had escaped to China and thence to the West. But in the process they had become separated from their son, who was captured by the police, who, after several weeks, threw him on to the streets.

Part of the grip over the people maintained by the Kim governments is the ruthless punishment of the entire family of an escaper. Parents, siblings, offspring – all are arrested and sent to concentration camps if anyone tries – let alone succeeds – in escaping abroad. Wishing to leave at all is a crime.

Released from police custody, the child became one of those who are called 'fluttering swallows'; street urchins who live rough, sleeping in alleys, scavenging for food, receiving no education. This was far from the capital, so no tourist would ever see one. At eighteen, Song too tried to make a break for the Chinese border, crossed it in the pitch dark of a moonless night, but he was caught two days later, stealing food. Back then, the Chinese authorities handed refugees over to the North Koreans. Song was sentenced to a labour camp for life. There he was tortured, beaten and put to work. He suffered for eleven years before he made his breakout.

This time, he went with three companions and again made for the northern border with China, rather than the South Korean border, the Demilitarized Zone, or DMZ, far to the south. Far from being demilitarized, the DMZ is the most lethal border in the world: in fact, two borders with a mile-wide strip between them containing land-mines, spotter-towers and machine-gun posts. Very few ever make it across to the south.

The quartet got into China. One of them, having worked there, spoke good Mandarin. The other three kept their mouths shut while the Chinese-speaker secured them rides on trucks and the freight car of a slow-moving train. They moved further and further into China, away from the border, with its numerous patrols. Then they turned south and eventually reached Shanghai.

It is a very long time since Shanghai was a fishing village. Today it is simply vast. Its miles of docks, quays and jetties play host to merchant ships of every kind. Most are large container ships, but there are still coastal freighters and they found one bound for South Korea across the East China Sea.

They stowed away under the canvas covers of a lifeboat. Discovered at sea by a single crewman, they persuaded him to replace the canvas tarpaulin and say nothing. Half starved and weak with hunger, they slipped ashore at Busan, South Korea, and appealed for asylum.

Song Ji-Wei had a good brain. He recovered his health and got a job, which enabled him to make a living. Ten years later, with his life savings and some local financial backing, he began to fight back. He started the No Chain Movement. When he and Weston met after his talk he explained to Sir Adrian what he was doing.

The core of the bewildering docility of the broad masses of the people of North Korea, he said, was their utter ignorance of anything that happened in the outside world. The sealing of their country and their lives from everything elsewhere was total.

They had no radios to listen to foreign broadcasts, no TVs, no iPads. From morning until night, then through until dawn, and throughout their lives, they were drenched in pro-government propaganda. Without any standard of comparison, they thought their lives were normal, instead of thinking them grotesquely distorted.

Out of 23 million there were about 1 million of the state-privileged who lived reasonably well. They did not suffer from the periodic famines that saw bodies piled in the streets, with the survivors too weak to bury the dead. The price was total and absolute loyalty to the Kim dynasty.

About twenty per cent of citizens, children included, were informers, supported by about 1 million secret police, constantly vigilant for a hint of disloyalty or disobedience. They might change – they would change – said Mr Song, if they could be told what a wonderful life was possible with freedom. His task was to try to inform them.

Near the border he had posted several volunteers, waiting for a south-to-north wind. Then small helium balloons were released with messages and pictures describing life in the South. These balloons drifted north, rose until they burst and rained their messages on to the landscape. Though it was an offence to read them, he knew that many did.

Sir Adrian recalled the story he had heard of the now-dead Kim Jong-il and his private dread of the 'Ceaușescu moment', when the people stop cheering and, one by one, start to boo.

'What would you need to expand your operation?' he asked now.

Mr Song shrugged and smiled. 'Funding,' he said. 'The No Chain Movement gets no material help either from the South Korean government or from abroad. We have to buy the balloons and the helium gas. With funding, I could even look into moving from balloons to drones. These could be recovered intact and used again. Over and over.

'With drones I could move to small, cheap, battery-powered tape-players. The spoken word and the moving picture are much more persuasive, more convincing. The North Koreans could see life in the South for what it is. The freedoms, the liberty, the human rights, the ability to say what you think and what you want. But that is a long way off.'

'And you think your once-fellow citizens might change? Rebel? Rise up?'

'Not immediately,' said Mr Song. 'And it would not be the broad masses of the people. As in Romania years ago, it would be the generals who you see fawning upon the fat man. They really control the machine of suppression and enslavement. It suits them to live in wealth, ease and priv-ilege. At the moment, worshipping the Kims enables that to happen.

'Do not forget the age factor. In my society, age is venerated. The whole High Command is old enough to be Kim's father. They do not like being treated with contempt. The defection of General Li has shaken them badly. So Kim has to deliver, and go on delivering. The West being so gullible, believing Kim is one day going to abandon all his nuclear weapons, enables him to go on delivering. So the generals will stand by him ... until they are themselves threatened. Then they will strike, like the generals of Romania.'

'You are persuasive, Mr Song,' said Sir Adrian. 'Personally, I cannot help you. But I may know someone who can.'

He had no doubt the overburdened British taxpayer should not be saddled with yet another contribution to a foreign cause, but he was not lying when he said he could think of a possible donor.

No one will ever know what really went wrong in the heart of the holy mountain of Paektu that day in September.

The Hwasong-20 missile towered up from the base of its silo far below. It was truly enormous. With extreme care, component by component, the new RD250 power unit from Russia had been installed. With even greater care, the highly unstable propellant, the hypergolic liquid that would launch it halfway across the planet, had been inserted. There was no thermonuclear warhead yet and the high-tensile steel doors to the sky were still in place.

But all complex systems have to be tested. It was during the testing that something went awry. In theory, there was nothing that could go wrong. Switching circuits on and off, ensuring that connections will not fail at the moment of need – these should not be hazardous.

The blast tore the holy mountain apart. It made the deliberate explosions at Punggye-ri, so eagerly watched by the media and American observers, look like celebratory fireworks.

There were no foreigners at Paektu. But the North Korean generals were there, crouching in their bunkers. They had come to observe a triumph. They stumbled back to their limousines, brushing the rubble dust off their uniforms.

Far away, in several directions, seismic detectors noted a tremor somewhere in the north of Korea. It was identified as being from the only volcano in that part of the world. They concluded it must be Mount Paektu rumbling. But surely it was dormant?

The outside world, the watchers of seismic recording screens, could only speculate as to why a seemingly dormant volcanic mountain had suddenly rumbled. In the palace of The Marshal in Pyongyang, there was no enigma, just delay.

The generals who had been present at the disaster of Paektu returned to the capital in their limousines, sweeping through villages of rake-thin, under-nourished peasants who cheered them because they dared do nothing else. Once arrived, they dared not be the first to break the news. Only after repeated enquiry by the plump dictator did one of them admit there had been 'a problem'. When the full details emerged the hapless messenger lost his job and his freedom. He was sent to a labour camp.

In that culture, to scream with rage is to lose face, yet

scream was what The Marshal did. For an hour. The courtiers fled in terror. When calm returned he demanded every tiny detail and finally ordered a root-and-branch inquiry into what had gone wrong. Later analyses of the wreckage would ascertain that the flaw must have been inside the RD250 engine that had arrived from Russia, some manufacturing error that caused a tiny spark. Whatever it was, the propellant fuel had ignited. But that was several weeks away.

In the immediate aftermath, The Marshal knew only that his gamble had failed. The Hwasong-20 had been the missile that, tipped with the most lethal thermonuclear warhead he possessed, should have made him a true nuclear power, invited to sit at the highest of high tables. His scientists now told him it would take years, and astronomical sums of money, to recreate the missile and another silo in another mountain. That was when he summoned the Russian ambassador, who left ashen-faced.

Chapter Nineteen

I T TOOK SIR Adrian three days to find his donor for the Korean resistance movement, the No Chain volunteers working under Mr Song. He began with quiet talks with two old contacts inside the National Crime Agency. This used to be the Serious Organized Crime Agency and, although not part of the capital's Metropolitan Police, it works closely with the Met but has a nationwide jurisdiction.

It also has divisions that concentrate on narcotics and the known Russian underworld. He spoke with the heads of both those divisions before settling on Mr Ilya Stepanovich. He was a former high-ranker in the Russian underworld who, like the now-departed Vladimir Vinogradov, during the economic collapse of Russia years earlier, had used money, bribery and violence to acquire a controlling interest in an industry. This was his country's platinum business. Out of this he had become a billionnaire.

This enrichment enabled him to become a supporter in funds and influence of the Vozhd when he was rising through his first premiership; after he had snatched it in 'arranged' elections, his presidency had now become permanent. The linkage had never been broken. Stepanovich's tentacles still reached into both the Kremlin and the underworld. His criminal record had been erased and he had moved to London to live the life of the Russian megarich who had been permitted to settle as 'non-domiciled'.

He lived in a £20 million mansion in the city's wealthiest enclave, Belgravia, kept his executive jet at Northolt, and his social in, instead of a football team, was his string of racehorses trained at Newmarket. He had several nonsecret phone numbers for friends and contacts, and another that was very secret indeed and protected by firewalls installed by some of the best cyber-geeks on the market. He presumed it was untappable. Luke Jennings had cracked the access codes in days. Dr Hendricks, once more without a clue as to how Luke had done it, set up an untraceable listening watch which eventually logged a call to a number in Panama City. This was identified as a bank.

The mentor at Chandler's Court put the young genius back to work. Another few days saw the in-house database and its covert records of overseas-account holders penetrated. The database enquired of the caller, who was clearly identified as Mr Stepanovich himself, because the ID codes were all perfect, how much he wished to have transferred and to which account with which bank.

There was no actual telephone involved. This was computer talking to computer. Sir Adrian allocated the role of 'caller' to himself, sitting in the computer hub at

Chandler's Court with Dr Hendricks at the computer console asking for instructions. Sir Adrian glanced at a sheet of paper in his hand.

It bore the e-details of a new account in a reputable merchant bank situated in the British Channel Islands. Letter by letter and figure by figure, Sir Adrian read out the account details. Dr Hendricks tapped them into the keypad and the instructions went in a nanosecond to Panama. Then he looked up.

'Panama is asking how much of the contents of this account you wish transferred.'

Sir Adrian had not thought of that. He shrugged.

'All of it,' he said. In another second the transfer was made.

'Bloody hell,' said Hendricks, staring at his screen. 'It's 300 million quid.'

The phoney Mr Stepanovich terminated the connection. He had already ensured that reverse-engineered enquiries would never lead back to Chandler's Cross. Then Dr Hendricks started to giggle. Across the room on a chair, Luke Jennings smiled. He had done something that had pleased his friend, so he was happy. Sir Adrian drove back to London.

Of course, this was far too much for the needs of Mr Song in Seoul. Sir Adrian cabled him a handsome operating fund to drench North Korea in subversive propaganda and permitted himself to offer some large anonymous donations to charities involving abused or hungry children worldwide, and damaged or crippled soldiers.

Domestic staff at the Belgravia mansion, chatting to one another over off-duty beers at the Crown and Anchor around the corner, mentioned hearing a sound like that of a wounded animal coming from their employer's sitting room after dinner earlier that evening.

What they did not divulge, because they did not know it, was that the departed fortune did not belong to Mr Stepanovich. He had been sheltering it for the Vory v Zakone. It was the Russian underworld's cocaine money, and they have a reputation for being very sceptical of excuses when their wealth goes missing. Mr Stepanovich saved his life by repaying them, but the racehorses had to go.

The day after the cheerful beers beneath the rafters of the Belgravia pub there was a very closed meeting at Chequers. Among the politicians was the Prime Minister, who was in the chair but said little, preferring as ever to listen to the real experts: the Foreign Secretary, the Defence Secretary and junior ministers from three other ministries. But they were there to listen to some very senior civil servants.

These included the Chief of the Defence Staff, the Chief of the SIS, the Director of the National Cyber Security Centre and his colleague from GCHQ, and one representative each from the SIS and the Foreign Office who spent their careers studying Eastern Europe and Russia. News had come in from various sources, and none of it was good.

A team of Dutch scientists, after years of study, had

concluded that there was no viable doubt that the Malaysian Airlines Flight 17 shot down over Ukraine in July 2014 with the loss of 283 passengers and 15 crew had been downed quite deliberately by a Russian missile crew operating a Buk missile out of Russian-occupied eastern Ukraine.

Intercepted radio chit-chat had confirmed those responsible were not Ukrainian rebels and knew perfectly well that their target was a civilian airliner. Most of the passengers were Dutch.

'There must be retribution,' said the Chief of the Defence Staff. 'Or at least deterrence. The provocations are mounting and mounting, to intolerable levels.'

There were grunts and nods from around the table. The next speaker was from the Foreign Office, and he was followed by the man from the NCSC.

There had been a devastating cyber-attack on Ukraine, on her banks, her government and her power grid. It was now being called the NotPetya attack. It had masqueraded as a criminal attack aimed at extracting a ransom as a condition of its cessation, but no Western cyber-crime agency was in any doubt that the Russian government was behind it.

More to the point, said the head of the NCSC, the cyber-attacks on Britain coming out of Russia were becoming weekly more and more vicious and more and more frequent. Each one caused damage and each cost money to defend against. It was the Foreign Secretary, at the invitation of the Prime Minister, who summed up.

'We are living in an age more dangerous than any in our lifetimes,' he said. 'The headlines are dominated by globe-wide terrorism mounted by a weird, pseudo-religious death cult stemming from a perverted Islam. But that is not the main threat, despite the suicide bombers. ISIS is not a nation-state.

'A dozen countries now have nuclear bombs and the missiles to launch them. Four are thoroughly unstable. Three others are not only ruthlessly dictatorial internally but relentlessly aggressive externally. North Korea and Iran are two of these, but the league-leader by her own choice is now Russia. Things have not been this bad since Stalin's time.'

'And the national defence position?' asked Mrs Graham.

'I have to agree with the Foreign Secretary,' said the Defence Secretary. 'Attempts by Russian submarines and surface warships to penetrate our inshore waters and by their nuclear bombers to penetrate our airspace are constant – at least weekly. Our interceptor fighters and submarine defences are rarely not on alert. The UK is not the only target in Western Europe, just the main one. As the Foreign Secretary said, the Cold War is back, and not by our choice, but by Moscow's. The West is under covert attack, masquerading as provocations, at every level.'

'And inside Russia?' asked the Prime Minister.

'Just as bad, if not worse,' said the Foreign Office specialist in Eastern Europe. 'The grip of the Kremlin on Russian life becomes ever harsher. The Russian media are now mostly slavish towards the Kremlin. Critical journalists are routinely assassinated by underworld hitmen. The lesson has been learned: do not even attempt to criticize the Kremlin. The price will not be your career but your life. Other targeted murders of critics outside Russia have taken place – as we know. We seem to have no recourse but to keep on accepting the aggressions – short of open war, and that is unthinkable.'

The gloomy conference broke up thirty minutes later. The ministers and principal civil servants filed out for lunch. Those at the back awaited their turn. At the door, Mrs Graham caught Sir Adrian's eye and nodded towards the library. She joined him there a few minutes later.

'I cannot stop for long,' she said. 'You have heard the assessment. Your first thoughts?'

'They are quite right, of course. The prospects are very gloomy.'

'And the last speaker? Is she right? There is nothing we can do?'

'Nothing above the surface, Prime Minister. Though, if Russia sustained a truly catastrophic accident and the Kremlin was then quietly warned that, if the provocations stopped, so would the accidents, it might listen. But nothing can be out in the open. All governments have to save face.'

'Please let me have your thoughts, Sir Adrian. On paper. Special delivery. Eyes only. Within a week. Do forgive me. I must go.'

And she was gone. Sir Adrian slipped away and drove home. He had an idea.

Sir Adrian was a man who preferred to research thoroughly before he opened his mouth or put pen to paper. He came from a calling in which, if the seniors got it wrong, the juniors could die. He had prowled the sources of information about gas pipelines, how they were created and how they operated. He concentrated on the International Institute for Strategic Studies, or IISS, and the Royal United Services Institute. He settled, out of the former, on Dr Bob Langley.

'Russia is spending a savage amount of money and effort on TurkStream, and is going for broke. No one seems to be paying a blind bit of attention,' said Dr Langley. 'Which is odd, because it will affect the whole of Western Europe for decades.'

'And TurkStream is . . .'

'The biggest natural-gas pipeline the world has ever seen. They are at work now and the plan is to be finished in late 2020. Then our world will change, and not for the better.'

'Tell me all you know about TurkStream, Doctor.'

'Natural gas, also known as petroleum gas, is increasingly powering our industries, and this will increase yet more. Some comes from the Middle East by tanker as liquid petroleum gas, or LPG, but much now comes from Russia, flowing west through a series of pipelines. Germany has already become virtually dependent on Russian

LPG, which explains why Berlin is now servile to Moscow. The pipelines run across Ukraine, Poland, Moldova, Romania and Bulgaria. All are paid transit fees, and these fees play a significant part in their economies. TurkStream will replace them all. When the Russian LPG is really on stream, Europe will become gas-dependent on Russia and, effectively, her servant.'

'And if we don't buy it?'

'Europe's industrial product becomes uncompetitive in world markets. Which do you think will win? High principle or profits? TurkStream basically consists of two pipelines. Both come out of the heart of Russia and dive into the earth at Krasnodar, near the Black Sea coast, in western Russia. Blue Stream goes under the Black Sea to emerge in Turkey and heads for Ankara. That, plus reduced prices, is the buy-off for Turkey, which is why she and Russia are now firmly in bed together.

'The second, much longer pipeline, South Stream, also runs under the Black Sea but emerges in western Turkey, near the Greek border. That is where the sea island will be built to accommodate the fleets of gas tankers serving Western Europe. Then the dependency will be complete.'

'So the man in the Kremlin knows what he is doing?'

'He knows exactly what he is doing,' said Dr Langley. 'First, military threat, married to relentless cyber-attacks, and then energy domination. A predecessor used the Red Army. For "red star", read LPG.'

Bob Langley was in part a trained strategist; he was

also a technician. He explained to the non-technical Sir Adrian that, although the under-sea excavators were as yet only halfway, liquid gas was flowing through them already. But to do that, it had to remain liquid, and not be re-vaporized.

To stay liquid, to stay under pressure as it flowed, it needed regular compressor stations approximately every fifty miles along the route. There were three types of these compressors, but they all did the same job.

'How are they controlled?'

'Well, by computer, of course. The master computers are in a facility outside Krasnodar on the Russian mainland. Way underground and miles under the Black Sea, the chain of compressor stations receive the flowing LPG, re-pressurize it and send it on its way to the next station, until it eventually emerges on the Turkish shore. To power themselves, they take a "bleed" of natural gas and use that as the energy source for their own needs. Ingenious, wouldn't you say? Pays for itself, and far away in Siberia, the gas just keeps on flowing.'

Sir Adrian recalled the old saying: 'He who pays the piper calls the tune.' Or, in this case, he who keeps the wheels of industry turning. In his bunker in the Kremlin, the Vozhd might preside over a rubbish economy in consumer-goods terms but, with one single weapon, he aimed one day to bend the European continent to his will.

The elderly knight now had enough information to compose and send his missive to the Prime Minister. He then spent two more days in technical research then, having heard back from her, motored north to Chandler's Court. There, he would confer with Dr Hendricks.

Dear Prime Minister, my thoughts, as you requested.

The future of our part of this planet, Western Europe, and of our country depends not on security. That comes later because, first, we need to be able to afford it. Prosperity is the initial concern. People will fight if they are destined to perpetual poverty.

It was Germany's pending bankruptcy in the thirties that drove Hitler to invade her neighbours. He needed their assets to head off the national bankruptcy caused by his spending spree. The people would have stopped worshipping him if they had gone back to the conditions of the starving twenties. Nothing much has changed.

Today, the key to prosperity is energy – cheap, constant energy and masses of it. We have tried to harness wind, water, sunshine – ingenious and fashionable, but a mere scratch on the surface of our needs.

Coal, black and brown, is over. Wooden pellets pollute. Ditto crude oil. The future is natural gas. There is enough under our planet's crust for a century of heat, light and motive power. These create wealth, comfort and food. The people will be content. They will not fight.

We know where vast unmined deposits are to be found, and fresh ones are being discovered all the time.

But Nature, being a perverse lady, has not placed them right below the great concentrations of people who need them.

There has recently been a huge natural gas discovery off the shore of Israel. (It extends into three other national sub-sea territories, but its principal 'find' belongs to Israel.) There is a problem.

Over short distances, natural gas can be piped under its own pressure from source to consumer. Israel's new field is fifty miles offshore. With a few booster stations, close enough. For longer transits, the gas must be liquefied and frozen into LPG – liquid petroleum gas. Then it can be shipped in this form, like any other tanker cargo. On arrival, it is re-vaporized to many thousand times the volume of the tanker. Then it can be piped and used as cheap, clean power throughout the country.

It would make a lot of sense for the UK to conclude with Israel a long-term, exclusive deal. They have the gas but no liquification plant. We have the funds and the technology to build one on a sea-platform offshore. It would be a win-win partnership, liberating us from decades-long dependence on possibly hostile states. But this paper is not about Israel. There are even bigger deposits deep inside Russia, but these are many miles away from the potential treasure-house of Western Europe.

To bring this gas ocean to market, Russia – in the form of its oil/gas monopoly Gazprom – must build one *or two gigantic pipelines from her gas fields across Eastern Europe to convenient seaports whence the tankers can supply the western half of the continent.*

Smaller pipelines have been mooted to cross Belarus and Poland, and also Ukraine, with tanker ports on the coasts of Romania and Bulgaria. But Russia has virtually invaded Ukraine, and relations are strained with Poland, Romania and Bulgaria, all of whom are in the European Union and worry about the Kremlin's new aggressiveness. The new and final choice is Turkey – hence the ferocious wooing of that barely NATO country and her highly authoritarian President.

Russia has now pinned all her hopes of swamping Western Europe with her natural gas and thus becoming, through our energy dependency, our effective masters. They plan to do this via pipelines to Turkey. There are two under construction. They are called South Stream and Blue Stream.

The main problem is technical. Both, in order to reach Turkish territory from Russia, have to pass under hundreds of miles of the Black Sea. They are being excavated even as you read these lines.

The excavators are machines of bewildering complexity and, like all such machines nowadays, they are computer-controlled. Computers, as we know, can solve many problems, but they can also malfunction.

I remain, Prime Minister, your obedient servant, Adrian Weston.

At Chandler's Court, Sir Adrian briefed Dr Hendricks. 'It will be massively protected from interference,' said the guru from GCHQ. 'Even if we could get inside, what malware could we insert? What instructions could we give?'

'I have been advised on that,' said Sir Adrian. 'A single trigger malfunction that would entail unfortunate consequences.'

An hour later, the two men were talking with a diffident boy at his computer bank in the operations room.

'Luke, there is a master computer near a town called Krasnodar . . .'

A week later, far beneath the blue waters of the Black Sea, something happened in a reciprocating compressor in Blue Stream called K15. The 'K' was for the Russian word *Kompressor*. The desired and instructed pressure began to vary. It did not decrease. Just the reverse. It began to rise.

Three hundred miles away, at a computer centre in a low steel complex of buildings outside Krasnodar, deft fingers made a correction. It had no effect. The pressure inside a machine far under the Black Sea went on rising. In the computer centre, further and more urgent instructions were inserted. K15 refused to obey. A pressure indicator was rising towards a red line.

Inside K15, permissible tolerances were being approached. Seams strained, then rivets popped. Margins of tolerance had been built into the construction, but these were being exceeded. K15 was built like a gigantic car engine with pistons that rotated on a crankshaft. A crank-shaft needs lubrication in the form of heavy oil. It began to fume. It ceased to lubricate.

Outside Krasnodar, profound concern mixed with utter bewilderment morphed into panic. When the far-away compressor exploded, no one heard a thing. But at the deepest point of the Black Sea, where K15 happened to be situated, the water is 7,200 feet deep and the ambient pressure more than any machine can stand.

Through the fissures the seawater flooded in – saline, corrosive, powered by the insane strength of its own pressure. It forced itself down the pipeline, mile after mile, until every seal at either end had been closed.

It overtook and consumed the excavators, which stopped, ceasing to turn at the point they had reached. By nightfall, TurkStream had to be closed down.

'This,' said the senior scientist in the computer centre at Krasnodar, 'should not have happened. It cannot have happened. I built this system. It was foolproof. It was impenetrable.'

But post-mortem examination, as the disaster sub-sea was being assessed, revealed that the Krasnodar master-brain computer had indeed been penetrated and a tiny malware sown.

Chapter Twenty

THERE WERE TWO reports. One reached the most private office in the Kremlin in the morning, one in the afternoon. Between them, they inspired in the master of all Russia the greatest rage his private staff had ever seen.

When angry, he did not publicly scream or shout, nor rage or stamp. He became deathly white in face and knuckles, fixed and motionless. Those foolish enough to address him, having failed to note the signs, would be greeted with a reply in the form of a hiss and would be wise to leave the room.

The first report was from a weapons company called Energomash, a manufacturer of missile fuel and engines, specifically the RD250, which had powered Russia's intercontinental ballistic missiles until Defence Ministry policy had replaced the country's principal rockets with another type, from another supplier. It was the ministry that had passed the Energomash report up to the Kremlin for attention as a precaution.

The company reported that it had received a complaint

from a recent customer about its rocket engines. It had sold the RD250 to North Korea, and the customer there had complained. In consequence, a defective missile-engine component in a huge consignment transmitted in a sealed train to Mount Paektu had caused a catastrophic explosion during testing of the Hwasong-20 missile. The detonation had destroyed the missile and with it the silo in which assembly was taking place.

Energomash had conducted its own thorough examination and had concluded that there was only one viable explanation. Its quality-control computer database had somehow been penetrated and near-invisible changes made to the manufacturing sequence.

The firewalls protecting its computerized manufacturing database had been so dense that external hacking had been deemed impossible. Something had gone wrong that simply defied explanation. Someone had accomplished the technically impossible.

The result was a disaster for North Korea and its secret missile programme and its subsequent refusal to place any more orders with Russia. Concealing this humiliation from the tight-knit scientific community concerned with missiles worldwide would be nigh on impossible.

However, the report from Energomash paled into insignificance when compared with the news that came in the afternoon from Krasnodar, the operating centre of the TurkStream project. For the Vozhd, the malfunction deep under the Black Sea was truly disastrous.

He was not technically minded, but the layman's

language in the document was plain enough. Somewhere deep under the ocean, close to the midway point between the Russian and Turkish coasts, a compressor had gone out of control, despite frantic efforts to correct the malfunction. Once again, computers that had always worked perfectly had refused to accept commands.

The technical chiefs of TurkStream had determined that there must have been an interference and that it had been externally sourced. But that was out of the question. The controlling codes were so complex, involving billions of computations and permutations, that no human mind could feasibly break through those firewalls to the controlling algorithms. Yet what could not be done had been done. The outcome was damage that would take years to repair.

Over Moscow, a warm spell had generated a black-cloud storm, but the cumulonimbi, dark though they were, engulfing the golden domes of St Basil's Cathedral could not match the mood inside the office of the master of Russia. In a single day he had not only read a report, passed by the Foreign Ministry, detailing a truly horrendous interview with the dictator of North Korea, but also received this devastating news.

For the man in the Kremlin the restoration of his beloved Russia to her rightful place as the sole superpower on the continent of Europe was no mere whim. It was a life's mission. This supremacy no longer depended on Stalin's massed tank divisions but on utterly dominating the supply to Western Europe of Russian gas at a price that no other supplier and no alternate energy-type could match. And that depended on TurkStream.

For years, the Vozhd had personally authorized a steadily mounting cyber-war against the West. Outside his native St Petersburg stands a skyscraper inhabited from ground to roof by cyber-hackers. These had steadily and increasingly sown malware and Trojan horses into the computers of the West, but in those of Britain and the US especially. It was war without shells, without bombs, but most of all without declaration. But it was war . . . of a sort.

Billions of pounds' and dollars' worth of damage had been inflicted; healthcare, air traffic and public service systems had crashed; and the Vozhd had exulted in the hurt caused to the hated West, even though ninety per cent of cyber-attacks had been frustrated by Western cyber-defences. But the report from Krasnodar detailing the years of delay and the Tsar's ransom in treasure that repairing the damage would cost proved, if further proof were necessary, that someone was fighting back. And he knew who it was.

Someone had lied to him or been, themselves, completely duped. The Iranians had failed. Somewhere, that British cyber-genius was alive. The teenager who, in cyber-space, could do the impossible had not died in a villa outside Eilat. He sent for his spy chief, the head of the SVR.

Yevgeni Krilov was with him within an hour. The Vozhd thrust the two reports at him and, while Krilov read, he stared out over the Alexandrovsky Garden at the roofs of western Moscow.

'You failed,' he said. 'Your Night Wolves failed in England, and the Pasdaran failed at Eilat.'

Krilov sat in silence and reflected that this was not all that had gone wrong. He had not revealed that his rival had not fallen for his plan to incriminate the Assistant Cabinet Secretary as his informant in London – and he still did not know why – and that his real 'mole', in the form of the junior civil servant Robert Thompson, must be presumed not to have died in a car crash but had quite simply disappeared, along with the daughter whose kidnapping had purchased his treachery. He did not know the details, but he had long ago been forced to assume that the four Albanian gangsters charged with that operation would not be seeing Tirana again.

None of this he had shared with his boss in the Kremlin. Years spent climbing the career ladder had taught him that superiors like only good news, and that these instances of good news, unless repeated, are soon forgotten. Failures, on the other hand, are etched into the record.

After the news the chief of the SVR had just learned, there could be absolutely no doubt: Weston was the man he was up against. It was he who was foiling his every attempt to locate and eliminate the teenage hacker.

All spy agencies have their legends. Sometimes these legends are their heroes, perhaps long gone, but sometimes they are their opponents, often also departed. The British remember Kim Philby, the Americans Aldrich Ames. The

Russians still snarl at the recall of Oleg Penkovsky and Oleg Gordievsky. These were the great spies, of their own side the traitors. But, across the divide, those who recruited and 'ran' them were the heroes.

When he was a rising star in the old KGB, Yevgeni Krilov had heard of a British spy who had flitted into and out of East Germany, Czechoslovakia and Hungary, who had recruited and run a cipher clerk in the Foreign Ministry and a Russian missile colonel in Hungary.

Krilov also knew, though he could never prove it, that he had also been present at the ÁVO trap in Budapest set in order to capture this spy. After that the man had been withdrawn from active operations to a desk job in London and risen to Number Two in MI6. Then he had retired. Or so it had been thought.

Yes, there was the teenage super-hacker, but Weston was running him, selecting the damage, slamming in body blow after body blow at Russia.

His master was obsessed by the code-cracking youth. But the thwarting of Krilov's Liechtenstein deception, the unveiling of Robert Thompson and the deliberate selection of ruinous targets – that was down to another mind, and every bell in his brain rang out the name Adrian Weston.

The Vozhd was still glaring out at the clouds now drenching Moscow.

'What do you want?' Krilov asked of the figure at the window.

The Vozhd turned, strode across the room and placed

his hands on the shoulders of the seated Krilov. The spy chief looked up into two ice-cold, angry eyes.

'I want it over, Yevgeni Sergeivich, I want it over. I don't care how you do it, who you use. Find this boy and terminate him. One last chance, Yevgeni. One last chance.'

Krilov had his orders. He also had his ultimatum.

In the spy world, they all know each other. Or at least they know of each other. Across the great divide, they study one another as chess masters pore over the tactics and the character of the players they are going to battle at some future table where the weapons are queens and pawns.

Allies meet and dine, confer, consult and sometimes share. At diplomatic receptions, under the protection of the Vienna Accords and their diplomatic immunity, opponents smile and clink glasses, each knowing who the other is, what they really do and that, if possible, the one will wreck the other's career. Sometimes they even collaborate – but only when the politicians, in their stupidity, are going too far. In the Cuban Missile Crisis of 1962, they collaborated.

That awful October, as Kennedy ordered the removal of Soviet missiles from Cuba and Khrushchev refused, it had been the KGB chief for the whole American East Coast who sought out a CIA contact. The Russian proposed to the American that if the USA would give up her Turkish missile base at İncirlik, which threatened Russia, Khrushchev could save enough face in front of his own Politburo to abandon Cuba. A swap, not a humiliation. It worked. Had it not, someone was going to launch a nuclear missile.

Yevgeni Krilov, in the back seat of the limousine returning to Yazenevo, had not been born at the time, but he had researched the incident thoroughly. Later, racing up the promotion ladder in the KGB, he had studied the faces of the British, American and French department chiefs who opposed him across the chasm of the Cold War. And Weston had been among them.

Then came Gorbachev, the dissolution of the USSR, the abandonment of Communism, the end of the Cold War. Then years of humiliation for Russia, much of it self-inflicted, which was even now being avenged. And by the time that was over, the man he was thinking of had retired. Five years later, at fifty, Krilov had been promoted to the chieftaincy of the Russian Foreign Intelligence Service, the SVR. He had thought there could no longer be a clashing of swords. But Weston had come back and, since he had, things had never gone so wrong.

Far to the west, the man he was thinking of, ten years his senior, was having a drink with friends at the bar of the Special Forces Club. The bar was noisy, convivial with shared jokes and old memories. Sir Adrian sat in his corner chair nursing his glass of claret, nodding and smiling when addressed but otherwise lost in thought. He was thinking of a Russian far away whom he had never met but whom he had first clashed with, and defeated, over twenty-five years before. Thanks to the witless Vernon Trubshaw.

It was at the end of the Cold War, but no one knew that. Back then, when so much of the land behind the Iron Curtain was hard to get at, let alone operate within, it was common practice to ask innocent businessmen with a legitimate reason for going there to keep their eyes and ears open for any snippet that might interest officialdom, meaning the spook world. On return, there would be a friendly lunch and a gentle debriefing. Usually, these were sterile, but one never knew.

Vernon Trubshaw was the sales director of some company that was attending a trade fair in Sofia, capital of the iron-hard Bulgaria. He was asked for a BOLO, and Adrian Weston was tasked to debrief him. And Trubshaw, throwing back the government-paid-for wine, had an anecdote, probably valueless.

He had been included in an invitation to a reception at the Russian embassy and during it he went to the basement lavatory. On emerging, he found four men in the corridor. One of them, clearly the senior man, was tearing an almighty strip off a younger and very junior one. All in Russian, of which Trubshaw spoke not a word.

The younger man was nearly in tears of humiliation as the older man treated him like dirt. A week later, the thirsty Mr Trubshaw was asked to a second lunch. More government wine . . . and some photos. Adrian Weston had asked the British SIS team in Sofia for a small gallery of faces from the Russian embassy there. Trubshaw did not hesitate. His nicotine-yellow forefinger tapped two faces.

FREDERICK FORSYTH

'He was the one doing the screaming, and that was the one being roasted alive,' he said. Another week later, under diplomatic cover, Adrian Weston was in Sofia. The local British intel team helped him with identifications. The humiliated Russian was Ilya Lyubimov, a junior gofer at their embassy. The next day, Weston knocked at the door of the young Russian's apartment.

He knew it was a long shot and probably doomed to failure. But he had not the time to stalk the Russian, to catch him alone outside the embassy, then court him over several weeks until a friendship bloomed. Fortunately, he at least spoke fluent and rapid Russian.

The crash-bang approach to a recruitment rarely works but, once again, one never knew. Weston inveigled himself into Lyubimov's flat and made his pitch. And it worked. The humiliation the young Russian had been subjected to in front of two colleagues outside the lavatory doors had rankled deeply and still did. This was one profoundly dejected and disillusioned young man. And he was angry, very angry. An hour later, he agreed to 'turn' and spy for the West.

He was no real use, of course, but six months later he was returned to Moscow, still in the Foreign Ministry. Two years later, patience had its reward. Someone in Ciphers had a heart murmur and was invalided out. Lyubimov replaced him. The mother lode. All the ciphers of all the diplomatic cables, worldwide – London got them all and shared them with the USA. It lasted until Lyubimov, eight years later, on a visit to his widowed mother in

264

St Petersburg, was knocked down and killed by a drunk driver on Nevsky Prospekt. The diplomat screaming abuse in the Russian embassy in Sofia ten years earlier had been Yevgeni Krilov.

In London, the knighted veteran Sir Adrian signalled for a refill. In Yazenevo, Krilov decided how he would fulfil his commission from the Vozhd. It was that or the end of him.

There was a man. He had heard of him and his reputation but had never met him. A man of the shadows, of the Spetsnaz. Even among these he was something of a secret, and he preferred it that way. He was known only as Misha, and he was the best sniper they had ever had.

There was talk that, in Syria, he had nailed over fifty terrorists of the al-Qaeda or ISIS persuasion and another hundred Ukrainian fighters in east Ukraine after the Russian invasion posing as an uprising. He was being compared to the legendary Zaitsev of Stalingrad.

A sniper is different. In combat men kill men, in the air, at sea or by shell, grenade and mortar on the ground. But they hardly ever see them as other human beings. When they use a rifle, the enemy is still just a form, a shape that slumps to the ground when dead. The sniper studies every tiny detail of the victim, before squeezing the trigger and ending the life.

It is not enough simply to be a marksman. Such an ace, horizontal and squinting through a scope-sight at a target on a range, can win an Olympic gold, but that piece of cardboard is presented to him, clipped motionless in place, unprotected. The combat sniper is a true manhunter.

Both have the capacity for total concentration, but the sniper must add to that the ability to remain utterly motionless, if need be for hours. The competition marksman does not need to hide himself; the sniper must remain invisible. He must suppress the urge to ease aching muscles, twitch, scratch or relieve his bladder, unless inside his clothing.

Camouflage is his salvation, his lifeline, and it will vary. In a city, it will be brickwork, stone, timber doors, windows, shattered glass, rubble. In the country, his background will be trees, bushes, grass, foliage or fallen timber. Into this, adorned with leaves and tufts, he must disappear like a creature of the wild. And then wait, hour after hour, until the target appears from his foxhole or crawls into vision.

All that waiting, all that thinking. It makes for a very private man, rarely a conversationalist even off-duty. Zaitsev had been the son of a hunter from Siberia, crawling through the wreckage of Stalingrad, taking down German after German. Misha was similar. He came from the Kamchatka, a land of snow and trees, but he could disappear into the broken brickwork of Aleppo or the scrubland of Luhansk and Donetsk, across the Ukrainian border.

Yevgeni Krilov lifted the receiver of his office phone. He needed to make a secondment from the Spetsnaz to his own SVR.

★

There is surely no such thing as a sixth sense, and yet there must be. Adrian Weston was alive because of it, and he knew others like him. Such were the merry drinkers at the club bar. There is a moment to stay put and a moment to move. Pick the right one and you will see old age.

He recalled the time in Budapest, back in the Cold War, when he was heading for a meet with an asset in a riverside café by the Danube. He was 'on the black', no diplomatic immunity, his asset a Hungarian general who had lost faith in Communism and turned coat. As he came closer, the sweat had started to trickle.

There was always a moment of trepidation, perfectly normal, to be suppressed, but this was different. Something was wrong: it was too quiet for a busy street, the pedestrians too carefully studying the sky. He turned down another alley, emerged in another street, blended with the crowd, slipped away. An abort, perhaps for no reason. Later, he had learned that the general was taken, interrogated with extreme duress, and that the dreaded ÁVO had been waiting for him in strength. That was why the passers-by had been staring at the sky. They had seen the silent trench coats hovering.

Now he was feeling the same about Chandler's Court. Its location and its house-guests were known in Moscow. There had already been one attack. Captain Williams and his men had done what had to be done. Krilov would have known weeks ago that his team were never coming home. But Krilov's boss in the Kremlin had torn up the rule book long since.

News of the disaster of Paektu mountain and from Krasnodar must have reached the Kremlin and the correct deductions made.

Sir Adrian knew he had no proof, but he suspected the news from Korea and Krasnodar would have led the man in the Kremlin to deduce that Luke was still alive, and thus another attempt on his life was more than conceivable. It might be entrusted to Yevgeni Krilov, but Weston knew the man at the top would be the giver of the order. In a long life of many hazards he had trusted his gut instinct and, so far, it had not let him down.

Disruptive to Luke Jennings it might be, but it could not be helped. Better to be disrupted than dead. It was time to move the computer hub to a new and safer place. He sought and got another talk with the Prime Minister.

'Are you sure, Adrian?'

'As sure as one can ever be in an uncertain world. I now believe he will be much safer far away.'

'Very well. Permission granted. Anything you need?'

'I think I still need close protection from the Regiment. I can sort that out directly through the brigadier and the CO at Hereford. But I will need a budget, Prime Minister.'

'Well, this office has access to a reserve fund with no questions asked. You can have what you need. Have you any new targets in mind?'

'Just the one. But it's back to North Korea again.

Unfinished business. But I'll be very careful, Prime Minister.'

With clearance from the PM, Sir Adrian returned to this new quandary: where to go?

He hunted high and low, then recalled a Scottish officer who had served with him in the Paras long ago. He had been The Honourable something back then. His father had died and he had become Earl of Craigleven. The family seat of Craigleven was a huge estate in Inverness, in the Highlands of Scotland with, at its centre, Castle Craigleven.

He recalled a brief visit there when they were both young men. Castle Craigleven stood proud and stark, medieval granite with sweeping lawns, on a promontory amid thousands of acres of forest and sheep pasture, offering deer-stalking and pheasant shoots west of Inverness.

Back in 1745 when Charles Edward Stuart, Bonny Prince Charlie, had led the uprising against King George II, most of the clan chiefs had sided with the Stuarts. The cannier Craigleven of the time had stayed with the King. After the destruction of the Highland army at Culloden, many of the chiefs had lost their lands and their titles. Craigleven was rewarded with elevation to earldom and even more estates.

Sir Adrian traced his old comrade-in-arms and they lunched in St James's. Yes, the elderly peer spent most of the year at his London house and the south wing of Castle Craigleven stood empty, available for a modest rent.

The wing alone had twenty-two rooms, plus kitchens and stores. There was a live-in staff who would have something to do with out-of-season guests.

'The place might need a bit of attention,' said the laird. 'It's been empty for several years, since Millie and I moved down here. But if you can give it a lick of paint, it's all yours.'

A reputable firm of interior decorators from Inverness moved in the next day. What was needed was a bit more than a lick of paint, but Sir Adrian and Dr Hendricks flew north to supervise and instruct. The computer scientist would recreate the cyber-centre so that the operations room at Chandler's Court could be transferred with as little disruption and upset to Luke as possible.

Both men knew there was another chore, and that it had to be done right. This was to create an exact replica of the living quarters of the vulnerable Luke Jennings, who would notice the tiniest variation in his surroundings and be unable to concentrate.

The entire transfer was going to take a week. In the interim, Sir Adrian asked Luke to devote his attentions to a new task. It concerned an ultra-secret and fearsomely guarded controlling database situated deep underground in North Korea.

In Russia, other preparations were in hand. A man called Misha was transferred from the Spetsnaz to the service of the SVR and given a copious briefing on what would be his third foreign assignment.

He had fragmentary English, acquired from a compulsory language-skills programme included in the training of Special Forces soldiers. He was shown an array of photos of a manor house buried deep in the countryside in a place called Warwickshire in the heart of England. He was shown windows at one of which it was likely that a face would sooner or later appear, and he was shown the face, transmitted from Tehran. It was not the actual face, of course, but it was similar.

In London, the SVR Rezident Stepan Kukushkin was fully briefed on the forthcoming mission and alerted that two of his sleeper agents living as British among the British would be needed to chaperone Misha into and out of the country, to and from his target area. This would involve transportation between various airports and a temporary safe house where he could live unseen until he could be introduced into the Chandler's Court estate.

Sniping is a speciality of the Russian armed forces and the traditional weapons have long been the Dragunov or the Nagant sniper rifles. But Misha had chosen the more modern and much superior Orsis T-5000 with its DH5-20x56 scope-sight.

Every sniper in Russia is steeped in the history of the great aces over the years and most especially that of Vassili Zaitsev. He had been trained from childhood by his father to bring down marauding wolves and became skilled in hiding in snowdrifts. In snow-blanketed Stalingrad through the winter of 1942 he slotted over 300 German soldiers, notably the German ace Major Erwin König.

But he had used a standard Soviet infantry rifle. Since then, impressive advances have been made in sniper rifles and the latest, the Orsis T-5000, can bring down a target which to the naked eye is out of sight. The one Misha chose was carefully packed under his personal supervision, with scope-sight and ammunition, ready to be transmitted by diplomatic bag, unexaminable by British customs and lead-lined in case of X-ray cameras used by Britain's MI5, to the Russian embassy in London.

Chapter Twenty-One

THE TWO RUSSIAN sleeper agents did not need to meet. One was the meeter and greeter and host at the safe house, a rented flat in the suburban town of Staines. The other was the scout and guide.

Misha flew in from Poland on a Polish passport, perfect in every detail. Speaking with a Slavic accent and hailing from a fellow member of the European Union, there was no hold-up at Heathrow. At customs, his valise was not even examined.

If it had been opened, the customs officer would hardly have been alerted. A tourist and keen birdwatcher would have brought with him rustic clothing in camouflage design, scrim netting, hiking boots and a water canteen. Several bird books and binoculars completed the disguise of a harmless twitcher. But it all went through untouched.

Outside the custom hall, in the concourse, the greeter was waiting in the right jacket and tie, with the right meaningless exchange of phrases. And his car was in the short-stay car park. The greeter was, to all intents and purposes, a British citizen with flawless English. Only in the moving car with the windows closed did the two speak Russian. Misha was installed in his Staines apartment within two hours of landing.

An hour later the greeter had phoned the headquarters of Russian TV, the English-language broadcaster of pro-Russian propaganda, spoken to the right technician and used the right sentence. At the embassy, Stepan Kukushkin was informed the shooter was in place, waiting for his rifle. Using the usual diplomatic codes, he in turn informed Yevgeni Krilov of the safe arrival of the killer. Misha had been told not to leave his flat, which he had no intention of doing, as he was watching football on TV.

The scout did not have such a frictionless routine. He motored out to Chandler's Court to see how best he might infiltrate the sniper into the forest. Cruising past the barred entrance, he saw the barrier rise to permit the entry of a pantechnicon bearing the livery of a well-known removals company. This intrigued him. Who was moving? One of the chemists in the government laboratories, or someone from the manor house?

He spent the night at his own home two counties away, but was back at sunrise, on foot with car parked out of sight. Another huge removals van, same company but different number plate, was easing out of the estate on to the road through the village. He ran for his car and caught up with the lorry as it turned on to the M40 motorway, heading north. He followed it through Oxford, then broke off, drove back south and reported to his handler.

The following day, the Russians got lucky. A third pantechnicon came out of the estate and also headed north. This time, it was followed. At the first pitstop for the truck drivers, at a motorway service station, a radio-tracker device was attached under a rear mudguard, undetected.

It led them on an exhausting 450-mile haul to the wilds of Inverness-shire in the Scottish Highlands, and to the sprawling estate of Castle Craigleven. Through the usual cut-outs, the Moscow agents reported back to Stepan Kukushkin. He realized that, by the grace of a deity in whom he did not believe, the Kremlin's operation had been saved by the skin of its teeth. The birds had flown, but at least he knew where they had gone.

With some relief, he was able to tell his superior, Krilov, that he had caused his agent to scout the Chandler's Court site just in time to spot the departure of the target, and he was happy to claim credit for having ascertained where the boy and his entourage had gone. Far from being cancelled, Misha's operation would be only slightly delayed.

Kukushkin's territory was the entire United Kingdom but his only permanent operation in Scotland was centred on the Royal Navy nuclear submarine base at Faslane on the river Clyde, but that was nowhere near Inverness. However, tourists from the south visited the Highlands and the sleeper he was using as his scout would have to join them. The man was authorized immediately to purchase a camper van sufficient for two. That at least would avoid sudden hotel bookings in a landscape where strangers might be noticed.

Two days later, the Rezident of the SVR had the package containing the sniper rifle delivered to Misha. The scout had introduced himself at the Staines rented flat and both scout and sniper set off for Inverness.

For safety, Misha did not do any driving. He had no British licence. The scout, whose British name was Brian Simmons, ostensibly a freelance taxi driver based in London, had impeccable paperwork and drove all the way. He clocked just over 500 miles and took thirty hours, including a night in a roadside lay-by.

It was on a bright mid-October morning that the harmless-seeming camper van entered the Craigleven estate and they saw the roofs of the castle. Now, Misha took over. He was concerned only with distances and angles. Two public roads traversed the estate and they motored down them both, examining the castle from all angles. It was clear the south wing was inhabited by guests.

There were living rooms on the ground floor and on the south face picture windows offering access to a spread of lawns. These ended with a near-precipice where the ground fell away to a deep glen with a stream at the bottom. Beyond the burn the ground rose again to towering, forest-clad hills. The valley was, at a point opposite the lawns, a thousand yards wide.

Misha knew already where he would have to establish his invisible sniper nest: on the face of the mountain opposite the lawns and the bedroom windows three floors above them. Sooner or later, a gangling blond boy would appear at one of the windows . . . and die. Or he would join others on the lawns to take a coffee in the sun . . . and die.

The Orsis T-5000 is a remarkable weapon, capable of blowing away a human skull at 2,000 yards with its .338 Lapua Magnum rounds. In the calm conditions of the glen, with almost no windage, a mere 1,000 yards offered a no-miss guarantee.

Misha ordered his fellow Russian to drive on, round the curves and out of sight of the castle. In a lay-by he stepped out of the camper van with his equipment and literally disappeared into the forest across the valley.

The sniper had no intention that anyone would see him from that point. He would live in the forest for as long as it took, something to which he was wholly accustomed. In the van he had changed into his streaked camouflage one-piece coveralls. In a sack at the small of his back were iron rations, a canteen of water and multi-tool cutters. A combat knife in camouflaged sheath was strapped to one thigh.

His rifle was shrouded in camouflaged sackcloth and his pockets held spare ammunition, though he had no doubt he would need no more than a single shot, and that was in the breech already. He had not washed, nor cleaned his teeth, for two days. In his calling, soap and dentifrice can kill you. They stink.

The surface of his uniform was covered in small cloth loops. These would be studded with sprigs of surrounding

foliage when he had chosen his LUP – the lying-up position from which a sniper fires. He began to move silently
through the forest towards the face of the mountain
he knew overlooked the ravine facing the south wing of
Castle Craigleven.

The agent who had driven the motorhome up from
the south watched his charge disappear into the forest and
could do no more. The phone once more cutting out
intermittently, he informed Kukushkin in London and the
chief of the SVR in Yazenevo. From then on, both senior
spymasters were helpless.

Neither could know exactly where the sniper was,
what he had seen in the forest nor what he was doing.
They knew only that he was a skilled and experienced
wilderness dweller, wily as a wild animal in his own environment and the best marksman in the Spetsnaz.

When he had finished his mission Misha would abandon his rifle, revert to being a harmless birdwatcher,
emerge from the Scottish forest and call using a few coded
words for transport. Until then, it was a waiting game.

Captain Harry Williams of the Special Air Service Regiment was not a sniper, but he had been in combat and well
trained on the Regiment's preferred long-shot rifle, the
Accuracy International AX50 with its Schmidt and Bender
scope. That same morning, he was installing himself and
his men in their quarters above the computer team in the
south wing of the castle.

His close-protection team had been reduced to him

plus three – one sergeant and two troopers. Sir Adrian had assessed the risk to his teenage charge after the move north as minimal. No one had any idea they had been seen moving out of Warwickshire. In their isolated Highland castle, it appeared that peace reigned supreme. So, on the second evening, Captain Williams borrowed the unit's jeep and motored down to the only village on the estate. This was the hamlet of Ainslie, two miles away.

There were no more than fifty houses, but at least there was a kirk, a small corner shop and a pub. The social life of the village was clearly dependent on the third. Harry Williams was in jeans and a plaid shirt. No uniform – no need. The locals knew the laird had guests, although he and her ladyship were not present. The drinkers at their tables had lapsed into silence. Strangers were rare. Williams nodded in greeting.

'Evening, all.' He sounded like a policeman on TV. There were a dozen nods. If he was one of the laird's invited, he was acceptable.

The drinkers were scattered around the single room but there was one sitting alone at the bar, as if lost in thought. There was a spare bar stool. Williams took it. They exchanged glances.

'Nice day.'

'Aye.'

'You a single-malt man?'

'Aye.'

Williams caught the eye of the bartender and nodded towards the man's glass. The barman took a fine Islay single malt from his whisky array and poured a measure. The man raised an eyebrow.

'And the same for me,' said Williams. His new companion was much older, nudging sixty at least. His face was tanned with wind and summer sun, wrinkled, laughter lines at the corners of his eyes, but not the face of a fool. Harry might have weeks to spend at Craigleven. He just wanted to make friendly contact with the locals. He had no idea it was about to pay a huge dividend.

The two men toasted and drank. Now Mackie began to suspect that the laird's guests might not be mere tourists. The man sitting beside him reeked of soldier.

'You'll be staying at the castle?' he said.

'For a while,' said the soldier.

'Do you know the Highlands?'

'Not well, but I've taken salmon on the Spey.'

The ghillie was a shrewd ex-soldier. He knew how many eggs made a dozen. The man he was drinking with was not a regular infantry officer on leave. He was lean and hard, but most of the laird's other guests seemed to be civilians. So this one was their protection.

'There's another stranger just moved into the forest,' he said conversationally. The soldier stiffened.

'A camper? Tourist? Birdwatcher?'

Mackie slowly shook his head.

In seconds Harry Williams was out of the bar, speaking into his mobile phone. The man at the other end was his sergeant.

'I want everyone away from the windows,' he ordered.

'All curtains drawn. All sides. I'll be back shortly. We're all on alert.'

As chief gamekeeper, like his father before him, on the laird's estate, Stuart Mackie was much concerned with vermin and the control of them. Inverness is the home of the red squirrel, but the vermin grey version was trying to move in and he was concerned to stop them. So he set traps. When he caught both types he liberated the reds and put down the greys.

That morning he had been tending his traps when he saw something that should not be there. His eye had caught a flash of white in a wall of green. It was a twig, fresh cut at a slanting angle, the white inner wood glinting in the morning light. He examined the cut. Not broken, not snapped, not ragged. Sliced as by a razor-sharp knife. So . . . a human agent. A stranger in his forest.

A man in the forest cuts a branch, even a twig, only because it is in the way. But a twig cannot be in the way. It can be pushed aside. So the foliage was needed for something, and there is only one thing that could be. Camouflage.

Who needs camouflage in the forest? A birdwatcher. But the twitchers, with their field glasses and cameras, lust for the rare breeds, the exotic. This was Stuart Mackie's forest and he knew the birds. There were no rare ones. Who else hides himself beneath camouflage in the forest? In his youth, Mackie had served in the Black Watch regiment. He knew about snipers.

★

Harry returned to the bar and ordered two more single malts, though he never touched his own.

'The people I and my men are protecting are very valuable,' he said quietly. 'I think I may need your help.'

Stuart Mackie sipped his replenished glass and made a speech.

'Aye,' he said.

Now it was dawn again and Mackie stood in the forest silent as a tree, watching, listening. It was the creatures of the forest he was observing. He knew them all. Occasionally, he moved, soundlessly, a few yards at a time, close to the steep slope that ran down to the stream flowing along the bottom of the glen. A thousand yards across the valley was the south face of the castle, the windows, the lawns.

It was the fawn that gave him the tip. The little roe deer was also moving through the undergrowth, looking for a tuft of fresh grass. He saw her; she did not see him. But she jerked up her head, turned, sniffed and ran. She had not seen anything, but she had smelt something that should not be there. Mackie stared where the deer had pointed.

Misha had found a perfect nest. A jumble of fallen logs and trunks, a tangle of branches on the slope facing the south aspect of the castle. His loupe-shaped range-finder had told him a thousand yards, half the lethal range of his Orsis.

In this camouflage-striped jungle clothing, flecked with twigs and leaves, he had become almost invisible. The stock of his rifle was snug in his shoulder, the metalwork shrouded in hessian sacking. He lay motion-less, as he had through the night, and he would not move a muscle, or twitch, or scratch for hours yet to come, if need be. It was part of the training, part of the discipline that had kept him alive in the undergrowth of Donetsk and Luhansk as he had picked off Ukrainians, one after the other.

He had seen the little roe deer. She had been ten feet away when she spotted him. Now there was a squirrel, scampering towards his netting. He had no idea another pair of eyes fifty yards along the slope was looking for him, no inkling another motionless figure as skilled as he was in the forest.

Stuart Mackie tried to see what the deer had been point-ing at. Further down the scree, a jumble of fallen trunks. Nothing moved . . . until the squirrel. It was hopping over the pile of logs and fallen branches. Then it too stopped and stared. It too ran to save itself, emitting a chatter of alarm calls. At two-feet range, it had seen a human eye-ball. Mackie stared. The logs were still and silent.

Oh, he was good. But he was there. Slowly, a shape amid the foliage. Pine and broadleaf twigs drawn through loops on the camo jacket. Beneath them, an outline, shoul-ders, arms, a hooded head. Crouched behind a tree trunk, hessian sackcloth over dull metal, nothing to gleam in the morning light.

Mackie slipped silently away, memorizing the spot. Behind a stout oak he pulled his mobile phone from his

pocket and tapped in the memorized code. Across the valley in the castle, a connect, a whisper.

'Stuart?'

'I have him,' the ghillie murmured back.

'Where?'

Harry Williams was in a top-floor room on the south
face. The windows were open but he was back in the recess
of the room, invisible from outside in the daylight. He had
his Zeiss field glasses to his eyes, his phone to his ear.

'See the white rock?' asked the voice down the line.

He scanned the mountain face across the glen. One
white rock, just the one.

'Got it,' said Captain Williams.

'Ten feet above it. Track fifty feet to your left. A jumble of fallen tree trunks. Hessian sacking, extra foliage.'

'Got it,' Williams repeated.

He disconnected and laid down the binoculars. He
shuffled on his knees to the upended armchair and the
rifle laid across it, took the stock into his shoulder and
squinted down the Schmidt and Bender scope-sight. The
cluster of fallen trunks was as clear as through the Zeiss. A
tiny adjustment. Clearer still. Could have been ten yards
away.

Hessian sacking – no place in a forest – and deep in the
sacking a hint of glass. Another scope-sight, staring at
him. Somewhere, an inch above the glass, invisible under
the hood, would be the squinting face of the marksman.

Down below he heard voices. The computer technicians, picture windows being opened. He had warned

them to stay away from the lawns and keep the curtains closed, but someone was coming out for a breath of air. It might be Luke. No time for mercy. The trigger of the AX50 was under his forefinger. A gentle pressure. A slight thump in the shoulder.

The .50 cal. round crossed the valley in three seconds. The Russian saw nothing, heard nothing, felt nothing. The incoming slug flicked off the upper surface of his own scope-sight and went into his brain. Misha died.

Inside the castle, Luke Jennings was not moving towards the lawns. He was in the computer centre, staring at his screen. Dr Hendricks crouched beside him. They had been up all night. For the Fox there was no night or day, just the flickering ciphers on his screen and the keys under his fingertips.

Nine time zones to the east, in a cavern beneath a mountain far north of Pyongyang, the technicians guarding the secret of Kim Jong-un's missile programme suspected nothing. They did not realize their firewalls had been penetrated, their access codes conceded, their control yielded to the high-functioning brain of a blond English boy far away.

In another semi-dark cavern in a Scottish castle, at Luke's side, Dr Hendricks, watching the cyber-doors open in front of him, merely whispered, 'Bloody hell.'

An hour after the shooting at Craigleven Sir Adrian had received a full report from Captain Williams, and it posed a quandary. What the Russians had done was a naked act of aggression and, if the media ever got a sniff of it, there was no way a massive scandal could be averted.

Moscow would deny all knowledge, of course. In the case of the Skripals, father and daughter, there had been two barely alive Russian asylum-seekers and the very Russian nerve agent Novichok had been found smeared on their door handle. Against a tower of evidence, Russia had still denied all knowledge and the scandal had raged for months.

Now there was a very dead body with certainly Russian-identifiable dentistry. But that too could be denied. There was an equally Russian Orsis T-5000 sniper rifle – but the UK would be accused of acquiring that from specialist sources outside Russia. Additionally, Sir Adrian had been specifically ordered by Marjory Graham not to start a war.

And, finally, the entire affair might lead to the exposure of the fragile youth lodged in Castle Craigleven, and that was something he wished to avoid at all costs.

He knew perfectly well who had ordered the sniper attack in the Highlands. But for the intervention of a very astute Scottish ghillie, the shooter might well have succeeded. Over a solo lunch at the club he hit upon an idea that might resolve all problems and inflict long-due retribution upon Yevgeni Krilov. On a safe line he called Captain Williams and issued his instructions.

As for Krilov, sitting in Yazenevo waiting for news, let him stew . . . for a while.

★

A week later, the British Foreign Secretary confronted the Russian ambassador, who had been summoned to King Charles Street. The minister remained standing to indicate he had no time for jollity. This was a formal rebuke.

'It is my forlorn duty,' he told the diplomat, 'to inform you that British security forces have captured a member of the Russian Special Forces, the Spetsnaz, on a mission of aggression in our country. Her Majesty's government takes the dimmest possible view of this outrage.

'The man in question was in possession of a sniper's rifle which he had every intention to use to commit murder.'

At this point, he turned and gestured to a table at the back of the room on which some object was covered by a green baize cloth. An underling swept the cloth away. On the table, on its twin legs, with scope-sight mounted, was an Orsis T-5000. The ambassador, who had been pink with anger and ready to deny all, went pale.

'I am required to inform you, Your Excellency, that the man in question has decided to confess all in the greatest detail and has requested asylum. In short, he has defected. Offered the choice, he has elected to emigrate and seek a new life in the USA. This request has been granted. He left this morning. That is all, Sir.'

The Russian ambassador was escorted out. Though visibly in control, he was inwardly seething with rage, though not at the British. His anger was reserved for the fools back at home who had inflicted on him this humiliation. His report later that day mirrored his mood in every aspect. It did not go to Yazenevo, headquarters of the

SVR. It went to the Foreign Ministry on Smolenskaya Square. And thence it went to the Kremlin.

When they came for him they were four and they were in full Kremlin Guard uniform. The Vozhd wished to make a point. They were led in silence up to the seventh floor but not impeded. Yevgeni Krilov did not protest; there would have been no point. Everyone knew whose orders were being carried out. Doors remained closed as he was escorted to the lobby and out through the main door. The ZiL limousine was not available. He was not seen in the silver birch forest again.

Chapter Twenty-Two

FOR MANY PEOPLE, walking the mountains and glens of the Highlands of Scotland is a pleasurable vacation. But it is also a challenge, demanding a high level of physical fitness.

Every mountain over 3,000 feet high is called a Munro, and there are 282 of them, including one on the estate of Lord Craigleven. That October, the weather had not yet broken; the sun still shone and there was still warmth on the wind, which was why the hill-walk was undertaken.

There had been much debate as to whether Luke was strong enough, fit enough, to join the group. He had been the keenest in assuring them all that he was. His mother had been dubious, but the weather was so fine, the air so bracing, that she conceded a five-mile march might do him good. She had long been concerned about the hours he spent in semi-darkness, tapping at his computer. So, it was agreed: he would go.

Perhaps it was being in the countryside, or it might have been the company of soldiers and computer men, but

Luke was gaining in personal confidence. On occasion, he volunteered a personal remark rather than waiting shyly to be spoken to or remaining in silence. She prayed he might be developing an awareness of a world away from a computer screen and the blizzard of ciphers which for so long had been his whole universe.

There were six in the party. It was led by Stuart Mackie, who knew every inch of the hills and valleys, and Sergeant Eamonn Davis of the Regiment, who was accustomed to the Brecon Beacons of Wales, his native land. The other four were two of the remaining soldiers, one of the computer specialists and Luke Jennings.

For the ghillie and Sergeant Davis, the hike was no more than a stroll in the park; both men were ultra-fit. The same applied to the SAS troopers. They could all have marched, or 'tabbed', a lowlander off his legs, so they bracketed the technician and Luke Jennings in Indian file.

The soldiers were accustomed to huge 'Bergen' rucksacks but for this march they needed only light knapsacks containing energy bars, water canteens and spare socks. They even carried the needs of the two computer experts, who bore nothing but their marching clothes. It should all have been so uneventful.

After an hour they paused for a break, then started the climb up Ben Duill. The gradient became steeper, but the path was a yard wide and easily navigable. To one side was the flank of the Munro, towering upwards to its peak. On the other was a quite gentle slope down to the valley.

There seemed no reason why Luke should lose his footing on a patch of loose gravel. It all happened so quickly.

If the man behind him had been a soldier, he might have grabbed him in time. But it was the computer engineer. He made a lunge for the falling boy but missed. Even then, Luke fell only a few feet, crashing through the heather until he stopped. But the single rock was unforgiving. It was concealed by the heather and the boy's head hit it with a low crack. Sergeant Davis was beside him in two seconds.

Of course, he was first-aid trained. He examined the grazed dent on the left temple, swung the limp figure over his shoulder and scrambled up the ten-yard slope to the path. Hands reached down to haul them both over the edge. On the level, he was able to have a closer look.

The bruise was swelling and turning blue. Sergeant Davis swabbed it gently with water, but the boy was out cold. He could have put him over his shoulder in a fireman's lift and carried him back to the castle. The other two soldiers could have spelled him, but that would have taken time. He did not know if he had time. He looked up and caught Stuart Mackie's eye.

'Chopper,' he said.

The ghillie nodded and pulled out his mobile phone. The nearest mountain rescue unit was at Glenmore, forty miles away, and they had a helicopter. In forty minutes the party on the mountainside heard the snarl of the engine of the Glenmore Coastguard's S-92 coming down the glen.

A stretcher was lowered and the limp body of Luke

Jennings lifted aboard. Within sixty minutes, still unconscious on a gurney, he was being wheeled into Accident and Emergency reception at Raigmore Hospital in Inverness, the nearest major city.

They did a brain scan and the verdict was that the patient should be transferred to the Edinburgh Royal Infirmary, way down south. The ERI has an acute unit that includes a specialist brain wing. The journey south was by plane.

Luke was lucky. Just two days back from his annual holiday was Professor Calum McAvoy, rated the best brain surgeon in Scotland. He did a second scan and did not like what he saw. External appearances, which had caused Sergeant Davis to underestimate the damage, were deceptive. The crack on the temple had caused a brain bleed. McAvoy decided to operate without delay.

He ensured his patient was in a deep induced coma before opening the skull, performing a hemicraniectomy in which a substantial section of the cranium is removed. What he discovered was what he had feared, and the only good news was that he was just in time.

It was an extradural haematoma – bleeding on the brain – and any further delay might well have led to permanent damage. McAvoy was able to stem the bleeding, quietly thanking Inverness for sending the lad to his 'acute' unit in Edinburgh, despite the time loss involved.

After suturing the bleed he kept Luke in the coma for three more days before bringing him back to consciousness. In all, the teenager spent two weeks in intensive care before, still swathed in bandages, he could be sent back to Castle Craigleven.

He was accompanied by his mother and Captain Harry Williams. Sue Jennings had been staying in a small hotel in Edinburgh so that she could visit every day and sit with him. Harry Williams had flown south to be with her and Luke.

Apart from the bandages, Luke seemed much as he had been before the fall. He still looked to his mother for support in social situations, but he was perfectly lucid. He seemed relieved, on his arrival, to be back in familiar surroundings where everything that belonged to him was still placed exactly where he insisted it must be.

For an hour he stayed in his room on the south face, overlooking the sweep of lawns and the spectacular view of the valley where, still unknown to him, he had nearly died for the second time. No one had told him there was now a Russian sniper buried deep in the forest across the valley.

Dr Hendricks fussed over him, eager to reintroduce him to the computer room, his preferred environment. Over their spring and summer together their relationship had developed to the point where the man from GCHQ was now almost a surrogate father figure, to such an extent that Luke's memory of his real, late father seemed to be fading. Not that his real father had even shown a flicker of interest in Luke's only interest – the mysterious world of cyberspace.

But Dr Hendricks noticed that even as the youth

patrolled his room, checking over and over again on the position of all his possessions, he did not evince much interest in returning to the computer room. It will come, he thought, it will come. After the brain damage, he just needs time.

The first warning bells began to sound after Luke had spent an hour back at the keys of his favoured computer. He was competent, like any young man of the modern age. His fingers flickered over the keys. He passed a few simple tests of dexterity. Then Dr Hendricks set him a more complicated challenge.

Far to the south, in the north-western quadrant of London, is the suburb of Northwood. Beneath its streets, with their rows of calm, tree-lined avenues of commuter dwellings, out of sight and largely out of mind, is the operations headquarters of the Royal Navy.

The Admiralty may be in central London, the warships moored in Devonport, the great aircraft carriers *Queen Elizabeth* and *Prince of Wales* still undergoing sea trials off Portsmouth and the nuclear-missile-bearing submarines in the Clyde estuary off Faslane, but the navy's computerized-war heart is at Northwood. This is where the database flickers deep beneath the suburban streets. And the database is protected by fearsome firewalls that guard its vital access codes.

Sir Adrian sought and received the permission of the First Sea Lord to see if the cyber-genius could possibly secure those access codes. Luke tried for a week but was repelled at every attempt. The sixth sense, or second sight, or whatever he had had, seemed to be missing. On theoretical exercises, others from GCHQ had made more progress, though none had ever reached the sacred core.

Sir Adrian flew from London to Inverness and was brought by car to the castle. He had long, gentle conversations with Luke and his mother, and more technical ones with Dr Hendricks, who explained that something seemed to have changed. The boy who had set off for his mountain walk two weeks earlier was not the puzzled youth now dabbling at his keyboard.

Again Sir Adrian consulted Professor Simon Baron-Cohen in his Cambridge offices. The academic and cerebral specialist was not encouraging. Despite all the expertise in the world, the effects of brain damage were still unpredictable.

What had happened to Luke Jennings was not simply a tap on the skull causing very temporary unconsciousness, what the layman calls 'knocked out' or 'knocked cold'. That happened to many people – in the boxing ring, at the work site or in the home. Recovery was speedy and permanent.

But it seemed what that Scottish rock on the mountainside had done was more serious. The professor confirmed that permanent brain changes could take place as a result of cerebral damage. There was simply no guarantee that time alone would change a damaged human brain back to the way it was.

★

Sir Adrian flew back to London to inform the Prime Minister that Operation Troy based on the incredible skills of the Fox was over.

'Is this lad damaged in any other way, Adrian?' she asked.

'No, Prime Minister. Indeed, since his return from hospital to the Highlands, he seems to be developing into a much more well-adjusted young man. But we have to accept that this astonishing talent he had for slicing through the world's most complicated firewalls has deserted him.'

'So our secret weapon is no more?'

'That is the case.'

'Who knows that it ever existed?'

'Very, very few, Prime Minister. Among our allies, the White House and a few very senior Americans. This side of the Pond, you, two or three Cabinet members and some senior executives in the intelligence community. We are all sworn to secrecy and accustomed to it. I do not foresee leaks if the whole hub is dismantled and dispersed. As to the Kremlin, I very much suspect they will wish to let this sleeping dog lie.'

'What about the Jennings family? Surely we have wreaked havoc among them?'

'I have a suspicion that Mrs Jennings wishes to remarry. I suggest they all sign the Official Secrets Act and that funds be allocated to find a job for Luke and to complete the education of Marcus, with an ex gratia payment for their spring and summer of dislocation.'

'Very well, Adrian. I rely on you to put the matter to

bed. In short, it never happened, or at least it had nothing to do with Her Majesty's government.'

'As you wish it, Prime Minister.'

The close-down would be very quiet and very discreet. With the Prime Minister's permission, Sir Adrian instructed Dr Hendricks in his Highland castle to begin the dismantlement of the computer hub and the restoration of the staff to their posts at Cheltenham.

As Weston had predicted, Sue Jennings and Captain Harry Williams decided to marry. She would settle down as a soldier's wife, using the proceeds of the sale of the Luton residence to purchase a family home outside Hereford, close to the base of the SAS regiment.

She put the decision to both her sons. They already got on well with Harry Williams. Marcus was philosophical about yet another move of school, since he still had a couple of years until he took the exams in the British system known as GCSEs. To Sue's surprise, even Luke accepted the decision. The most challenging variations of behaviour caused by his condition seemed to be abating. All he wanted was his computer room, where he could play his cyber-games, and it now seemed he could cause no more havoc among the databases of either friend or foe.

That left Dr Hendricks with one last quandary as the headquarters at the Scottish castle were being dismantled. He was still in possession of the information yielded by Luke's last triumph before he was injured. This was the access codes to the inner heart of the North Korean missile programme, its acquisition still unsuspected in Pyong-yang. He passed the decision to Sir Adrian.

The old knight had had an eventful but tiring seven months. He had wearied of London; of the noise and the pressure, the fumes and the bustle. He longed for his cottage in the landscape of unspoiled Dorset. His spaniel had been cared for by a neighbour; now, he wanted to walk the woods again, with dog at heel, to live among his books and his memories, to have a log fire on a winter's night. However, he had one last chore to do before he left the metropolis.

The United Kingdom was still capable of taking covert control of the guidance systems of the North Korean rocket programme. He decided it would be a pity to waste such a chance.

That autumn, the North Koreans tested another missile. It was not the Hwasong-15 but the smaller and older Taepodong-2. Their reasoning was simple. Despite all Pyongyang's promises, secret development on the miniaturization of nuclear warheads had continued at unknown research laboratories well below ground. Ostentatious demolitions had taken place at ground level to justify the trade benefits being permitted by the USA.

After the disastrous experience with the Hwasong-20, it had been decided to carry out fundamental improvement to the earlier Taepodong and fit it with the smaller atomic warhead when it was ready. The cover story was that the four-stage Taepodong was destined for space research only; thus the test-fired missile had no warhead.

It was launched from the Tonghae facility to avert suspicion. Tonghae had earlier been used to launch non-weaponized missiles.

The latest Taepodong performed perfectly – at first. It rose vertically and sedately into the stratosphere. It was designed to climb through the stratosphere into the exosphere before turning east towards the Sea of Japan. After crossing the Japanese island of Hokkaido it was intended that it run out of fuel and crash into the western Pacific. At the zenith of its climb, however, something went wrong. It wavered, tilted and turned west. Towards China.

In Tonghae, the scientists at their computer banks feverishly tapped in the commands to turn the missile back on course. The sensors failed to respond. When it became plain the Taepodong was out of control they frantically programmed in the codes to ensure self-detonation. It flew on, trembled, tilted and began to fall.

It fell in open countryside, causing a huge explosion and an enormous crater, but no casualties and little damage other than sending tremors through a dozen nearby peasant cottages just north of Beijing. But Chinese defensive radar systems had been alerted and countermeasures moved to code red. In his office inside the Forbidden City in Beijing, President Xi was informed both of the alert and the rapid false alarm.

By coincidence, that morning riots broke out in three

provincial cities of North Korea. Desperately hungry citizens raided the food stores of officialdom and the privileged few. The praetorian inner army intervened with brutal reprisals, but several generals ordered their commands to stay in barracks. This was reported to Beijing. Among the reports were allegations that for some weeks the people had been drenched with pamphlets borne by helium balloons on the autumn south-to-north winds.

President Kim withdrew to his fortified luxury compound on Wonsan Bay on the east coast. A whole division of ultra-loyal presidential guards was posted at all access points.

A week after the missile fell, elite Chinese amphibious troops landed on the west coast of Korea Bay. The landings were not opposed. Most of the North Korean Army, advised by repeated messages in fluent Korean on all the airwaves they used to remain in barracks for their own safety, did so.

For the dictator of North Korea, the Ceauşescu moment referred to by his late father in conversation with Condoleezza Rice, had arrived: the moment when the ranks of brainwashed serfs finally ceased cheering and began to boo.

A week later he emerged from his Wonsan Bay fortress under close arrest. Photographic drones operating off two US Navy warships close to the South Korean coast broadcast the events to the world.

★

Near a castle in the Scottish Highlands, a cottage in Dorset and close to the SAS base at Hereford, walkers heard
frequent gunfire. The pheasant season was in full swing.

List of Characters and Organizations

UK

Professor Simon Baron-Cohen, academic and specialist in mental fragility

Lucinda Berry, Commissioner of the Metropolitan Police

Sir Richard Dearlove, Head of MI5 until his retirement in 2004

Professor Martin Dixon, Royal United Services Institute

Mrs Marjory Graham, Prime Minister

Dr Jeremy Hendricks, GCHQ computer scientist and mentor to Luke Jennings

The Jennings family: Harold, Sue, and their two sons, Luke (18) and Marcus (13)

Dr Bob Langley, International Institute for Strategic Studies

Julian Marshall, Assistant Cabinet Secretary

Mr Ciaran Martin, Director of the NCSC

Jessica Thompson, Robert Thompson's daughter (10)

Robert Thompson, Personal Private Secretary to Home Secretary

Sir Adrian Weston, Security Adviser to PM
Captain Harry Williams, CO SAS bodyguard team

British National Cyber Security Centre (NCSC), based
    in Victoria
Cabinet Office Briefing Room (COBRA)
Government Communications Headquarters (GCHQ),
    based at Cheltenham
International Institute for Strategic Studies (IISS)
Royal United Services Institute for Defence and
    Strategic Studies (RUSI)
Secret Intelligence Service (SIS), or MI6, based at
    Vauxhall Cross
Security Service, or MI5
Special Air Service (SAS)
Special Boat Service (SBS)
Special Reconnaissance Regiment (SRR)

Europe

Herr Ludwig Fritsch, banker at Vaduz Bank,
    Liechtenstein

USA

Graydon Bennett, State Department
Wesley Carter III, US Ambassador in London
Detective Sean Devlin of the NYPD
John Owen, Legal Attaché (FBI representative)
President (the POTUS), President of the United States

Central Intelligence Agency (CIA)
Department of Homeland Security
Federal Bureau of Investigation, the Bureau (FBI)
Immigration and Customs Enforcement (ICE)
National Security Agency (NSA), based at Fort Meade
Special Activities Division (SAD)

Russia

Captain Pyotr Denisovich, captain of the *Admiral Nakhimov*
Yevgeni Krilov, head of the SVR at Yazenevo
Stepan Kukushkin, head of station of Krilov's SVR unit
  in the Russian embassy in London
Oleg Politovski, deputy to Kukushkin
Ilya Stepanovich, former high-ranker in the Russian
  underworld, now billionaire
Viktor Ulyanov, Russian criminal in New York
Vladimir Vinogradov, former gang boss and professional
  criminal, now oligarch and billionaire living in London
Dmitri Volkov (Mr Burke), leader of Russian sleeper
  network in the UK
The Vozhd, President of Russia
Yakovenko, Russian ambassador to UK
Bujar Zogu, Albanian killer contacted by Vinogradov

Department V, or Otdel Mokrie Dela, trained killers,
  formerly Department 13
FSB, renamed Second Chief Directorate of the KGB
KGB, USSR security agency (1954–91)

Foreign Intelligence Service of the Russian Federation, or SVR, based at Yazenevo

Night Wolves, attackers and killers

Spetsnaz, Special Forces soldiers

SVR, foreign intelligence arm of the Russian Federation, based at Yazenevo

Vory v Zakone, or 'thieves in law', organized criminal underworld

Energomash, manufacturers of the RD250 rocket engine

Israel

Avigdor (Avi) Hirsch, Israeli ambassador in London

Meyer Ben-Avi (codename Cufflinks), Director of Mossad

Duvdevan, infiltrators of enemy countries

Kidon ('Bayonet' or 'Speartip'), overseas assassins

Mossad (the 'Institution'), secret intelligence agency

Mossad LeAliyah Bet, former name of Mossad

Sayanim ('the Helpers')

Sayeret Matkal, Special Forces unit

Shmone Matayim, or Unit 8200, cyber-brain think tank

Iran

Ali Fadavi, head of the Pasdaran Navy

Colonel Mohammed Khalq, Taeb's head of operations

Ayatollah Khamenei, Supreme Leader

Hossein Taeb, head of intelligence for the Pasdaran

Al-Quds Brigade, inner kernel of the Pasdaran
Basij, Pasdaran volunteer reserve
FEDAT, nuclear weapons research and development HQ,
    operating under the Defence Ministry
Pasdaran, Islamic Revolutionary Guard Corps
SAVAMA, secret police
VAJA, Iranian Secret Intelligence Agency

Fordow, uranium processing plant

Korea

Song Ji-wei, founder of No Chain movement
Jang Song Thaek, uncle and mentor of Kim Jong-un
The Kim dynasty: Kim Il-sung, Kim Jong-il, Kim
    Jong-un
General Li Song-Rhee, four-star army general, defector
    to South Korea/USA

Koryolink, nationalized mobile phone network
Paektu, sacred mountain, supposed birthplace of Kim
    Jong-il
Punggye-ri, nuclear testing site, now destroyed

ABOUT THE AUTHOR

Former RAF pilot and investigative journalist **Frederick Forsyth** defined the modern thriller when he wrote *The Day of the Jackal*, described by Lee Child as 'the book that broke the mould', with its lightning-paced storytelling, effortlessly cool reality and unique insider information. Since then he has written twelve novels which have been bestsellers around the world: *The Odessa File*, *The Dogs of War*, *The Devil's Alternative*, *The Fourth Protocol*, *The Negotiator*, *The Deceiver*, *The Fist of God*, *Icon*, *Avenger*, *The Afghan*, *The Cobra* and, most recently, *The Kill List*. He recently published his autobiography, *The Outsider*.

He lives in Buckinghamshire, England.